THE ANGEL

'Jess Walter is a national treasure'
Anthony Doerr

'A glorious addition to the oeuvre . . .
So. Damn. Funny . . . Prepare for delight'
Kirkus Reviews (starred review)

'Fans of Walter's seminal *Beautiful Ruins* will fall hard for the
swoony title story . . . Wise, poignant and generous of spirit,
these stories remind us that Walter is a national treasure'
Esquire

'Even great short story collections normally contain a miss or two
in the lot. But not this one. Every single offering in Jess Walter's
newest collection is a poignant, heart-filled gem. His subjects range
from Italian actresses to besotted teachers, surprising one-night
stands to overheard diner conversations. He delights equally
whether bringing to life a minor moment or an epic love story'
Daily Beast

'Empathetic yet unsentimental [and] intensely affecting fiction'
New York Times Book Review

'Jess Walter's new collection of stories gives us characters as
diverse as an actor in recovery, an exchange student in Rome, a
teenage girl grappling with the loss of her mother and a young
gay man struggling to connect with his elderly father. Walter is
sure to bring his poignant touch to these stories as he did with
his previous books, *Beautiful Ruins* and *The Cold Millions*'
Literary Hub

'The tales in *The Angel of Rome* aren't easily
categorized, but each one provides a refreshingly
honest glimpse into what it means to be alive'
BookPage (starred review)

'Jess Walter's intriguing and witty collection of short
fiction stories shines a light on the lives of a diverse range of
characters experiencing existential crises while searching
for inspiration . . . unequivocally relatable and insightful,
perhaps even encouraging the reader to do a little
bit of their own introspective thinking'
Town & Country

'*The Angel of Rome* is the mark of a profoundly talented
writer who can capture the internal lives of a twenty-something
barista living in Bend, Oregon, an older man glaring at
kids from his window in Spokane and an Italian actress
reflecting on how she never got her dream role in
equally persuasive and poignant ways'
Seattle Times

ABOUT THE AUTHOR

JESS WALTER is the author of seven novels, including *Beautiful
Ruins*, which was a *New York Times* bestseller, *The Financial Lives of
Poets*, *The Zero* and *The Cold Millions*. His story collection, *We Live
in Water*, was one of Barack Obama's books of 2019. Walter lives
in Spokane, Washington with his family.

THE
ANGEL OF
ROME

And Other Stories

JESS WALTER

PENGUIN BOOKS

PENGUIN BOOKS

UK | USA | Canada | Ireland | Australia
India | New Zealand | South Africa

Penguin Books is part of the Penguin Random House group of companies
whose addresses can be found at global.penguinrandomhouse.com.

First published in the United States of America by Harper,
an imprint of HarperCollins Publishers 2022
First published in Great Britain by Penguin Books 2022
001

Printed and bound in Great Britain by Clays Ltd, Elcograf S.p.A.

The authorized representative in the EEA is Penguin Random House Ireland,
Morrison Chambers, 32 Nassau Street, Dublin D02YH68

A CIP catalogue record for this book is available from the British Library

ISBN:978-0-241-99822-9

www.greenpenguin.co.uk

CONTENTS

THE ANGEL OF ROME

Mr. Voice

MOTHER WAS A STUNNER.

She was so beautiful men would stop mid-step on the street to watch her walk by. When I was little, I would see them out of the corner of my eye and look back, my hand still in hers. Sometimes I'd wonder if the ogling man was my father. But I don't think the men ever saw me. And my mother didn't notice them, or pretended not to notice, or had stopped noticing. She'd simply pull my hand toward the Crescent, or the Bon Marché, or the fountain at Newberry's, wherever we were going that day. "Come on, Tanya, no dawdling."

This could have been my mother's motto in 1974: no dawdling. I was nine then, and Mother thirty-one. She had four or five boyfriends at any given time; she eliminated them like murder suspects. We lived in a small apartment above a jewelry store where mother worked as a "greeter." I think the owner's theory was that men wouldn't dicker over carats if my tall, striking, miniskirted mother was looking over their shoulders. ("Oh, that's beautiful. Your wife is very lucky.") She seemed to have a date whenever she wanted one, at least three or four a week. I knew them by profession: "I'm seeing the pilot tonight," she would say from a cloud of hair spray, or with a dismissive roll of her eyes, "The lawyer's taking me to Sea Galley." Mother left me alone in the apartment when she went on these dates and I fed myself and put myself to bed. But she was always there when I woke in the morning, sometimes hurrying the pilot or the lawyer out the door. After one of the men spent the night, I'd wonder if he might stick around for a while, but the next day he was gone and in his place was a fireman or an accountant.

Then, one day, Mother stopped dating entirely. She announced that she was marrying one of the men—a guy she'd been out with only three times by my count—"Mr. Voice." He was a short, intense man with buggy eyes and graying hair that he wore long and mod, his face framed by bushy sideburns and a thinning swoop across his big forehead.

"You're marrying *him*?" I was confused. Mother always said that one day my father would return, that he was her "one love," that what they had was "special," and these other boyfriends were just "placeholders" until he came back. I didn't remember my father, and she wouldn't talk about him—where he lived or who he was—but she'd get this faraway look and make pronouncements like "We'll always be together" and "He'll come back." Until then, she was just biding her time, or so I thought. But then Mr. Voice came along.

"What about my father?" I asked. We were packing up the apartment into grocery-store boxes.

"Your father?" She smiled gently. "Your father has got nothing to do with it. This is about making a home, a family for us." Wait. She was doing this for me? I didn't want her to make a family for us; I wanted to wait for my father.

She set down the dishes she was packing and pushed the hair out of my eyes. "Listen to me, Tanya. You're a very pretty girl. You're going to be a beautiful woman. This is something you won't understand for a while, but your looks are like a bank account. You can save your whole life, but at some point, you'll have to spend the money. Do you understand?"

It was the only time I ever heard Mother talk about her looks this way. Something about it gave me a stomachache. I said I understood. But I didn't.

Or maybe I did.

Mr. Voice was fifty then, almost twenty years older than my mother. Although his name was Claude Almond, everyone knew him—and I mean, *everyone knew him*—as Mr. Voice. This was the name on his business cards, the name in the phone book, the name on the big sign outside the studio he owned, the name people greeted him with on the street, mimicking his basso profundo: *Hey, Mr. Voice*. By the summer of 1974, when my mother married him, Claude was famous in our town, on every radio station on the dial, on TV commercials, at civic events, hosting variety shows. Mr. Voice's rumble narrated our daily life in Spokane, Washington.

Looking for AM/FM-deluxe-turntable-8-track-stereo-speaker sound with psychedelic lights that rock to the music? Come to Wall of Sound Waterbed on East Sprague, next to the Two Swabbies—

Starlight Stairway is presented once again this week, in vivid color, by Boyle Fuel—if you need coal or oil—call Boyle—

This weekend, at Spokane Raceway Park, we've got the West's best funny cars—Kettleson's Mad-Dog Dodge Dart, Kipp's Killer-Cuda, and the Burns' Aqua Velva Wheelie Truck. Your ears are gonna bleeeed—

That was Mr. Voice.

Even now, I remember their wedding more clearly than I

remember either of my own: Mother wore a magenta minidress, and she put me in a dress that matched it—in hindsight, perhaps not something a nine-year-old should wear. "I think people can see my underwear," I said.

"At least you're wearing them," she said, tugging at her own skirt. Our long brown hair was fixed the same, too, smooth as poured syrup behind headbands high on our heads, bangs shiny and combed straight. I got to wear lipstick for the first time: a lacquered coat of pink that made my lips look like two candles. I was Mother's only bridesmaid. Claude had four children from his first marriage, but only his youngest, Brian, who was sixteen, stood with him, in a chocolate tuxedo that matched his father's. He had these sleepy eyes behind big, black-framed glasses and a shock of hair that looked like a wave about to crash.

They were married at the end of the 1974 world's fair in Spokane—such was Claude's celebrity that the TV stations covered it and there was a picture in *The Spokesman-Review*: "Local Radio Host Married at Expo." The wedding was in a little outdoor theater-in-the-round on Canada Island, and a judge friend of Claude's performed the ceremony.

While we waited for the bride to emerge, Claude stood smoking a pipe in his chocolate tux and ruffled white shirt. He was talking to a couple of businessmen in gray suits when he saw me. He walked over and looked down at me with those bug eyes of his. "Listen, Tanya," he rumbled. "I know this happened fast for you. I just want you to know, I'm not trying to replace anyone. You don't have to call me Dad. You can call me Claude if you want. Or Mr. Voice."

This was the first real conversation we'd ever had and it was confusing—that omnipresent radio voice telling me I didn't have to call him Dad. Then Claude kissed the top of my head and re-turned to the men in suits.

Behind me, someone spoke, mimicking Claude's thundering bass. "Listen, whatever your name is." I turned. It was Claude's son Brian, doing a practiced impersonation of his father. "You can call me Dipshit if you want. Or Dickhead Douchebag." Then he smiled and rolled his eyes.

Mom and Claude had written their own vows, New Age hippie gibberish about being "mate and muse" to one other and "sharing soul and sinew"—not until death do they part, but "as long as we grow and glow."

The judge pronounced them man and wife; they shared an un-comfortably long kiss and then they walked down the aisle to applause. I tugged at my skirt and followed with my new step-brother, who gracefully offered his arm. I took it. "Don't mind me," Brian said, "I always puke at weddings."

CLAUDE HAD A big, sprawling rancher on the back end of Spo-kane's old-money South Hill, with an open floor plan and a built-in hi-fi system connected to intercoms in every room. He loved that intercom system. You could hear every word spoken in that thin-walled house, but Claude still insisted on using the intercoms. I'd be reading, or playing dolls, and there would be a hiss of static, and then: "Tanya, have you finished your language arts? . . . Tanya, *Wild Kingdom* is on . . . Tanya, dinner's ready, London broil." We ate in a mauve kitchen overlooking a shag-carpeted, powder-blue sunken living room. On the other end was a hallway with three bedrooms lining it: Mom and Claude's, mine, and, every other weekend, Brian's.

In the A-frame center of the house, the walls didn't go all the way to the ceiling—contributing to the open feel of the house, and to some of the worst memories of my childhood. Such was the combination of Claude's vocal power and 1970s home construction that I could hear every sordid thing that happened in the master bedroom the first year of their marriage. Claude's voice must have been key to their foreplay because he narrated their sex life the way he did the weekend stock-car races.

"Dance those ripe tomatoes over here . . . Mm, baby . . . Yeah, Mr. Voice digs his little hippie girl . . ."

Claude apparently liked to role-play, too, because sometimes I'd hear bits and pieces of various bedroom radio dramas. Like pirate-and-wench: "Prepare to be boarded, m'lady." Or stern British headmaster: "Oh, someone has *bean* a bloody bad girl." He'd play Tom Jones or Robert Goulet records—miming them, I think—and then pretend Mother was a groupie: "*What's new, pussycat?* Did Kitty like the concert tonight?"

I never heard my mother's voice during these sex games, and based on how quickly Claude emerged from their bedroom in his short silk robe afterward, the sex itself was less involved than Claude's narration leading up to it. Sometimes I hid under a pillow to block the actual words, but there was no hiding from the rumble of his voice in that house.

Mr. Voice was everywhere then; in my tenth year I couldn't escape him informing me there was "strawberry shortcake for whoever cleans their plate," or on the hi-fi radio telling me to "git on down to Appliance Round Up for the rodeo of savings," or calling my mother "my foxy cheerleader."

One night they were playing some kind of Roman orgy game ("Pluck another grape into my mouth, house-girl") when my bedroom door flew open. This was Claude's custodial weekend, and in the doorway stood my stepbrother Brian, looking alarmed.

Without a word, he took me by the hand, pulled me into his bedroom, and sat me on the floor in front of his stereo. "Listen," he said, "any time I'm not here and that shit starts up, you can just come in my room, okay?" Then he put his black stereo headphones on my ears and cranked up the music: Crosby, Stills & Nash.

I closed my eyes and played with the springy cord while I listened. Halfway through the song, "Wooden Ships" became, in my mind, the story of Brian and me—*Go, take your sister then, by the hand . . .*

I opened my eyes. Brian was sitting on his bed, cross-legged, filling some kind of pipe with brownish-green mulch that I intuited must be marijuana. I took the headphones off. Immediately, I could hear Claude's voice, more distant than it had been in my room, but still sonorous and rich. "Oh, you like that, naughty girl?"

"Honestly, it's not the sex," Brian said. "It's the acting that offends me."

Then he looked up at me and cocked his head. "You really *do* look like her," he said.

Back then, I heard this a lot. I would stare at my face in the mirror and wonder—*did I really?* Everyone said she was beautiful. Did that mean I was, too? Would my father recognize me if he saw me? Would I have fifty boyfriends and then, one day, cash out my good looks like a bank account? What made a person beautiful, anyway? Mother had two eyes, eyebrows, a nose, a mouth—just like anyone. I felt chubby and had a spray of freckles across my nose. Would I get tall like her? Would the spots on my face go away? Would her face become mine? What did that word even mean, *beautiful*?

But that day, I was ecstatic to be told that I looked like her. I put the headphones back on, smiled, and closed my eyes to listen to the song—*We are leaving*—and I smelled pot smoke for the first time that afternoon—*You don't need us*—as Claude finished his business with his intransigent servant girl.

NOT LONG AFTER it started, no more than a year, the sex part seemed to end for Mother and Claude, or at least the loud over-acting that often preceded the sex ended. I wondered if my mother just had enough. Or maybe Brian said something to them about the thin walls.

Having been married twice myself in the forty years since that time, I know that a marriage can just settle into a domestic lull, too, and maybe that's what happened with Mother and Mr. Voice. Still, I can't recall a happier, more peaceful time than the second year of my mother's marriage to Claude. Unlike in our old routine in the apartment downtown, she was home every day when I returned from school and every night when I went to bed. She had quit her jewelry store job and she embraced the domestic life, cooking, cleaning, doing laundry; she even dressed like a mother, her skirts slowly moving down her thighs to her knees. One day I got dressed for school and asked what had happened to the jumper I was wearing. It was strangely stiff. "Oh, I ironed it," Mother said.

Ironing. Who knew?

Claude seemed happy, too, or at least busy. He had just started a brand-new business—"Mr. Voice is going national!"—in which he read and recorded books: Bible stories, westerns and thrillers, mostly for long-haul truck drivers. "Every new semitruck has a cassette tape player," he said. "And I will be in all of them."

Claude worked with a partner named Lowell, a lawyer whose job it was to secure the rights to the books. I loved Claude's new job because it meant I no longer heard him on the radio or TV all the time. He was not Mr. Voice anymore, but my stepfather, helping with my homework and pulling the last of my loose teeth. I don't know if it was the new business, but Claude seemed to age a decade in the year he developed Mr. Voice's Stories on Cassette—his swoop of hair disappeared in front, what was left on the sides and back was long and gray. With the round glasses he'd begun wearing, Claude looked like Benjamin Franklin. He and my mother began to look more like father and daughter than husband and wife.

That year, Brian spent more time at the house, too, which I liked a great deal. He'd started out being distant toward Mother, but she was nothing if not persistent and nothing if not charming, and she instituted a campaign to get him to like her, complimenting his clothes and his hair, and making his favorite food, tacos, at least once a week. She called him "Bri-guy," and ruffled his hair at the dinner table. Brian played guitar in a little two-man band with a high school buddy, a drummer named Clay, and Mother encouraged them to set up a practice space in the garage. Clay was tall and dark-haired, with an intense stare, and something about the attention that Mother showed him made me a little uncomfortable. "Well, if it isn't young Clay," she'd gush, or "Clay, how is it that you get handsomer every time I see you?"

That spring Mother set up guitar lessons for Brian with a guy she knew named Allen, who was the guitarist in a local band called Treason. I remembered Allen as one of the men she'd dated during her "No dawdling" phase—one of the murder suspects, as I used to think of them—the musician: a greasy guy with long blond hair who would come pick up Mother on a motorcycle and take her to a downtown club called Washboard Willies.

But he must've been a great guitar teacher because Brian really improved. I loved it when Brian got serious about the guitar. I'd sit on the floor of his bedroom while he played the beginning of "Stairway to Heaven" or the intro to "Layla." Brian's voice was, unlike his father's, thin and reedy, but I still held my breath when he sang, and sometimes he'd sneak my name in there, in the chorus to the Allman Brothers' "Melissa." *But back home he'll always run to sweet Tanya . . .*

One day, I was in my room doing homework when I heard Mother and Brian come in the door from guitar lessons. I hopped off my bed and ran toward the hall just as the door slammed. Brian stomped past me and threw his guitar in his bedroom closet. Mother went into the kitchen and lit a cigarette. I lingered outside Brian's door, waiting to hear him play whatever song he'd worked on that day with Allen but he just sat on his bed and opened a book. He said he was done with guitar.

"Why?" I asked.

"Because guitar is for assholes," he said, looking up from his book and glancing past me, toward the kitchen.

"What about Clay?" I asked. "What about the band?"

"There is no band!" he snapped. I backed out of his room.

That night at dinner Brian couldn't bring himself to look at Mother. And she seemed nervous around him. They both stared at their plates while Claude rambled on about the story he'd taped that day—a novel about a sheriff who shoots an outlaw and ends up caring for the dead man's horse. Claude was clueless about whatever was going on. Meanwhile, I was furious with Mother. Something had clearly happened, and I sensed it had something to do with her. If she drove Brian away, I would never forgive her.

The next day, Mother searched Brian's room, found his marijuana pipe, and confronted Claude with it when he got home from work. From my room, I could hear them arguing. "I won't have this in my house," she said. "What if he's smoking it around Tanya?"

"I'll talk to him," Claude said, "it's a confusing time for young people."

"Confusing?" Mother scoffed. "Your son is a druggie. And I don't want him around Tanya. That's final."

"Linda, be reasonable."

They went back and forth like this. I walked down to Brian's room, ran my hand over his guitar, put on "Wooden Ships," and settled under his headphones.

SOMETIMES YOUR LIFE changes in big, dramatic ways, as though you've been cast in a play you don't remember auditioning for. Moments have the power of important scenes: being paraded in a tiny purple dress at a wedding, someone putting headphones on you and playing a rock song. But other scenes occur offstage, and you wake one morning and understand that one thing is now something else.

This was how it happened that, in the summer of 1976, just before my twelfth birthday, Mother ran off with Brian's guitar teacher, Allen. I don't recall anyone telling me that it happened, or any great argument or a fight between her and Claude. I didn't even get to say goodbye. I just recall suddenly understanding why Brian had quit the guitar and knowing that Treason was going on the road to open for a larger band and that Mother was going with them.

I was furious with her, much angrier—it seems to me now—than Claude was. But there's a fogginess I feel about that period, too, a disorientation that makes it hard to remember. Maybe it was the shock of what happened, or maybe it was the fog of adolescence. Since that time, I have witnessed this transformation in my own daughters—that intense dawning of self-awareness that causes teenagers to tune out the rest of the world. A child's powers of observation must be strongest, I think, between eight and eleven; by thirteen we can't see past ourselves.

Whatever the cause, I just remember smoothly moving from living with my mother and Claude to living alone with Claude. We developed a quiet, easy relationship. We ate dinner and watched TV together. On Tuesday nights, after I finished my homework, Claude would make popcorn and we'd watch *Happy Days* and *Laverne and Shirley*. When Marshall Doyle asked me to "go with him" at school, Claude explained what that meant and gave me the words to tell him, No, thank you. When my period arrived, Claude took me to the store for tampons and explained the basics of female reproduction and human sexuality to me, something Mother had failed to do. Thankfully, in his sex talk, he didn't say anything about pirates or naughty schoolgirls or Robert Goulet.

Brian came over a lot that year. He was taking classes at Spokane Falls Community College, and we all had dinner together at least twice a week. I was in middle school and could feel myself changing. My arms seemed to grow overnight, my shirts became tight, cuffs of my pants rose off the floor. I retired my Teenform trainer and rummaged through Mother's box of old Playtexes and Maidenforms until I found a few that fit—a soft white one, a sheer lime-green one and a flesh-colored 1960s bullet bra that I only wore once. It was around that time that I also became aware of boys and men watching me more attentively. There was a heaviness in their stares, a pressure that I recognized with both discomfort and familiarity, as if I'd been expecting it all along. This was how it felt to be her, to feel as if you were onstage. I recalled her mannerisms, the way she managed the attention while feigning indifference, and I worked to master each of her old moves: a glance away at just the right time, a tilt of the head and a lift of the eyes, a laughing flip of hair from my shoulder.

But as boys began to notice me, the one I most wanted to see me, Brian, still thought of me as a kid. He called me "Little T" and "Turd-bird." I thought of him as I dressed each morning—would Brian like this skirt, this blouse, these jeans? When I started wearing makeup to look older, he made it clear he wasn't a fan: "You got some shit on your face, Turd-bird." Tall, intense Clay had started hanging around again, too, and if Brian didn't notice me, Clay certainly did. "Man, someone's growing up," he'd say, and Brian would look at me as if this couldn't possibly be right. Then he'd grunt reluctantly: *I guess so.* Or *Yuck.*

That's how I started flirting with Clay. It was another thing I'd seen Mother do—charm a man through his friend. I'd hear them setting up Clay's drum kit in the garage and I'd put on a pair of shorts and go out to the garage, get on my bicycle, and pedal slowly away. "Bye, Brian. Bye, Clay."

Clay would watch me ride away, smiling with half of his mouth, while Brian tuned his guitar. I could sense their eyes moving, Clay's to me, Brian's to Clay, then Brian's to me. It was not a plan, as such. But I'm sure some part of me intuited that the way to Brian was through jealousy of his best friend. I also knew it was weird to be in love with your own stepbrother, and I held the secret deep inside, ashamed and worried it meant I was a pervert.

I was usually home alone for a couple of hours after school, and sometimes I'd go into Brian's room and look through his clothes and albums, imagining he was there. I was doing that one day when I heard the doorbell ring. I ran to the front door, opened it, and there was Clay.

"Hey, Tanya," he said, his eyes traveling up and down like he was watching a yo-yo.

"Brian's not here," I said. "He's at his mom's." I tried to be cooler than usual, since Brian wasn't around to make jealous. But later I would wonder: Did I tilt my head, shift my hip? Was it my fault?

"Oh," Clay said. Then, "Shit." He glanced back at his blue Nova, skulking in our driveway. "So you're here alone?"

I stared at my shoes. "Um yeah . . . But Claude will be home from work pretty soon."

He asked if he could use our phone, and when I said yes, he followed me into the house, a bit too close, it seemed, and when we got to the kitchen, I took the phone off the wall, turned and handed it to him. But he hung the phone up. "I forgot the number." Then he moved closer to me, backing me up until I was against the wall.

"Clay . . ." I put my hand on his chest, the way I remembered Mother doing—a way of touching someone that also kept a bit of distance.

But he just kept coming closer, pressing me against the wall. He kissed me, not the way boys my age kissed, but as if he was trying to pry me open with his tongue. I closed my eyes and tried to imagine I was kissing Brian, but it wasn't right. I didn't imagine Brian kissing like this. Clay's hands moved all over me, squeezed and pinched.

And I thought: Does he know I'm only thirteen? What nineteen-year-old boy wants to do *this* with someone who's only thirteen? Wasn't that gross? I pushed a little harder on his chest. "Clay, I don't . . ."

But he just kissed me harder, mashing my lips against my teeth. He sucked at my neck and said, "Don't tell me you don't want it. The way you look?"

I couldn't make sense of his words. *Don't tell? Want what? Look how? What?*

Later, of course, you question yourself: Was I allowing this? Did I do something? But it was so fast, his hands insistent, quick, aggressive, like I was fighting a war on two fronts. I would stop his right hand from mashing my left breast and his left hand would be moving up my right inner thigh, the whole time his tongue was stuck deep in my mouth. *Don't tell . . . don't want . . . way you look.* He pulled me to the kitchen floor, his weight on top of me. I tried to deflect him long enough to think, but there was no time for thoughts, just the battle of those hands: I stopped the right and the left undid my bra; I stopped the left and the right jammed itself down the front of my jeans. I gripped his right forearm but his fingers moved over my pelvis. I gasped. No one had ever touched me there. Thankfully my jeans were very tight, and I squeezed my legs together and that's when a clear thought formed, *I DO NOT WANT THIS*, but the distance between my mind and my mouth seemed daunting and his tongue was keeping me from talking and I felt a panic go through me, that he would choke me with his tongue, and that's when I heard the voice of God descend from heaven and rain down upon the carpeted floor of that 1970s mauve kitchen.

"You little creep!" In my memory, the dishes rattled and the windows shook and birds scattered at the very moment Claude came home from work, opened the door from the garage to the kitchen, and saw Clay wrestling with his stepdaughter on the floor. Clay recoiled from the thunder of Mr. Voice, his wrist catching on my zipper as he yanked his hand out of my pants. "Get your hands off of her! She's thirteen, for God's sake!"

There was much scrambling, one swift kick (Claude's) and a great deal of apologizing (Clay's) and a bit of crying (mine) and then Claude grabbed Clay around the back of his neck and shoved him toward the door. "Don't ever come to this house again!"

I ran to my room and curled up on the bed as the Nova rumbled to life and backed out of our driveway.

I was in there alone for what felt like a long time; I think Claude had a stiff drink to fortify himself—I could smell it on him when he appeared in my doorway. "Hey. Are you okay?"

I nodded.

"Look, I didn't . . . I don't know if . . ." He looked pained. "I have to ask . . . is that something . . . you wanted to happen?"

"No." I started crying. "I don't think so."

"That's what I thought." He nodded. "You don't ever have to do that, you know. With boys. They can be . . . insistent. You just say no. And keep saying no. He doesn't have the right to—"

But before he could finish, I was crying harder. "It was so confusing. He said . . . I wanted it. The way I looked." I wept into my hands.

Claude came in and sat on the bed.

"He's wrong. You know that?"

I nodded, but I couldn't stop crying.

"Do you want to know what you look like?" Claude lifted my chin. "You look like Tanya. This is *Tanya's* face. Understand? It doesn't belong to some boy. And listen: it's not *her* face either."

We both knew who he meant by *her*.

"This is Tanya's face."

I stared up into his bulging eyes, the veins traversing his balding forehead, the gray hair wiring off in all directions. "Claude?"

"Yes?"

"Do we have to tell Brian about this?" I asked quietly.

"Brian? What's—" He cocked his head, looked at me, and, not for the first time, I could see that Mr. Voice knew a lot more than he ever let on. "Oh," he said. "Oh. Brian."

"I don't want him to think I did something wrong."

He smiled, and if he thought I was a creep for having a crush on my stepbrother, Claude certainly didn't show it. "You didn't do anything wrong. And don't you worry about Brian."

Of course, it wasn't long after that day that I came to realize something else, again without much fanfare: Brian was gay. Claude must've already known. He was much more open-minded than many of the men of that period: he accepted this fact as easily as he had once accepted that Brian might like girls. And so, when Brian started bringing his boyfriend around the house, Claude welcomed him without so much as a hitch in that deep voice. "More London broil, Kevin?"

We talked about this quality the other day, Brian and I, at Claude's funeral, how Mr. Voice was constantly surprising you, how his goofy looks and odd manner could cause you to miss what a good man he was. There was an obituary in the newspaper, not as big as the story of his wedding, but still nice, which focused on the period when he was known as the voice of Spokane. Claude's book-on-tape business turned out to be a failure, mostly because his lawyer partner hadn't secured the rights to every book that he read. Claude settled the lawsuits and spent the next twenty-five years doing voice work, but his heyday was clearly behind him. He got remarried late in life, long after I was gone (to college, Denver, two marriages, a career) to a nice woman named Karen, who always talked in a whisper—as if there was only enough vocal power for one of them—but who sobbed loudly throughout Claude's funeral.

There was a reception after the service, and I sat with Brian and his husband, a tall, quiet man named Dale, and their two adopted kids. My second husband, Everett, couldn't make it to the funeral and my older daughter, Brittany, was away at college so I brought Meaghan, who was seventeen, and who did me the favor of taking out her various piercings and wearing a dress that covered most of her tattoos.

"What a beautiful girl you are," Dale said to Meaghan. "Like your mother."

I looked at Brian and we smiled at each other. I was filled with nostalgia and warmth for my stepbrother, my first love. I thought, too, of how many times I'd heard that phrase myself growing up—*you look like your mother*—and how it had suddenly stopped.

It's another of those things that I barely recall. I was fourteen and it was not long after the incident with Clay. I remember Claude picking me up from school and taking me home in his Lincoln Continental, but a teacher or my principal must have already broken the news to me because I seemed to know when I got in the car; all I remember is him telling me *how* it happened.

She'd been gone two years by then. We had talked on the phone a few times, and she'd apologized for leaving without telling me. There was even some discussion of my going to Los Angeles for the summers, but Treason was doing well in Southern California and it was clear Mother wasn't coming back to Spokane anytime soon, and that the road was no place for a girl.

Allen wasn't driving. Claude thought maybe it was the drummer who fell asleep at the wheel. Whoever was at fault, the Treason tour van crossed the centerline and hit another car on the highway outside a town called Victorville. For years, I would say it in my head, like an incantation: *Vic-tor-ville*. Three people died in the accident, the driver of the other car, the bass player, and my mother. "She was killed instantly," Claude said, which, I could tell by the way he said it, was supposed to be good news.

She was cremated and we had a small service in Spokane. Mother's two cruel sisters came up from Oregon. I'd met them only a few times; they hadn't bothered to come for the wedding. They clucked and disapproved: "Linda never did have her shit together." They stared at me and said, "It's crazy how much you look like her," and "Spittin' image," as if this meant I was destined for trouble, too. They offered to let me come live with them. I asked Claude if I had to.

"Of course not," he said. "Tell them you have a home."

There's not much else, at least not to Mother's story. My own story isn't hers, just like my daughters' stories aren't mine, just like—as Claude said all those years ago—my face isn't hers, and their faces aren't mine. You make a life for yourself and mine has been a good one—I became a special-ed teacher, then an assistant principal, and now I am the principal of a middle school. I had one not-so-good husband, one good one (in that order), lots of friends, excellent health—what can you say about a good life?

Mother's loss affected me less and less as the years went on and I probably thought of her most when my own daughters got older and came into the family looks—that same thick brown hair, same sharp cheeks, arched brows and stage-light eyelashes—the same stares from strangers. I vowed never to say anything like Mother had said to me, about their looks being a bank account, especially not to Meaghan, who has the other thing Mother had, a danger, a smoky allure that stops men in their tracks.

When Meaghan got the tattoos and piercings, I was angry at first—I had to be, it's a mother's role—but I can't say that I blamed her.

But back then, when I was fourteen, I still wasn't sure. I saw Mother's face in the mirror, in my dreams at night. And then, a few weeks after she died, Allen brought Mother's things over to Claude's house—clothes, jewelry, a purse, some pictures, a makeup bag. It wasn't much. Allen was wearing a cast with pins through his arm and shoulder, jeans and a denim vest. One of his eyes was messed up from the wreck, all red and bleary. He kept pushing his shaggy, dirty blond hair out of his eyes and staring at me. "Goddamn, you look like her," he said. "Freaks me out how much. There's maybe a little bit a me in there, but not as much as she always said."

And that was it. Somehow, it didn't really matter, finding out. Two years earlier, it would have changed my life. But on that day, I suppose the only thing I felt was some small measure of contentment for her: that he had, indeed, come back for her, just like she always said he would. They were *special* after all, destined to be together. I thanked Allen for bringing her things, watched him ride away on his motorcycle, and went inside to have dinner with my father.

Fran's Friend Has Cancer

"FRAN'S FRIEND HAS CANCER," says Sheila.

"Who?"

"Fran's friend. Has cancer."

"I don't know who you're talking about."

"I'm telling you. Fran's friend."

Max looks up from his menu. "I'm hearing the words, Sheila. I don't know who that is?"

"You don't know who Fran is?"

"No, I don't know who Fran is."

"You don't know your cousin Fran?"

"*Frannie*? Since when does Frannie go by Fran?"

"Are you asking me since when your cousin, who has always gone by the name Fran, started going by the name Fran?"

"Hmm." Max blinks. "What are you gonna have?" Now that he thinks about it, he *has* heard Frannie go by Fran.

Sheila squints through her bifocals at the large menu. "I always wonder who would order a poached egg."

"Millions of people eat poached eggs."

"I'm not saying I wouldn't eat a poached egg. I'm saying I don't know who would order one."

"Presumably, the people who eat them."

Max hates going to plays in the afternoon, and more than that, he hates going to lunch before afternoon plays. He doesn't like being around so many *old* people, so many people—he hates to admit it—like them. The average age at a Wednesday Broadway matinee is dead.

Max slams the menu shut. "There are too many choices!"

"That doesn't make sense."

"I don't trust places that make too many things."

He looks around the restaurant: shin-to-ceiling windows, small round tables packed too close together on cold subway tile. Outside, tourists and theatergoers float ghost-like down 46th Street. The whole day has felt off—the wrong turn on the West Side Highway, trouble finding parking, a hazy walk through midtown—all of it surreal and familiar, like a recurring nightmare, as if young, healthy Max were in bed somewhere, tossing and turning in the midst of an unsettling dream of old age, this bitter drift toward obsolescence.

Sheila hums as she reads the menu, her dusty blue eyes set like sapphires in that creased face. Max wonders for a moment if she is pondering aging as well. But no, after so many years, he knows exactly what she's thinking.

He says: "So you're going then."

She looks up from the menu. "I told you I was going. You know I'm going."

"Right. I'm just saying, you've definitely gone past the planning stage and you're going."

"What does that even mean? Yes, Max. I am going."

"No. Of course. You *should* go. All I'm saying is that when I was getting radiation, did Brad come to visit once?"

"God, Max. He'd just started a new job. And the girls were little. It's not easy traveling with children."

"So he just sits at home and pouts until his mommy comes to see him?"

"Max—"

"He's a child, Sheila!"

"He's *my* child, Max."

"He's forty-eight years old!"

"So you're saying you don't want me to go."

"I'm saying . . . when I was sick last year, did Brad come to visit one time?"

"So your position is that I should not go."

"My position is that when your mother's husband is getting treatment for cancer, what a decent person would do is go and visit—for his mother's sake at least. I don't care if he doesn't like me—"

"Of course he *likes* you, Max."

"He always resented me."

"He resented you when he was nine! What nine-year-old wants his mother to remarry?"

"Well, he's not nine anymore."

The waiter ducks in. "Have you decided?"

"Please, we just opened our menus! Can you give us a minute?"

"Of course, I'll be right back."

He shakes his head at the retreating waiter. "They should put a turnstile on the door if it's going to be like that." Max opens the menu again. "Breakfast, lunch, dinner—it's too much. What kind of cancer?"

"Breast, I think. This is the woman who lives on the first floor of her building, the one Fran went to Greece with three years ago, remember?"

"For God's sake, Sheila, why would I remember who went to Greece with my cousin?" He flips to the lunch page. "Everybody's always so proud of their Reuben. Like there's some trick to piling meat on kraut."

"Fran is helping during her treatments. Bringing her food. Taking her to appointments. The woman lives alone."

"Frances was the only one of those kids ever worth a damn."

"She's hardly a kid, Max. She's our age."

That's right. Max shakes his head. He kissed her one time, when they were, what . . . nine, ten? Maybe that's why she's still Little Frannie in his mind. A family vacation on Block Island, aunts and uncles dealing pinochle inside the beach house while the cousins played wedding outside, none of the boy cousins willing to be the groom until Max said, *I'll do it*. And the kiss, his first, although when he told the story back at school, he left out the fact that she was his cousin. "Frannie was always nice. Her siblings I wouldn't throw a rope if they were drowning."

Sheila sets the menu down. "Maybe the Cobb salad."

Of course she's having the Cobb salad. Sheila always has the Cobb salad. All that meat and cheese on a salad—it's perverse. He flips to the front of the menu again. "I just pray I don't relapse while you're gone."

"You're not going to relapse because I go to Oregon for a couple of weeks."

"*A couple of weeks?* I thought it was ten days."

"It's all the way across the country, Max! Should I go for an hour? Take a cab and leave the meter running?"

"I'm just saying, ten days is not two weeks."

"Or maybe the Caesar."

"Doesn't matter. I don't think the waiter is coming back. It's rush-rush-rush then disappear."

"I wonder if it's her lover."

"The waiter?"

"Fran's friend. I wonder if the sick friend is her lover." Sheila leans forward and whispers. "She's a lesbian, you know."

"My cousin is not a lesbian."

"Of course she is."

"You watch too much television."

"No, we talked about it years ago, during the whole gay marriage business. She said she was secretly glad she hadn't been able to marry any of her girlfriends."

"Really? Frannie?" Max didn't know that he knew any lesbians. And it turns out he's kissed one? "I always thought she was just plain."

"Oh God, Max!" Sheila sits back. "That is the worst thing I've ever heard."

"*That's* the worst thing you've heard? What a life you've led."

Sheila shakes her head and sighs into the menu. "Maybe the pasta special."

"I'll bet he doesn't even ask about me."

"Brad?" She looks up again. "Of course he'll ask about you."

"Yes, but he'll do it like he's asking about a chronic condition you have. 'And how . . . is *Max*?'"

"He'll say, 'How is Max?' and I'll say, 'Well, Brad, thanks for asking. Max is fine. The cancer's in remission and Max is once again able to say the most horrible things about lesbians.'"

"I did not say all lesbians are plain. I said my cousin is plain. And I thought my cousin was plain long before I knew she was a lesbian!"

"It's definitely breast. I remember now." Sheila starts over with the menu, like a book she's decided to reread. "She's had a double mastectomy. Fran's friend."

"Well, I imagine lesbians don't care as much about breasts anyway."

"Good God, Max. The things you say!"

"Is Brad even taking time off work while you're there?"

"We haven't talked about it."

"It would be just like him to coax you all the way across the country for a month and then be too busy to actually see you."

"We're going to the coast one day. I do know that. And I'm going to see the girls' school."

"Well, great. It sounds like you have the whole thing planned. So you're definitely going."

"Yes, Max. I am definitely going."

"That's good. You *should* go." He looks down into the menu again. "Maybe Fran can come take care of me while you're gone. Sounds like she isn't above helping someone in need."

"You're going to be fine, Max."

"Who knows, maybe I'll turn her back."

"Turn her? Oh dear God, Max! What's the matter with you? Honestly." She flips another page of the menu, sighs deeply. "Do you think the Cobb salad is named after anyone in particular?"

The waiter flashes behind them, and drops drinks off at another table, Max turning in his chair. "Excuse me. We've been ready for some time."

But the waiter is practically on skates, and he blows past them, no time for their order.

No wait—it's the opposite of that, the waiter has *all the time*. He is young and this is what the young do with time, they hoard it, waste it, slop it over the sides of their cups, the young so cavalier with time—a bit for this table, none for that one, careless and slapdash with Max's wrenchingly precious time—who knows how many lunches he and Sheila have left, how many trips to the city, how many walks and matinees and looks and breaths and—

and—

Max notices something odd. The young man at the table next to them. He's acting strangely.

He's on the bench side, next to Sheila, but at his own table. He has on black, round glasses. Arrogantly thick brown hair. Hipster messenger bag on the booth next to him. He's been there the whole time, not far from Sheila, but seeming to ignore her, drinking his expensive foamy coffee. Writing in a black journal. But now he's paused, as if waiting for inspiration, or—

The young man shoots a quick sideways glance at Sheila, at *his* Sheila, and Max feels suddenly protective of his wife, of them both. Max tries something: "I think it's named after Ty Cobb. That meat salad of yours."

The young man with the pen writes in his journal.

Max stands.

"Max?" Sheila asks. "What is it?"

Max leans over the young man and snatches the black journal from his hands. He looks up, startled. "Hey—"

Max reads the open page: messy but legible, a half-print, half-cursive script. He reads: *I think it's named after Ty Cobb. That horrible meat salad of yours.*

"Are you eavesdropping on our conversation?"

The young man looks too stunned to say anything. Max flips back several pages. He reads: *Fran's friend has cancer. Who? Fran's friend. Has cancer.*

Then: *Couple in late 70s, woman in bifocals, once pretty, man balding, voice whistling through false teeth. Having lunch before a matinee.*

Max tries to keep his voice from whistling. "What the hell is this?"

"It's nothing." The young man holds out his hand for his journal. "I'm a writer, that's all."

"And you're writing about us?"

"Well, no, not really. It was a prompt."

"A what?"

"A writing prompt? My professor gave it to us. A prompt is, like, you know, an idea, or an assignment to get you going. Like, um, it might be a first line, or a name, or a suggestion about how to get started."

"And what was this particular *prompt?*"

"That we go somewhere and observe people and write down a conversation we hear. Then create a story around it."

Max flips through the pages. *Sounds like you're going. I told you I was going . . . All I'm saying is when I was getting radation did he come to visit even once.*

"You misspelled radiation, you dipshit."

"Oh, yeah, it's—" The writer adjusts his glasses. "It's just notes. It's rough." He looks at Sheila, as if for help. "I'll work on it later."

"You're scavenging our lives for your entertainment?"

"Max!" Sheila says. "Give the man back his book."

"It's a journal, Sheila. And he's writing about us in here. This vampire is sucking the life from us." He hands Sheila the journal so she can see.

The writer looks from Max to Sheila. "No, it's just an exercise. To create . . . you know . . . characters."

Max feels himself flush. "We're not characters. We're people!"

"I mean, for, like, a short story or something."

"A short story?" Max doesn't know what to say. "What's the matter, you can't write a whole novel?"

The young writer rubs his jaw. "Can I just have my journal back?"

Sheila is squinting into the pages. "I can't read this. Whatever happened to penmanship?"

"We are not characters in some story." Max points at the journal in Sheila's hands. "I *said that*—about radiation. I *had* radiation! We are real people."

Sheila says, "Does this say, *once pretty*?"

"You're not a writer at all," Max says. "You're a goddamn pick-pocket."

The writer winces. "Look, I'm sorry if—"

"Why us?"

"What?" The writer seems unprepared for this most basic of questions.

"Why not that couple over there? Or the goddamn waiter?"

"What you were talking about, I guess."

"What we are talking about is private. Between us. This is not some play you bought tickets to see. Everything in the world to write about: terrorists and bank robbers and you choose us?"

"It was just interesting," the writer says, "her wanting to go visit her son and you not wanting her to go—"

"*Not wanting her to go!*" This is too much for Max. "I said she *should* go! I told her to go! If you're going to eavesdrop at least get it right!"

The writer rubs his temple. "And the stuff about cancer, and the lesbian stuff."

"Dear God, Max. Did he put those awful things you said about Fran in here?"

Max reaches down to take the journal back from Sheila, but when he stands again, he feels the blood in his face, like he has risen too quickly. His breath is short and tastes chalky. "This is *ours*! You can't just . . . just—"

Max opens the journal to another page. He reads about his cancer, about Block Island, about kissing Frannie, about the waiter hoarding time.

A shiver runs through his chest.

He did not say those things out loud.

He looks at the writer again, who suddenly seems inscrutable behind those big glasses. Did the writer just guess, or—no. No, that's impossible. Maybe Max didn't think those things after all, maybe reading them now is suggesting thoughts he didn't actually have or—

He flips back a few pages and sees his idea of this day being like a recurring dream and then he reads this about aging: *a bitter drift toward obsolescence.*

The writer's face seems to shift slightly, to the beginning of a smirk, like Brad used to have when he was a kid, those moments when he was caught misbehaving but knew there was nothing that Max, as the stepdad, could do.

"Max?" Sheila asks.

The waiter has arrived. "Sorry for the delay. Are you ready?"

But Max can't catch his breath. "We are not eating here. Come on, Sheila."

"But I'm starved."

"Come on. We're going."

"We won't have time to eat."

"I'm sorry," the waiter says. "It got busy and—"

Is this it, Max wonders. The end? His hand quakes as he reaches into his wallet and crumples a twenty-dollar bill on the table. "Sheila. Please."

She begins gathering her things. Coat. Purse. Umbrella. Max's shallow breath stinging as it whistles in and out.

The writer holds out his hand again. His expression is cold now, unreadable. Max looks down at the journal in his hands. He flips forward a few pages, past the last line he read, the bit about Ty Cobb. He prays for empty pages but there is more writing. He closes the journal before he can read it, before he can see what happens to them now, how many pages they might have left.

No. This is insane. A delusion. Is he having a stroke? Max steadies himself against the table. Sheila has gathered her things and risen onto shaky legs, her knee still sore from the day she twisted it at their friend's cabin on the North Fork. He wills himself to stop thinking such things, as the journal no doubt reads now: *her knee still sore from that day at the North Fork.* Sheila looks up at him. She must see the fear on his face because she touches his arm. "Max?"

It is her touch that brings him back. Connects him to life, rights him. And the absurd banality of it all brings back his anger. *You finally get to meet your Maker and He turns out to be a twenty-five-year-old Dipshit in a creative writing class?*

"Hey," Max says. "There's something you should know. It's not like this."

He waves the journal in the face of the writer, who has profoundly failed to capture the *feeling* of it all, the ache in Max's sternum that long-ago summer day, Frannie's hand on his chest as she kissed him on the beach, the other cousins in two applauding lines, playing groomsmen and bridesmaids—then, twenty-five years later, *a finger snap*, Max at a real wedding, his own, and another ache as another hand presses on his chest, beautiful Sheila on the day they kissed at her family's church, and in the front row, surly, quiet, nine-year-old Brad in a rumpled suit, watching his mommy get remarried—and another finger snap and almost forty more years passes and Sheila's hand on Max's chest as he finishes his last radiation treatment—and Christ, the shame he feels for trying to guilt her into staying with him now, the fear that he might get sick while she's gone, that he will lose her forever, the dread of dying alone—what words exist for that?

Of course she should go to Oregon to see Brad, of course she should see her son and her granddaughters, of course, of course, of course. It's just—

Sheila is standing next to him now. "Max, is everything okay?"

No. Everything is not okay. There is cancer and there is death, and there is this idiot with his prompt, his notes, his dream within a dream. Max gathers his strength and bends until he is at eye level with the writer. "Listen. It's not like this. Getting old. You need to know. It's so much worse. You won't find it eavesdropping on people in a restaurant. It is not a drift or a dream or a story. It is an unimaginable loneliness. The loss . . . of everything." He slams the notebook into his creator's thin, empty chest. "And it's coming for you too, bub."

Magnificent Desolation

I HAVE A CRUSH on the mother of my worst student.

I suppose *crush* is a funny word for someone my age, fifty. And it's an odd word to describe a person I've only just met—but it's strangely appropriate. I feel like a teenager, goony and shy, *crushed* by this person who suddenly appears in my classroom doorway to talk about why her son is failing seventh grade science.

It turns out I have seen this particular woman in the parking lot of our school, six or seven times, waiting for her child to finish a sport or some other after-school program. Before today I didn't know who she was or which child she was attached to; she was just a striking face sitting in a white SUV, all drastic cheekbones and dark eyes, and I confess to a double-take or two in response to her sharp profile as I made my way from the school building to my own car.

Now, in person, I must say: Abigail Cullen is ethereal. She floats through the door in a long white skirt and a dark blue top that reminds me of the upper atmosphere, where the stratosphere meets the mesosphere.

Hey, I'm a science teacher, not a poet.

"Hello, you must be Jacob's mom," I say, and I close my laptop and push back my chair. I rise and gesture toward my humble kingdom. "Please, come in."

I HAVE TAUGHT middle school science for twenty-six years. I always planned to sharpen my focus and eventually get a PhD in some narrower field, become a professor. But by the time I finished my bachelor's degree, I was buried in debt. So I took enough education classes to get a master's, got certified, and then this job came open in my hometown and I applied, got it, and half a life later, here I still am.

This is not a major disappointment. Turns out I enjoy teaching adolescents. It is the closest we have as humans to a metamorphic or larval stage. I find the average twelve-year-old's awkwardness surprisingly endearing. And not entirely unfamiliar. In fact, I get a visceral reminder of it every year on the first day of school, when I rise in front of them and feel a version of low-level social terror more fitting to their developmental stage than mine, when my own internal monologue (*Does this shirt match my pants? Was that a stupid thing to say? Do I have a booger in my nose?*) seems unchanged from when I was in their unlaced tennis shoes.

My older sister, who is the marketing vice president for a regional bank, calls my job "teaching cats to fetch." And she's not wrong. It can feel that way at times—the utter disinterest coming from all of those Brendans and Britneys. I will finish a section on igneous rocks (going so far as to bring in a hunk of local basalt) and I will think to myself, *Hey, not bad, Edward, not a bad lesson at all.*

Then I will look up to meet twenty-five dull-eyed, comatose stares.

But it is this very unlikelihood of success, long odds that they are, which can make the rare victories feel so special, the warm feeling I get every once in a while when a student lights up over a lesson on tectonic plates, or a fourth-chair clarinetist raises her hand and says, "Like music?" during our section on the properties of waves. "Yes, Morgan," I will say with a smile. "Exactly like music."

It is then that I remember why I do this job, when I think: *Maybe I have awakened a soul.*

"I'M JACOB'S MOM," says Abigail Cullen. Her arms are so tan. "Thank you for agreeing to see me, Mr. Wells."

"Of course," I say. "Jacob is . . ."

Jacob is what? Difficult? Challenging? Loony tunes? I draw a blank staring at his mother's face. I really should have had a word at the ready to describe Jacob before she came in. Instead, I stare at her, the juvenile voice in my head grilling me: *Do my pants match my shirt? Do I have a booger in my nose?*

"Right." Mrs. Cullen smiles and looks down after my silence. "I suppose that's why I'm here."

I THINK I was destined to teach science. I was born July 20, 1969, the day men first walked on the moon. While my father sat watching news reports of the lunar landing on the waiting room television, a surgeon delivered me from my dying mother, who had a blood clot in her lung. After that, my dad raised my sister and me alone. I came into this world as my mother left it, as Neil Armstrong stepped onto the chalky surface of a *new* world and said, "That's one small step for man. One giant leap for mankind."

Armstrong later claimed that what he actually said was: ". . . one small step for *a* man . . ." This upset some people because that article *a* seemed to diminish what was a vast human endeavor. But I always believed that *a* man made more sense. If Armstrong had meant *man* in the broader sense, he would've in essence been saying, *That's one small step for mankind, one giant leap for . . . mankind.*

Few people remember what was said by the second man to walk on the moon, my hero, Buzz Aldrin.

"Beautiful view," said Buzz.

To which Armstrong replied, "Isn't that something? Magnificent sight out here."

Then Buzz uttered the two words which still give me goose bumps, expressing the paradoxical nature of what it is to grasp humankind's miraculous and unlikely existence on a life-giving rock in the exurbs of a cold, hard universe.

"Magnificent desolation."

"WE DON'T BELIEVE in that," Jacob Cullen said the first week of class. He was explaining why he couldn't do the assignment on plant life cycles. (It was nothing controversial: photosynthesis, vascular vs. nonvascular structure, that sort of thing.)

"You don't believe in plants?" I said.

"Sex," Jacob said. He was a slight twelve-year-old with intelligent eyes and a constant smirk. From what I gathered, he had recently moved to our school and hadn't made friends yet. I was predisposed to like him, the way I tend to like any kid who doesn't quite fit in.

"You . . . don't believe in sex?" I asked.

"You're not allowed to teach it to me."

"I am most assuredly *not* teaching you about sex, Jacob."

"You said sperm."

I explained that the lesson was about *angiosperms* and *gymnosperms*, plants that reproduce using flowers and fruit versus plants that use cones.

"We don't believe in that," Jacob said. "God made the plants."

This became a pattern. Whatever I taught—cell structure, heredity, geology—Jacob Cullen would approach my desk after class. "We don't believe in that."

"You don't believe in rocks?"

"You said some rocks are four billion years old. How is that possible when the Earth is only six thousand years old."

My unit on the moon and tides was the last straw.

I looked up to see Jacob at my desk. "What don't you believe in now, Jacob? The moon? Tides?"

"God hung the moon," Jacob said. "And the moon landing was faked."

This is when I had finally had enough. That night I emailed Jacob's parents.

AND NOW? WELL, whatever clever intercession I had planned on behalf of science has fled my addled mind. I can't stop staring at Abigail Cullen, her jet-black hair tied back tight against that smooth, elegant forehead.

"Please, have a seat," I say, and my hands shake as I gesture to a student's desk. "Is Mr. Cullen coming?"

"Jacob's dad is playing golf," she says. Then she clears her throat. "We recently got divorced."

"Ah. I'm sorry," I say, then blurt out, "Me, too. Divorced, I mean. Not golfing. Clearly." I indicate the room around us, which another sweep of my hand is meant to reveal is obviously not a golf course but a seventh grade classroom. So suave, so clever. Sweat breaks on my forehead. What's the matter with me?

I might also have corrected that *recently* when mentioning my own divorce. Anya left eight years ago. I have not attempted to date anyone since. I meant to. But human beings like me, it turns out, are as subject to Newton's First Law of Motion—that a body at rest will remain at rest unless an outside force acts upon it—as is anything else. And it's surprising how few outside forces are lining up to act upon a fifty-year-old middle school science teacher.

Re: my divorce, another saying pops into my head, *It feels like yesterday,* which conveys nicely how the memory of a distant event somehow is sharper than one might expect given the passage of time. But I would argue that Anya's leaving is *not* like that for me. The particular day my wife left feels *exactly* like it was eight years ago. In that I can't really remember it with any real clarity. I know we talked, the last of a conversation we'd been having for a month. I remember being surprised that she was all packed. But I can't conjure a single image of her car leaving, or the weather, or what either of us was wearing. It is the days and weeks and years preceding her departure which feel like yesterday to me, close enough to touch, to breathe. I walk into the living room after work and I am stunned to not feel her there, to not see her curled up on the couch, legs folded beneath her, a cup of tea on the table. I open the garage door and wonder where her car went. I slide the closet door open and fully expect to see her coats and blouses, her work slacks draped neatly over plastic hangers.

Why did Anya leave? Some problems don't have easy answers. We didn't fight. We liked going on hikes together and playing cribbage and trying new restaurants. I believe we were fairly well-suited. There were things she said before she left, about wanting to find herself and about passion and about the brevity of life, but I always felt like the things she *didn't* say were equally as important. Our inability to have children. The death of her mother back in Minsk. And a quality in me that Anya called "your distance," a description—and one that I cannot argue—suggesting that I could be emotionally unreachable at times.

I wish I could argue that, but in truth I have always had difficulty expressing emotion. The more intense the feeling, the harder it has always been for me to talk about, i.e., growing up without a mother, or my father's alcohol-fueled dementia. I'm certain that I do repress things, as Anya said, but as I responded to her: I certainly don't do it consciously. Or intentionally. What can you do when someone's complaint about you is so elemental? That you are too tall. That your eyes are too blue.

My sister is just as stoic in her bearing. We are not criers or huggers. When I told her that Anya had left, my sister considered what I'd said for a moment and then asked, "Will you be selling the house, Edward? I know a good agent."

I have always been Edward. As a baby, Edward, as a six-year-old, Edward, as a college freshman, Edward, as a teacher, Edward. Only Anya ever called me Eddie. From our first date—outdoor symphony concert with fireworks—after which I walked Anya home and she kissed me, she teased me about how many dates it might have taken for *Eddie* to kiss *Anya*. Twenty? Forty? I put the over/under at six.

"Goodbye, Eddie," she said that first day, after she kissed me. She said the exact same thing nine years later, when, without the kiss, she left for good. "Goodbye, Eddie."

Maybe this is why, in my classroom now, after my inane chatter about golf and divorce, I stick out my hand and officially introduce myself to Abigail Cullen this way: "I'm Eddie Wells. It's nice to meet you."

"Abigail Cullen," she says. And a jolt of electricity goes through my arm as our hands touch. Seriously, what is this? A kind of temporary insanity? Some latent adolescent hormone stored up in my body somewhere? She's just a human being, her hand just a hand, her skin just skin. Why is my face flushed? Why is my palm suddenly damp with sweat as I gesture toward a seventh grader's desk.

And why does my voice crack when I ask her, "Can I get you something?"

Abigail Cullen looks around. "Like . . . what?"

This is a fair question. We are in a science classroom, not a martini lounge. I honestly do not know what's the matter with me. I reach for a chemistry beaker. "Liquid volcano?"

EVERY TEACHER FINDS it necessary to deal with fundamentalists from time to time. Especially science teachers. I have had parents request that I teach intelligent design or creationism alongside what they call the "*theory* of evolution." Other parents get agitated if I go anywhere near reproduction. But try teaching biology without the concept of procreation. You simply can't. Our seventh grade curriculum, because it is so general, is about as inoffensive as you can get, but that doesn't stop some parents from being suspicious of my motives, as if I'm trying to indoctrinate their children with, I don't know, socialism, or paganism, or pornography.

I try to be patient, but to be honest, sometimes it gets to me.

If a parent brings up such concerns during conferences, I have a respectful speech I give about science and religion. I think having people see you as a human is key to these engagements, so I always talk about being a shy kid myself when I was their child's age, how science was my favorite subject, how I was born the day men landed on the moon. Then I tell them an anecdote about my hero. "Do you know the first thing Buzz Aldrin did when he landed on the moon in 1969? He took communion. You see, he believed science and religion complemented one another, because both seek to understand the great mysteries of existence—one through hypothesis and experimentation, the other through parable and metaphor."

It usually softens the parents but every once in a while this strategy backfires and makes everything worse. "The Bible is *not* metaphor," an angry father said to me once. "It is the absolute word of God."

I smiled. "But you have to admit, even Jesus spoke in parables."

"Jesus spoke in truth," the man said. "And as far as I'm concerned, you and your science class are part of Satan's PR department."

How do you respond to *that*?

This may be another reason why Buzz Aldrin is my hero. He spent much of his life being harassed by conspiracy theorists. In 2002, one of them was haranguing him outside a hotel, insisting the moon landing was faked, and that Buzz should confess to it. Several times, Buzz asked the man to leave him alone. He turned away repeatedly, but the man kept hounding him, yelling at his back, "Liar! Coward!"

I have watched the video of what happens next maybe a dozen times: the seventy-two-year-old former astronaut keeps turning his back on the man until finally he can't take it anymore. He stops, faces him, and throws a compact punch into the lunatic's jaw. This is the moment Buzz Aldrin became the hero of science teachers everywhere, the patron saint of *Not-taking-any-more-of-this-bullshit.*

"LET ME START by saying that I am not trying to demean anyone's faith," I tell Mrs. Cullen. "What I'd like Jacob to learn is the difference between *belief* and *knowledge*."

But I am lost in her eyes. I clear my throat. "For instance, you could choose to not believe in gravity, but it won't change what happens when you step off a curb, right? It is the same with evolution. Or climate change. These are not opinions to be retweeted or given thumbs-up, but complex series of processes that have been widely observed and studied, proven over decades and centuries through scientific method—whether a certain church or politician agrees with them or not."

She cocks her head as if she's not quite following. I think of giving her the Buzz Aldrin speech, but instead, I try another tack.

"That's why I don't believe it's wise, or fair, to limit a child to the knowledge that was available two thousand years ago," I say, "just as it wouldn't be right if Jacob got an infection to give him frankincense because that was the only medicine available in biblical times. Does that make sense?"

That's when I see the Cullen smirk on Jacob's mother's face. "Frankincense," she says.

And this is when all hope drains from my body.

This is no longer simply about a boy and his religious parents.

This is about what's wrong with our whole fractured and digitized country, the divisions created by people who cherry-pick facts, or who ignore them altogether, who choose for their reality paranoid videos fed by social media algorithms, the cynical tools of the greedy and lazy, the willfully ignorant.

And what I do next is unlike me.

I plead. "Ms. Cullen," I say, leaning forward. "Abigail. I'm sorry to be so familiar, but if two intelligent people like us can't get past these medieval fears and superstitions, past centuries of bigotry and backward thinking, what chance does humanity really have? I mean, with the serious threats that we all face—real, existential threats—we can't be wasting our time arguing over whether God made plants, or whether the moon landing was real!"

At this, Abigail Cullen bursts into laughter. "Did he say the moon landing wasn't real? Mr. Wells, I think my son is having some fun at your expense. We are not religious. At all. Jacob hasn't been to church since he was baptized. He is, however, about to get crucified." She smiles. "Metaphorically, I mean."

APPARENTLY, JACOB HAS told his parents that he is failing science because his teacher is a well-known drunk. Mr. Wells forgets to assign readings and doesn't grade tests. He sits at his desk, often asleep, or hungover. He doesn't allow people to ask questions and will not see students after school. He assigns readings and gives tests that don't even correspond to the homework. He leaves early every day to go to the bar. Because of his problems, in fact, everyone in class is failing.

"Everyone?" I ask. "Well, that's quite a curve."

"Oh yes. It's an open secret," Mrs. Cullen says. "No one says anything about it, though."

"And why is that?"

Mrs. Cullen leans in herself, as if confiding a juicy bit of gossip. "Apparently, Mr. Wells was in a terrible accident last year."

"An accident!" I almost admire Jacob's creativity. I hope he's doing better in English than in science.

"Oh yes. His wife and children were killed," she says. "So. He drinks to forget."

"Sure. Can I ask, How many children?"

"Two."

"Ah yes," I say. "The twins. Hope and Reason."

She laughs and shakes her head. "I am sorry, Mr. Wells. Since the divorce, and the move, he's been acting out like this. I found out earlier that he told his P.E. teacher that he can't play floor hockey because he has lupus."

"In his defense, it is floor hockey."

We are still laughing when Mr. Cullen comes in.

"What's so funny?" he asks. He is tall and balding, thick like a former football player. He is still wearing his golf clothes. His face is flushed and I suspect he has been drinking, working up his anger, which is likely made worse by seeing me laughing with his ex-wife.

He strides across the classroom toward me. "I don't care what happened to you," he says, "you have no right to take it out on these kids."

"Mike, calm down—" Mrs. Cullen rises.

"I'm not gonna calm down!" He is coming around my desk.

I rise, too, hands in front of me in a peaceful gesture. "It seems there's been a misunderstanding."

"Mike," Mrs. Cullen says. "Jacob is pretending to be some kind of fundamentalist. He says he doesn't believe in science. He told his teacher the moon landing was faked."

Mike Cullen looks confused. He is standing right next to me. "So what." He smells like beer. "The moon landing *was* fake," he says. "I saw a video on it. They couldn't have flown through the Van Allen radiation belt without getting—"

I don't even remember throwing the punch.

AFTERWARD, ABIGAIL INSISTS on driving me to the emergency room, even though I could easily drive myself. The injury looks worse than it is—a broken zygomatic arch, the narrow piece of cheekbone between the jaw and the ear. It will be a quick fix, maxillofacial surgery, like popping the dent out of an old car.

The whole thing sobers Mr. Cullen up rather quickly. I could be fired, of course, if my principal found out I took a swing at a parent, but luckily, my weak blow missed, and Mr. Cullen feels so badly for the damage his resulting counterpunch caused that he agrees not to file a complaint against me.

"Thank you," I say. "I honestly don't know what got into me."

"I really am sorry," Mr. Cullen says as I press paper towels against my bleeding nose.

"No, it's my fault," I say. "I can't believe I lost it like that."

"I can," says Abigail, shooting a look at her ex-husband.

But before we leave for the hospital, I feel compelled to tell Mr. Cullen one thing. "Listen," I say. "While it's true that lengthy exposure to the Van Allen belt could theoretically cause a human being to suffer health issues, simply flying through on a spaceship is harmless and would expose you to roughly the same amount of radiation as an X-ray—like the one I'm about to get."

He stares at me for a long time. "Okay," he says finally.

"I'm so humiliated," I tell Abigail on the drive to the hospital.

"I go fifty years without taking a swing at anyone and then I lose it over the Van Allen radiation belt?"

She smiles. "It's okay. Mike can be an ass. And he was drunk. I kind of wish you had better aim."

I promise her I will train harder for my next defense of the scientific method.

Later, with a bottle of pain pills in my pocket and my surgery scheduled for later in the week, Abigail drives me back to the school. We have a nice talk on the drive, about kids and science and the pain of divorce. *Ask her out,* my internal voice says. Of course, this is the same hormonal voice that had me trying to punch someone two hours earlier, so the adult voice, the careful voice, reminds me that asking out a parent would be as inappropriate as the near-punch I almost landed.

I put the over/under on me asking out Abigail Cullen at *not happening.*

But then, sitting in the parking lot, in the leather passenger seat of her white SUV, I find myself thinking about Buzz again. About Anya and about passion and about the brevity of life.

"Abigail," I say, "I hope this isn't inappropriate, but I wonder, would you like to have lunch with me tomorrow?"

She looks at me, then at the school. "In there?"

Ah, right. How stupid of me. It is Thursday. A school night. "Right," I say. "Yes, tomorrow, I *will* be eating lunch in the teachers' lounge. I guess the weekend would make more sense for such a thing."

She smiles kindly. And whatever teenage hormones I'm feeling are immediately familiar with this particular smile. The gentle letdown. She explains that her divorce is still fresh, that she is trying to break a pattern of "fixing one problem with another," and that, right now, her kids need her attention. "I'm not really ready for anything . . ."

She doesn't say the word, but we both know it: romantic.

But then she surprises me by reaching over and taking my hand. "But it's so nice that you asked. Thank you. And actually, I could use a friend. Maybe we could, I don't know, go on a walk sometime."

"As it turns out," I say, "I am an accomplished walker."

After my surgery we agree to meet at the botanical garden at Manito Park. The sting of *I could use a friend* has largely worn off and I am very glad to be out walking with her. I am the one who suggests she bring Jacob, so that he can do an extra credit assignment on plant reproduction. Abigail tells me I look good, that the swelling has gone down, that I look like myself again. I explain how I brought my X-rays to class and how it turned out to be one of those rare expansive teaching moments; looking at pictures of my skull, a few of the students making the cognitive leap that they, too, were a collection of bones that a scientist might one day study.

Abigail tells me another good thing has come out of our meeting: her ex-husband has agreed to see a therapist about his temper. She's glad for the kids, she says, especially Jacob.

As if on cue, he yells, "Angiosperm?" I look down to where he is examining the bursting crimson leaf of a Japanese maple. "That's right, Jacob," I say. "Very good." His mother and I are standing above him, on a wooden footbridge, life everywhere around us in the dappled sunlight.

"Magnificent," I say, "isn't it?"

Drafting

AFTERWARD, SHE DROVE—PAST BARS, restaurants, coffee shops, the library. She crossed the river, back and forth. She drove past her apartment in Brownes and finally she parked outside the Baby Bar, and that's when she decided to call Boone. She fingered the screen but before she could call him the phone buzzed and the word Mom flashed. She let it go to voicemail.

She had erased Boone's contact information in a fit almost a year ago—but she had the number memorized. Two rings.

"Hey there," he said. "Long time no fuck."

"I need to see you," she said.

"I like to hear *that*."

Then she told him.

"Ah shit," Boone said.

He met her at the Baby Bar. He hugged her and she lost her breath when his arms roped around her.

They ordered. Beers came but when he reached for his wallet, he came up empty. "Ah shit, Myra."

"It's okay," she said, "I got it."

She paid with a ten and they took their cans of Rainier to a booth. The Baby Bar was empty and dark. She loved the place: best juke in town.

"Look, whatever the doctors say, do it," he said. "Just do your fuckin' treatment, whatever it takes. When it's over, me and you, we'll go on a trip."

"Go where?"

"America."

"We're in America, Boone."

"You know what I mean. We'll just go."

"What about Carla?"

"I really think it should just be the two of us."

She laughed. "You know what I mean."

"This has got nothing to do with Carla."

"You and I going on a trip has nothing to do with your wife?"

"Not this time."

Boone's hair was long again, curly in front, the way she liked it. He ran his hand through it, pushed it back, but it fell forward over his eyes.

"I always liked your hair like that."

"Shit." He riffled his hair again. "I'm an old shoe."

She smiled. "What does that mean?"

"Most of what I say don't mean anything." He waved for another beer, then seemed to remember he didn't have any money.

"It's okay," she said. "I got it."

He was twelve years older than her, thirty-six. His birthday was April 9. His favorite food was tacos. He still rode a skate-board. He worked in construction for his uncle, who was a con-crete finisher; Boone built the wooden forms. He said that in an earlier time he would've made his living as "an outdoorsman," but it seemed to Myra that his idea of being outdoors was to buy a case of beer, drive into the woods, build a fire and sleep in his car.

He had been on-and-off with Carla for a decade. They had a little boy together, Dylan. Boone and Carla happened to be off, or so he said, when he met Myra in a bar almost four years ago. That night, she couldn't look away from him. He had thick brows and a dent above his cheek from a fight he didn't remember. People always said he looked like a younger, scruffier version of a famous actor but they could never come up with the name, even though it was obvious to her. After they broke up, she watched Clive Owen movies and wondered if two people could look more alike and be more different.

"Isn't there a good kind and a bad kind?" he asked her now.

"Yes," she said, but that was all she said about it.

"Shit, Myra. I'm sorry." He looked down at the beer can again. He seemed to see something in the beer, her future maybe.

"Are you high, Boone?"

"Oh yeah."

THE SURGEON SEEMED pleased with himself.

THE SECOND WEEK of radiation, she didn't think it would be so bad, dying.

SHE WOKE NEXT to the toilet. She couldn't breathe. Everything was on fire. Spinning. She clutched at her hair and it came out in a fistful. She retched fire, like lava through her esophagus. Each jagged breath was a prayer: *please don't puke; please don't puke*.

Her stomach buckled but nothing came up. She gagged and a

dribble of bile fell from her lip. She spat. Panted. Spat. Panted. One time with Boone she'd had a bad reaction to shrooms and vodka and had been up all night, vomiting, but that was like a warm bath compared to this.

"Myra?" Her mother stood in the doorway.

She panted over the toilet. Her mother set a glass of water on the floor. "Thank you."

Her mother's eyes drifted to the clump of hair on the floor. "There's a nurse on twenty-four hours. I can call."

"I'm fine." She sipped at the water, but it was like lighter fluid going down. Her mom set something else on the ground next to her. Her phone.

"You left this upstairs." On the screen it said Message and Boone's phone number.

"Myra, I hope you're not getting back into it with him—"

"Mom—"

"Do you remember how unhealthy that whole time was for you—"

"Of course I do. I just wanted to tell someone. He's checking to see how the surgery went."

She waited until her mother went back to bed to open the message. Before this, the last time she'd heard from Boone was more than a year ago, when she'd texted to tell him she'd gotten into law school, and he texted back a blurry picture of his dick. He'd typed, Your witness counsler, misspelling counselor so badly it took her a minute to get the joke. When they were together, he had teased her about wanting to be a lawyer. He said he was using her, *not* for sex, but for future legal representation.

Now, lying on the floor sick, she opened the new text. It was a blurry picture of his ass. He'd written, thinkin of u.

THE LAST TREATMENT nearly wiped her out. She slept for two days afterward. When she woke, she imagined the terrible heartburn was the cancer itself, even though she knew better. But it was helpful to have some feeling—this burning—to think of as the cancer. It hurt more than she could imagine was possible, like someone pulling a hot wire brush up and down her esophagus. She wanted water, but water made it worse. She wanted milk, but milk made it worse. This is cancer, this is love, this is everything: *it makes it worse.*

She slept in the basement of her parents' house. She'd given up her apartment downtown right after she was diagnosed. Her dad must have taken care of the lease because she never heard from the landlord. This was her father's way, the old litigator working behind the scenes—he would deal with her surgeon, her oncologist, her landlord, her supervisor at the law firm where she'd worked as a paralegal, her advisor at Gonzaga. All taken care of. This was her dad's way: take care of everything but her.

While her parents were both at their offices Myra went upstairs and watched TV, but by mid-afternoon she'd make her way back downstairs, into the guest room. The rest of the night she'd pretend to sleep. She'd hear her mother's footsteps on the carpeted staircase and then in the doorway, and she'd breathe heavily in the dark until her mother went back upstairs. Then she'd hear her father come home, talk to Myra's mother and the rest of the evening would be noises from upstairs: phone ringing, doorbell, dinner dishes, TV, the creak of her father's shoes. Morning and her mother's light steps on the stairs again.

"Myra?"

"Mmm."

"I made a quiche. Are you hungry?"

"No."

"You should eat."

"I'll have some cereal later."

Her mother came over, sat on the bed, and put her hand on Myra's forehead. Myra puffed out a little laugh. "Are you checking to see if I have a fever? Think I should stay home from school?"

Her mother laughed, too, and then covered her mouth. "Oh baby," she said, her voice cracking into tears, "I don't know what else to do."

"I know, Mom." Myra sat up. She reached over and put her hand on her mother's forehead. "I don't know what to do either."

MYRA TRIED ON clothes but nothing fit right. She settled on a pair of striped tights. Her hip bones jutted like holstered guns. Her boobs were empty wind socks. She fingered the scar. She put on a sports bra and pulled a dress over the tights, and a sweater over the dress and a jacket over the sweater. If she just kept layering maybe she could build a whole person. Her sister had given her a reddish-brown wig, as close to her own color as she could find. She put it on. She looked like a pencil with an eraser cap.

The heartburn had cooled to a hard, metallic thing in her throat. Nothing tasted right; she was swallowing foil. This was the cancer now: a cold blade from tongue to lung.

She came upstairs and saw the pills her mother had left out for her. She took them with orange juice and felt them slide by the icy knife. She poured herself a bowl of cereal. It seemed like all she'd eaten for two months was cereal.

Her father came in straightening his tie. "You feeling better?"

"I think so," she lied.

"Well, you look good," he lied.

"Thanks, I feel good," she lied.

"I made a lunch for you," her mother said. As if to prove that here, finally, was some truth, she held up a sack lunch. "A sandwich." Like Myra was nine.

"Thanks, Mom. I'll put it in my cubby with my mittens."

Her mom laughed. "Are you going out today?"

"No."

She watched her parents leave for their separate offices. One day she overheard her mother say that "Myra's sickness" had aged her ten years. When she was sure their cars had pulled away, she texted Boone.

The rest of the morning she watched TV. *The View. Family Feud.* It was crazy—if you died, these shows would just keep going. New hosts. New commercials. New credits. The mail would come just like yesterday.

Her phone buzzed. It was a text from Boone. It read: guess who and contained a picture of what she finally figured out was his blue-jeaned crotch.

Myra got up quickly and felt dizzy. She sat down, took a deep breath and stood again. She felt something else in her stomach— anticipation.

HE WAS DRIVING a beat-up 1970s El Camino, a car with a pickup bed. She slid in. She liked the feel of the cracked bench seat. She liked the old-school window crank and she put the window down and up and down again. "I like this!" she said.

"*And* . . . it plays cassettes," Boone said. "I had to scrounge some old tapes from my brother." He reached in a box between them and held up a few: Pearl Jam, Blind Melon, Gin Blossoms, Sting. It was a 1993 time warp. He laughed. "I fuckin' hate Sting."

He drove them west on I-90, toward Seattle. They came out of the valley and up Sunset Hill, trees giving way to hunks of basalt jutting from wheat fields. She reached down and felt her hip bones again. She'd packed only a couple of things. Another dress and a pair of tights. Toothbrush. Makeup. Antinausea medicine. At the last minute she'd grabbed the lunch her mother made.

A little lake appeared out her window. Right next to the freeway. There was only one house on it, a rancher built on rocks above the shore. "You think those people own that lake? Their own lake? How wild would that be?"

"That would be fucked-up," Boone said.

"I think it would be peaceful."

"Peaceful. Fucked-up. Same thing."

"Peaceful and fucked-up are not synonyms."

"Cinnamon?"

She laughed. "You're stoned."

"Asked and answered, your honor."

He had a six-pack of Miller High Life at his feet, and he offered her a can. She shook her head. He opened it, took a swig and put it between his legs.

She leaned back, her head on the bench seat. She closed her eyes. She could feel the freeway beneath them, rolling away, like they were gathering it up and spitting it out behind them. The door didn't quite seal right and there was a hiss of wind at her temple. Miles passed.

She opened her eyes. They were driving past Sprague Lake, a big acidic-looking lake with basalt boulders and no trees around it. It looked like some mysterious Scottish loch. Boone had opened another beer. He offered her a drink.

"What did you tell Carla?"

"I said"—he took a swig of beer—"so long, sucker!"

THE CAR BEGAN to overheat. They were almost to the Columbia River gorge overlook, where Boone said he wanted to stop anyway. "I think we can make it."

As it got hotter, the car started making a kind of grinding noise. To cover the sound he cranked the volume on the Sting cassette. Little wisps of smoke came from under the hood.

"Ooh, I kinda like this one." He started singing, "*I'll have the fish and chips, man. A bottle of Dewar's and some oats and chives.*"

She fell against the car door. "Those aren't even close to the lyrics."

He had this way of laughing, eyes going slack and one corner of his mouth rising. Like nothing in the world was worth taking seriously. "Sting doesn't sing real words," he said. "He just makes noises."

She opened the tape case and unfolded the liner notes to read the lyrics: "*There's a bloodless moon where the oceans died.*"

"That's what I said."

She fell forward, and when she could talk: "You said oats . . . and . . . and . . . chives." It hurt her chest to laugh this hard. She thought: fuck you, knife.

"And Dewar's. You forgot the Dewar's."

THEY SAT ON a boulder overlooking the canyon and far below, the massive slate-colored Columbia. The river snaked below cliffs, twisting toward Oregon, toward the bloodless moon where oceans die. They ate the lunch Myra's mom had packed.

He offered her a pull on his beer. Then he put his arm around her.

"Boone, I don't know . . . I don't think we should . . . I mean, I don't even know if I can . . . and . . . and Carla."

"Hey, I ain't trying to fuck you. I'm just putting my arm around you. Trust me, you'll know when I'm trying to fuck you."

"Yeah. How?"

"Well, for one, it will involve my dick."

"Wow. Sounds dreamy."

He squeezed her shoulder. "I'm just doing *this*. This is okay, right?"

"Yes." She leaned her head on his shoulder. "It's okay."

She had a geology teacher once who told her to think about geology as the science of time. This mountain range, this river gorge—they were clocks. The whole world was a clock face, with a gliding osprey rising on a secondhand updraft, as if being called to heaven.

"I'll have the fish and chips, man," she said.

SIX CARS IN the overlook parking lot, three with Washington plates, an Oregon, an Iowa and a Montana. "See, America," Boone said. He had the hood up, and eventually a trucker came over with radiator sealant and a few extra gallons of antifreeze.

Boone paid the man in home-grown weed. A fuzzy bud from a

freezer bag full of them in a black backpack behind his seat. The only thing he'd packed.

And just like that they were back on the road, sun over the river gorge. Boone had finished most of his six-pack and so Myra volunteered to drive. She knew he couldn't afford another DUI. She wrestled with the wheel; the car pulled hard to the right.

"Yeah, sorry. Alignment's for shit." Boone flicked his cigarette ashes out the open passenger window. "Dude warned me that it was in rough shape. But what do you expect for eight hundred bucks? It's a classic."

Myra's phone kept buzzing. Her mom must've come home for lunch. And she would have called her dad, her sister. All of them calling now.

Her iPhone vibrated on the seat between them. "Can you turn that off for me?"

He swept it up and tossed it out the window.

"Boone!"

He opened his hand. The phone was still in it.

She looked down at the screen. The words Missed Call and Mom.

"Do it," she whispered.

His eyebrows. Jesus, those thick black brows. They rose just a fraction of an inch, his eyes widening—that dark mischievous thing he could pull off with nothing but his eyes. He held the button down until the phone went off, Mom the last thing she saw on the screen.

"That's an expensive phone," he said. "I ain't throwin' it away. Your parents hate me enough."

She used to bait him sometimes—play against their roles, usually after he called her rich girl or counselor, or your honor, or genius or whatever. He set the phone down again on the bench seat between them, facedown so she couldn't see the screen. Then he took a drink of his beer and looked out at the steak-knife peaks of the Cascade Mountains.

"Pussy," she said quietly.

He swept her phone up again and this time it went right out the open window.

THEY GOT TO Seattle around seven. He had her drive south on I-5, then take the bridge into West Seattle. But they got lost trying to find his buddy's house. "It's by a community college," he said.

"That's helpful," she said.

Boone's flip phone was dead, so he couldn't call his friend. They tried to find a pay phone but there didn't seem to be one anywhere.

They finally found one outside a convenience store, but Boone remembered that his friend's cell number was on his dead phone. "Shit." He sat outside the store asking everyone who pulled up if they had the right kind of phone charger, but no one did. Myra watched him sit on the hood of the car, drinking a beer, as happy as if he were on a deck chair on that little private lake. Maybe that was why she'd wanted to see him after she got sick, that quality. No one could make more of a disaster than Boone.

Finally, a girl in a Subaru Outback had the right car charger for Boone's phone. Boone climbed in her car while they charged it up. Myra watched them talk. The girl played with her hair and chewed her lip. Boone told some story and the girl put her hand on his arm and laughed. Myra thought it was like watching herself four years ago. The girl in the Subaru wanted to sleep with him. Girls always wanted to sleep with Boone. He had that quality.

In the girl's car, Boone leaned forward, made his call with the phone still plugged in, gestured, and then closed his crappy old flip phone. He nodded thanks to the girl and started to get out of the car, but the girl said something, and he stopped. They talked for another minute. Boone shook his head and gave that easy smile of his, and the girl said something else. Then she handed over her car charger. He shook his head, tried to say no, but she wouldn't hear of it, and he nodded his thanks again and took it.

He walked around the car and climbed back in the El Camino. Myra glanced over at the girl in the Subaru—thick brown hair and lots of makeup, no more than twenty. Myra tried to look unthreatening, like Boone's sister or something; because she didn't feel threatening, not like she used to, when she would get bent out of shape about Boone sleeping with every other girl in Spokane. He wasn't hers. He wasn't Carla's either. How strange, this desire to possess people. Myra thought about tipping her wig, showing her bald scalp. But the girl had already looked away.

"We're in business! Tony lives just a few blocks from here. I knew we were close." He held up the car phone charger. "What am I gonna do with this?" Then he cracked the last beer. "Gonna be some earthshakin' tonight."

BOONE'S FRIEND TONY had also been a concrete worker, but he'd moved back to Seattle, gotten married, gone to trade school and was getting certified as a journeyman carpenter. They lived in a duplex.

Myra thought the carpenter's wife was beautiful: tall, blond and full-figured, with bright red cheeks. She didn't catch her name.

"Couch okay?" Tony asked.

"Okay for *you*," Boone said. "Fuckin' A, I didn't teach you nothing about entertaining, man? You always give the guests the bed."

The carpenter grinned. "How about I give the guest a boot up his lazy ass."

Boone gave the carpenter's blond wife his most charming smile. "Thank you for your hospitality. Myra here will sleep on your very comfy sofa. Maybe you can bring me a sleeping bag and I'll crash on the floor?"

The wife went to get a sleeping bag.

Boone hit Tony in the shoulder with the heel of his hand. "Dude, she's fuckin' awesome. How long you been married?"

"Year and a half." He lowered his voice, chewed his lip. "She miscarried."

"Aw right." Boone seemed to recall his friend's hasty wedding. "I forgot about that . . . right. Shit."

THE CARPENTER AND his wife had four plastic chairs around a Formica kitchen table. They sat with kitchen glasses of red wine, all but the wife, who apparently didn't drink. She kept looking sideways at her husband.

Myra sipped at the wine, but it tasted metallic and bitter.

"Once you get the van, you could maybe get some jobs over here," Tony said to Boone. "Pay's better. I could probably hook you up." His wife cleared her throat.

"I mostly want the van for camping," Boone said. "But yeah, maybe."

BOONE AND THE carpenter went to pick up the van.

The wife sighed deeply and looked at Myra across the Formica. "Look, this might not be my place."

Myra wondered if Tony's wife knew Carla. They were probably friends.

The wife sighed again. "I just want to say, I know what you're going through. I was drinking by the time I was twelve and was using at fifteen. This disease stalks you. It becomes you, right? And you think you're keeping it together . . . but you aren't. You get to a place where you can't enjoy life anymore. Not like other people do. It's messed up."

Myra stared across at the carpenter's wife. She was so pretty. Her cheeks seemed to have little bulbs in them, and her eyes were bursts of blue and green; she was so *alive*. Myra had never wanted to kiss a girl before, but she imagined kissing the carpenter's wife, drawing her healthy breath from those big apple cheeks.

"What are you on?" the wife asked.

Myra opened her mouth to say she wasn't a junkie, but a little noise came out, like a laugh, or a whimper.

"Look, I'm not judging you," the wife said. "I just wanted you to know . . . if you want to go to a meeting, or just talk, I'm here."

"Thank you," Myra said.

"The first thing is to admit that you're powerless over it."

Myra smiled. "Oh, I feel that."

"MYRA? YOU AWAKE?"

She rolled over.

Boone was sitting up in his sleeping bag. "I've been meaning to ask. Are you gonna go back to law school?"

"Yeah. I hope so."

"You should."

The house was quiet.

"Your mom called me," he said.

"Oh."

"I told her you were fine. I said we'd be back tomorrow."

"Will we?" she asked. It was dark and she couldn't see his face, but she imagined it, those devilish eyes doing the caring thing. That's what had gotten her. At first, it had been the dark eyes that drew her in—the adventure, some negation of the way people saw her: the smart, careful, responsible one—but once she'd seen those other eyes of his, that's when she got hooked.

"I should get back, too," he said. "I'm supposed to pick Dylan up after preschool. Carla's gotta work." And then a laugh. "He lost a tooth."

"Did he?" Sure, Dylan was old enough to lose teeth. Of course he was. "Sure. We should get back."

"Cool." Boone put his head back down.

She kept staring at him, a lump on the floor. "Thank you, Boone."

From the floor, he gave her the thumbs-up sign.

IN THE MORNING, the men walked around the van that Boone had bought. They were drinking Bloody Marys. Myra folded up the blankets and put them on the couch. She watched through the front window as Boone danced around the van. She tried to see him dispassionately, like a stranger: the floppy long hair, the Vans, the leather jacket. It would not end well, this look; he was straining at the very edge of it now, flecks of gray in that bushy hair. Skate-dude was not a good look to take into your forties, fifties, sixties.

The carpenter's wife came in behind Myra and handed her a cup of coffee. "God, I am so, so sorry for what I said," she said. "Tony told me——"

"It's fine."

"No, I can't believe I thought you were——" She covered her mouth. "It was so wrong of me."

"I should have corrected you." Myra turned and faced the carpenter's wife, looked into those blue-green eyes, arched in the center, warm and wet at the corners. "As soon as you say that word, people look at you like you're a ghost. They tell you how their mother survived breast cancer or how their friend had it and now she's fine or now she's dead, or I don't know." Myra felt herself run out of steam. "I just . . . I get tired."

"No. I totally understand." The wife smiled generously. "I didn't even know women so young got it."

It was the same thing Myra had said to her oncologist. It's becoming more common, he'd told her, or more commonly diagnosed anyway. And then he told her the rest: the aggressiveness, and even if you beat it, low fertility rate, high rate of reoccurrence, early menopause, *bloodless moon where the oceans die.*

The carpenter's wife swallowed hard and put her hand on Myra's arm. "Can I ask . . . the prognosis?"

"Good, I think," Myra said, more for the carpenter's wife than because she knew that to be the case. Even though it was small and localized, the surgeon had wanted to do a full mastectomy, but Myra had talked her into just taking the lump, what the doctors euphemistically called *breast-conserving* surgery. "It'll be a few weeks or maybe months before they know. And they have other options." More arrows in our quiver, as her oncologist said.

The carpenter's wife opened her mouth to say something but stopped.

Myra smiled. "You were going to tell me that your sister had a mastectomy and now she's fine."

"My sister-in-law! I'm sorry."

They both laughed.

And suddenly the woman pulled her into a hug. It was jarring, and she almost spilled her coffee. But she felt this other body through her layers of clothes, felt her arms, her heavy boobs, her warmth, and she breathed in the woman's shampoo and felt dizzy. She cried into the woman's shoulder.

BOONE HAD APPARENTLY paid for half of the van using his deceased stepmother's prescription drugs. The van had no license plates. The back had nothing in it, just the metal ribbed floorboards covered with awful stains; Boone said the owner had used it to haul butchered meat. It was gray and white and rust-colored and dented and pocked like it had been in a hailstorm. Boone made a phony temporary license plate by tracing the carpenter's plate with a Sharpie. He taped it to the window.

"There," he said.

In front of the carpenter's house, they hugged goodbye. The wife put her warm hand against Myra's cheek. "Come back sometime."

Myra said she would.

It was four and a half hours from Seattle to Spokane. "I'd let you drive the van, but it doesn't have heat," Boone said.

So she drove the El Camino and they left West Seattle in the rain, the city falling away into a blur of suburbs and lakes and then the sudden tree-blanketed mountains. Myra drove behind the van, wrestling with the El Camino's bad alignment, listening to Sting sing about kingdoms turning to sand, and suddenly he seemed like the greatest lyricist in the world: *I'm mad about you.*

She looked down and noticed that the gas gauge was on empty. She flashed her lights at Boone and he pumped his brake lights and they drifted together over to the side of the road. He walked backward on the shoulder from the crappy van, ignoring the semis blowing past him in wet bursts. They were on their way up Snoqualmie Pass, probably twenty miles from the peak. There was a little swirling snow, nothing serious yet.

He stuck his head through the open window and looked at the gauge. "I think we can make it," he said. "There's a gas station at the summit."

"We're going uphill," she said. "We'll use a lot of gas. Maybe we should go back to North Bend."

He nodded, chewed that lip. She remembered that he wanted to get back to pick his son up at school and she was suddenly filled with sweetness for that little boy, whom she'd never seen. She pictured a little Boone, losing a tooth, stuck with this hapless father and his dangerous eyebrows.

"We can make it," she said.

Boone grinned. "I tell you what we're gonna do. You're gonna draft off me."

"What?"

"Draft. Like race cars. Or bike racers. Get real close, like three feet, so you can't see any road between our cars. Just stay right behind me, and draft off the van. You'll use, like, half the gas. We'll go slow, exactly fifty."

It was a terrible idea. It was surely illegal. Maybe insane. "Okay!" she said.

He winked. And then he leaned inside the car, and for the first time in probably three years, Boone kissed her. He smelled like beer and pot, smelled like Bloody Marys and cigarettes; he smelled great.

Just before they left the carpenter's house, his wife had asked Myra what she saw in Boone. "You do know that everyone thinks he's kind of—" She didn't finish.

"A fuckup?" Myra said.

The carpenter's wife had laughed.

So Myra told the carpenter's wife how, during radiation, there was a moment when she thought it might be okay to die. "In fact, it was like I was already gone—like I was looking back at my life. And I could see the whole thing laid out, like, I don't know, a straight line. You're a kid. You go to school. And you see where the line is supposed to go: boyfriend, job, husband, baby, whatever. But when I really looked at the line . . . the only parts that really meant anything to me were the jagged parts . . . the parts that everyone else saw as mistakes."

There was something else, too. In the El Camino she hit rewind on the cassette player and settled in behind the van. During treatment, it was as if she had gone away somewhere, out of necessity, and now she needed to be yanked back, pulled back into the world. She got closer to the van. Closer. Closer. At first she could see Boone in the side mirror, nodding, *Yes, yes*, and she inched closer, closer, and then she was so close she couldn't even see the side mirror anymore, or him, just the back of that crap-van, and the whole world became the back of that chipped, pocked gray van. People in other cars kept passing them, and looking over, probably assuming the van was towing the El Camino, then seeing that it wasn't. Myra glanced over at one man in a Jeep and smiled. *That's right, motherfucker; we are doing this!* And the snow swirled and he pulled her up the hill and Sting sang, *I'm mad about you!* and she rolled down the window to keep the car from steaming up, and the cold air burst inside of her, into the hole where the knife used to be, and she sang in puffs of steam as they ascended together, the road fell away and the cold clear summit rose into view.

The Angel of Rome

I met the Angel of Rome on a cool autumn evening in the year of my reinvention, 1993.

I was what you might call a work in progress then, a shy, sheltered twenty-one-year-old, in Europe for the first time, with a once-in-a-lifetime opportunity: to study Latin at the Vatican.

This was in part because of my devout mother, who always dreamed that her only son might one day become a priest. Mom was the office secretary for our Catholic diocese back in Omaha, Nebraska, but she was also an unmarried mother who lived in a cloud of shame that she imagined my entry into the priesthood might lift for both of us. Like a two-for-one redemption deal.

As a kid, I lived to please this quiet, melancholic woman, so I went along with her plans. But like a badly made cake, Catholicism had failed to rise in me, and by high school—around the time I began noticing girls—I was having serious doubts about a life of Jesuit celibacy.

I could only afford community college after high school, so I lived at home and worked weekends and summers at Dillard's department store. After two years, I commuted to the University of Nebraska-Omaha, and was just finishing my junior year when Mom showed me an item in the parish bulletin that would end up changing my life: a year in Rome paid for by the Omaha Chapter of the Knights of Columbus, which was offering a scholarship for a local priest novitiate or Latin scholar.

"Um, you do realize," I told Mom, "that I am neither of those things."

Yes, I had taken two years of Latin in high school and repeated Latin I and II in college, but this no more made me a scholar than taking Biology 101 and 102 would've made me a doctor.

For my mom, though, the optimal word was *Vatican*. "It can't hurt to apply," she said. "And who knows, maybe your faith will be renewed."

But another faith had been rising in me in those years. Writing. In high school and college, books began to provide the thing that religion couldn't, a sense of meaning, a path to understanding the world.

In fact, I likely would have ignored this Roman scholarship altogether if I hadn't just bumped into an old friend from English class.

Clarissa Mills had been the most interesting person in my high school. She wore army jackets over her plaid school uniform and combat boots under. She called everyone by their last names. She listened to punk, wrote poems, and knew all the best movies and songs the second they came out. She was pretty and rich—her parents were doctors—but wore her popularity lightly, and managed to be friends with everyone, even the lowly scholarship kids who had to wash dishes in the cafeteria to get a break on private school tuition. Kids like me.

After graduation, the wealthy kids from my high school went to private Catholic colleges: Creighton for those who stayed in Nebraska, Marquette and Notre Dame for those with the money to venture out. Clarissa went all the way to Georgetown. And that was the last I heard of her until the end of my junior year in college, when I went to work at the mall one day and saw her coming out of Waldenbooks. "Rigel!" she yelled.

We went to the food court to have a soda and catch up. It was as if the once-insurmountable class divisions of high school had dissolved. We were both just English majors now, geeking out over literature. She was reading Dickinson; I was into Dos Passos. She wanted to be a poet; I admitted wanting to be a novelist. We had both just turned twenty-one; she'd gone to a few bars; I hadn't yet. I sensed an opportunity, and I asked how long she was in town. But she was leaving in a few days and was spending the next year studying abroad in Italy.

"What about you?" she asked. "What's next for Jack Rigel?"

Something about that question crushed me. What *was* next for me? Spend the summer working at a department store a mile from my house? Commute to the only college I could afford? Live the rest of my life in Omaha, sitting next to my mother every Sunday at Mass? So much for dissolving class distinctions.

I don't remember what I told Clarissa. We said a hurried goodbye without exchanging addresses or phone numbers. But that summer, when Mom came home with the application for the Knights of Columbus scholarship in Rome, I began to see it as my ticket out.

A year in Rome was perhaps the only chance I'd ever have to remake myself—into a *New Jack Rigel*. To transform shy, unworldly Nebraska Jack, still in the navy-chinos-and-red-polo uniform of his parochial high school, into Continental Jack: dashing, sexy, a mysterious ex-pat writer and scholar.

I could practically see this *New Jack Rigel*—sitting all day in cafés, sipping espresso in dark sunglasses and the black leather coat he bought with what he intriguingly called his "rather small inheritance," quoting Sartre and Nietzsche, smoking Muratti cigarettes like he owned the company.

Look! Through the café window, it's *New Jack Rigel,* shaking another cigarette from the pack as he laughs at some brilliant idea he has scribbled in his Moleskine journal!

I SUPPOSE EVERY person, at some point, tries to break free from the identity you are assigned as a kid, from the person your parents and friends see, from your own limitations and insecurities. To create your own story.

That's how I felt as I carefully filled out the application, exaggerating both my interest in the priesthood ("a calling too important to ignore") *and* my Latin education ("four years, college"). I felt poised at the edge of something, like an actor who has just walked onstage and stepped into the spotlight.

And then . . . Rome happened.

2

I rented a small apartment in the Trastevere neighborhood, a narrow room carved off the back of an old automotive shop. It was cold and noisy, and I barely slept there, nagged by a persistent cough and a severe case of jet lag, which was made worse by a group of unruly boys constantly kicking a soccer ball against my wall.

In Latin class, I was completely overwhelmed. I was a college senior in a grad-level seminar filled with classicists, Latin scholars, and novitiates from all over the world. Some had even published articles, and one—Nicholas Loughton, an insufferable Brit who talked through his nose—wasted no time in referencing his book contract: "Yes, but isn't it also true, as I suggest in my upcoming book . . ."

I was easily the youngest and least accomplished of the twelve students, and I sat off by myself, yawning, coughing and shrinking into my beloved leather coat. My plan to spend the days writing in cafés (where I imagined, improbably, I might run into Clarissa) turned out to be both expensive and impossible, waiters and baristas quickly sweeping away my empty cup and shooing me along.

So I studied alone in my small room, chewing on stale bread and drifting in and out of uneasy sleep, until the pounding of the soccer ball woke me yet again to find myself alone in a spartan room with nothing but a bed, a suitcase, and a portable typewriter, on which I had planned to write the ex-pat novel that would make me the next Hemingway. Instead, I mostly wrote homesick letters to my mother, ending each one with a plea for money.

But my sad letters weren't even making it to the States, entombed instead in the notorious Italian postal system—the very system I was relying upon to deliver my much-needed second scholarship check from the Omaha Knights of Columbus.

By October, I was nearly out of money, and limiting myself to a single meal each day.

This was my situation as I started my second month in Rome: *New Jack Rigel* somehow worse off than *Old Jack Rigel*—sleepless, sad and starving, alone in a city where I struggled to communicate at the level of a dull six-year-old.

Leaving class one day, I passed some of the other students talking in a huddle outside. The author Nicholas Loughton was explaining how he hoped to stay in Italy after our seminar ended. "I'll apply for adjunct teaching jobs," he was saying, "at the Italian campuses of Jesuit colleges: Boston College, Gonzaga, Georgetown—"

I stopped suddenly at the mention of Clarissa's school. "Georgetown?" The group turned in my direction. "Do you know where that is?"

Nicholas Loughton looked at me as if he'd never heard me speak before. Probably because he'd never heard me speak before. "Washington, D.C.," he said.

"No. I mean the Italian campus."

"Oh," he said. "It's in Florence."

Florence? I felt like my knees had been taken out.

That afternoon, I wandered the streets, trying to figure out why this news had been so deflating. Was I in love with Clarissa Mills? No. I had seen her exactly one time in three years. After that, I didn't even try to contact her. Instead, I moved to Rome and indulged in my simple fantasy: me in a café, tousled hair and leather coat, journal and cigarettes, and Clarissa coming in and seeing me: *Rigel, what are* you *doing here?* Yet, when I thought about this fantasy, I didn't even see Clarissa Mills.

I wasn't imagining her as my girlfriend.

I was imagining her as my *witness.*

I simply wanted Clarissa to *see me* and report back to the people at home how much I had changed. How pathetic! As if I'd never gone to Rome, never really left high school, as if I was acting for a bunch of rich kids who didn't even know me.

But more even than that—I could see it now—I wanted a witness to make my change feel real to someone else. *Me.* Even I didn't believe in *New Jack Rigel*.

This realization hit me, coincidentally or not, as I stood outside a travel agency, Viaggi d'Oro, Golden Voyages. And it landed on top of twenty-one years of insecurity, loneliness, and, in that moment, homesickness.

So, I gave up. I marched inside, past the beautiful photos of the Alps, Sicily and the Amalfi Coast, and I asked the young clerk how much it would cost to fly to Omaha, Nebraska. One-way.

She spoke impeccable English, and she smiled as she looked up the price on a big desktop computer. After some quick math, and a glance at my bank statement, we decided I was just forty thousand lire short of a plane ticket home. About thirty bucks.

I stared at the sheet of paper on which she'd written the price.

Only one other person was in the travel agency, a slender young man with a mustache whose English was less impeccable. "I give you fifty buck America for you coat," he said.

I looked down at my beloved black calfskin leather jacket. It had been the key to *New Jack Rigel*. In fact, it *was New Jack Rigel*. And honestly, it was just a little bit big on me, anyway, or, as the salesman had put it: "Your arms are too short for this beauty."

This is the problem with living in fantasies; we so often fail to account for *ourselves* being in them.

3

The man with the mustache didn't have the money on him so I agreed to meet him back there the next evening. The travel agency closed at seven and the clerk said I could be on a plane in less than a week.

I barely slept that night, and the next day in class, I girded myself to ask our brilliant but stern instructor, Monsignor Arturo Festa, for advice. I waited until class had ended and all the other students had left and then I approached his desk. He was just packing up his brown briefcase.

Monsignor Festa was tall and bald, stooped and severe-looking, as if someone had removed half his bones and left the rest to droop in disappointment. He was from the Lombardy region of Italy, but he'd spent six years in America before being called back to work at the Vatican in the Latin Letters section of the Secretariat.

Rather than acquire a fondness for Americans during those six years, however, the monsignor's time in the States seemed to have filled him with disdain. He once volunteered in class that Americans were a self-satisfied and incurious people, who showed little interest or facility in learning other languages. I was pretty sure he meant me.

"Monsignor, can I speak with you?"

He turned. "*Latine loqui, Discipule Rigel.*"

Yes, of course. Monsignor insisted everything be spoken in Latin. He said that since so much of our Western culture emerged from the language, nearly everything could be translated back. He challenged us to stump him with modern terms: computer, blue jeans, Walkman, all of which he deftly lobbed back in their Latin form.

"Television," someone said once.

"Interesting." Monsignor tapped his cheek with his index finger. "*Tele*—from the Greek, meaning 'far away,' or as we would say in Latin, *procul*—and *vision,* its Latin root, *visio* or *visionis,* not only the act of seeing, but the thing being seen, too. And what better way to understand television, the device *and* the programs, than *procul-visionis,* stories from afar."

In this way, he could make the mundane seem magical, and I felt like applauding every time he did it. But while he was brilliant, he was also the most intimidating teacher I'd ever known. And now I had to tell him that I wanted to give up and go back to America. And I had to do this in Latin. My mother, homesickness, the priesthood, my upbringing, the rich kids at home, Clarissa Mills studying in Florence—how could I translate these things? I stood there, frozen.

Finally, Monsignor spoke. "*Quaeramne ex te quaestionem?*" Could he ask *me* a question?

I nodded.

"*Quattuor annos Latine?*" He looked over the rims of his glasses. "Four years, Mr. Rigel?"

I looked down at my shoes. "No."

"*Quam multos annos?*"

"*Duo,*" I muttered into my chest.

"Ah," he said. And with his suspicions confirmed, Monsignor Festa shook his head, picked up his briefcase and started to leave. But he paused at the doorway. "*Vero nihil verius,*" he said.

Nothing is truer than truth.

4

I was bereft. When you think you're fooling the world, you're usually just making a fool of yourself. I vowed there would be no more pretending after that, no more posturing, no more hacking on harsh Italian cigarettes. From now on, I would be my authentic self, even if it meant giving up and going home. Starting over. I slinked back to my room and fell immediately into a deep, depressed sleep. When I awoke it was with a start, hours later; a soccer ball had predictably slammed against the wall. I looked at my watch: five-fifteen. I could still make it to the travel agency.

I hurried outside, past the indolent soccer boys and into the steady stream of chattering couples and families out for their evening promenade, toward the travel agency where I would sell my treasured coat to buy a ticket home.

Everywhere around me was the intoxicating smell of food: meat, bread, dry cheeses. I'd already had that day's meal and I could practically *taste* the air, thick with garlic, tomato, oregano. My eyes watered as I moved in this cloud of strangers.

The streets were a maze in Trastevere, the once working-class neighborhood separated from the Centro Storico by the Tiber River. I moved beneath ivy-covered arches, lines of shirts and pants hung to dry, past tables and chairs where old men sat drinking and smoking, until a few blocks from my flat, I realized I was lost.

After a month in Rome, this was not a new experience, of course. The strange street, the unknown piazza. Turning circles in search of a familiar landmark. You are never so alone as in a group of people speaking a foreign language.

A *carabiniere* was standing on a corner and I moved to ask this police officer for directions, but he ignored me and turned to light a young woman's cigarette. I stepped past him, into the narrow alley that I hoped would open into a street I recognized.

But at the other end of this narrow passageway, my path was blocked by a large group of people. I said, "*Scusi,*" to the back of a big wool coat. Beneath it, the man's legs were spread wide, his elbows out like a soldier standing at parade rest.

I repeated, in my stiff Italian, "*Mi dispiace, scusi.*" Still, the big man in the wool coat didn't acknowledge me, so I turned to his right to look for another way around the crowd.

And that's when I happened to look into the restaurant abutting this alley.

It was like looking into another world, the room so bright as to seem luminescent, like a religious painting, the sparkle of bejeweled patrons, swirl of silverware and wineglasses, gleaming white-shirted waiters carrying trays of rich food, every table filled with beautiful people. They laughed and gestured and smiled like movie stars.

It was as if some kind of dream had been constructed on the other side of this glass. And then I had the simplest realization: *I have always been outside.*

My life was a series of windows like this, rooms that I found myself staring into. On the other side were the rich, successful kids from my high school. On the other side was a world of private colleges, fraternities and sororities, of families with a mother *and* a father—all of it behind cool glass. Even television and movies, what were these but windows into other worlds? All the glamour and beauty that life has to offer would forever be in there, as I would forever be *out here.*

Inside was more than a dining room; it was an epiphany.

I continued to stare as a steaming bowl of *cacio e pepe* began making its way across the dining room, toward me.

I blame my hunger for what happened next, and for the unlikely turn my life was about to take. Through the window, my eyes followed the pasta down to a table for two just to my left.

And there she was.

The Angel of Rome.

Angelina Amadio, the actress and model, and one of the most beautiful women in the world, was sitting at this table, right below me. She looked up. Out the window. At me. An unreadable look passed over her face.

"Hey!" I said. "I know you." Then I put my hand against the window.

And before I could drop my hand and run off in embarrassment, the Angel of Rome smiled sympathetically, reached up, and put her own hand against the window. She spread out her fingers until her hand was the exact mirror of mine.

5

The past is a dead language, too. You can try speaking it into existence, translating it, explaining its context. You can coldly recite its objects and actions, master its vocabulary. You can say, *Here was a street and there a restaurant. Here was a hungry, homesick young man in a fine leather coat, there, a cool window, and on the other side of it, a striking Italian actress.*

But can you really speak the past? Feel it? The glow of that restaurant and the dark beauty of that woman, our hands together, yet separated by clear glass? "Angelina?" I said.

And that's when a voice grumbled from behind me. "Ahhh! *Che cazzo ai! Fermati!*" Stop! Then a bunch of words I didn't understand—machine-gunned Italian with a few uses of the word *fanculo* that I was unfamiliar with to that point.

I looked back over my shoulder. That crowd of people blocking the alley was horseshoed around lights and what looked like a small set of train tracks, ending just behind me, as if a kiddie carnival ride had been set up and abandoned.

Mounted on the tracks was a large camera dolly, and a man behind the camera, and more people behind him—all of them staring at me, and the camera pointing into the brightly lit restaurant at the Angel of Rome.

A man with a clipboard stepped in, pulled me away, and pushed me against a wall. "*Ma chi cazzo è sto stronzo?*"

"I'm sorry," I said. "I didn't know."

The man turned, his hand still on my chest while he yelled down the alley. That's when the police officer I had seen flirting with the girl came running up. Clipboard man berated him, his hand still on my chest, gesturing wildly toward the camera dolly.

The cop pointed at me and rattled off words that I couldn't catch, except *ladro*, thief.

"I didn't steal anything," I said.

What I had done, apparently, was wander onto an active film set, the restaurant lit like heaven because they were filming there, and now I could see the bright banks of light everywhere, and I understood that the people seemed as glamorous as movie stars because they were. Or actors anyway. I had stumbled into a shot that, I found out later, had taken the director three hours to set up, in preparation for what filmmakers call the Golden Hour, a period of dusky light that, like everything in the reductive world of filmmaking, turns out to be only a third that long.

"I'm sorry," I said again.

"Hey, you American?"

I looked up. It was the big man in the wool coat, striding toward me. I had missed the visual clues of his Americanness (were those cowboy boots under his wool coat?). His face was familiar, too, though I couldn't quite place it. His eyes were wide and green, a little too far apart on a square and unbelievably large head. There are only two places you encounter heads like that: Easter Island and Hollywood.

"Yes," I said. "I'm an American!"

He flashed big white teeth at the man with the clipboard. "It's okay, Fredo, kid's with me." Then he dragged me by the arm away from the restaurant window and the camera dolly, away from the clipboard man and the *carabiniere*.

"Do not piss off the crew," the big man said. "Rule number one."

"I didn't realize——" I said.

"You know Angelina?" he interrupted me, side-glancing as we walked.

"Oh. Yeah." I was about to explain that I didn't *know* know her, but recognized her from a movie, when he interrupted me.

"Where you from, kid?"

"Omaha."

"Nebraska!" He said it like he'd answered a particularly difficult trivia question. "Never been there. Hear it's shitty. Nah. Kidding. I'm sure it's great. What are you doing in Rome?"

I told him I was studying Latin.

"No shit?"

The big man led me down the street, to a small tent; on a table inside was a pot of coffee, a few bottles of water and a couple of half-eaten pizzas. "How about that? My third day in Rome and I bump into the very person I need."

I was trying to figure out why he would need a Latin speaker when my mind caught up to my eyes and I recognized him, or, rather, I recognized a character he'd played on a TV show my mother and I used to watch back home, *Tower and Bridges*. It was a 1980s cop show about two detectives, a by-the-book police officer named Dan Bridges, and a wild, rogue cop named—

"Ronnie Tower!" I said.

A smile crossed his square jaw and he growled, "Here's trouble!" This was his catchphrase from that old TV show, the thing he said when he and Bridges first showed up at the scene of a murder, or when their gruff sergeant called them into his office, or when he and Bridges went on a double date with blond identical twins on roller skates at the Santa Monica pier. You never knew when it was coming in a particular episode, but it always did—most satisfyingly when Ronnie Tower stood over some dead henchman he'd just shot—"*Here's trouble!*"

Now, he leaned in as if confiding something intimate. "Wow. I hate to admit it, Nebraska, but I needed that, someone recognizing me. I was starting to feel invisible, you know? My show isn't even syndicated here. It's like I'm *nobody* in Italy." I nodded, no translation needed for that particular feeling. Then he leaned in again. "Meantime, do you know what shit TV show everyone watches here?"

"No."

"Take a guess. What show has been dubbed and syndicated across this whole continent and is on every time I turn on my stupid hotel TV?" Before I could answer, he said, mockingly: "*Super Macchina!*"

I shrugged.

"*Knight Rider!*" he said. "You believe that? David Hasselhoff and a talking car? I mean, I'm no Olivier, but at least I get better lines than a freaking Pontiac."

Then Ronnie Tower pulled me away from the food-and-coffee tent, before I could grab so much as a slice of cheese. "Listen, Nebraska, I got an idea. My agent negotiated a translator for me on set, but two things: A, I like you better, and two, she's not even that hot, and C, I don't trust her, know what I'm saying?"

I did not.

"Also, she works for the producers. So B, I get the feeling she's watching me. Waiting for me to do something that violates my contract. And three, what if I need something the producers don't want me to have. Something off the books. Know what I mean?"

I said nothing.

"Like, I don't know . . . cocaine."

"Oh, I . . . " I stammered, "I wouldn't have any idea—"

"I don't mean *actual* cocaine, Nebraska. I just mean something the producers wouldn't approve of . . . *like* cocaine." He lowered his voice even further. "Unless you happen to know where I might . . . get . . . some—"

I shrugged.

"No. Right! Good. That was a test. You passed." He winked, then gestured back at the window. "But mostly what I need you to do is talk to my costar in there."

He explained what his agent had told him about Angelina Amadio. That she refused to speak English now because the one time she'd been in an American film—I nodded, *yes, I'd seen it!*—her performance had been panned, her accent so heavily mocked she stopped speaking English altogether. "That's why I need you."

That's when it dawned on me that when I'd said I was in Rome studying Latin, Ronnie had *heard* Italian. Or worse, that he somehow believed the language spoken in Italy *was* Latin.

"Wait." I looked into the window at the Angel of Rome. "You want me to talk to *her*? To say what?"

"Clear up a misunderstanding we had yesterday."

"What kind of misunderstanding?"

He rubbed his head. "Oh man, where to start. Well, see, there's a tradition on TV and film sets. At least in America. A sort of romantic amnesty." He looked for another way to explain himself. "You ever go to summer camp, Nebraska?"

I nodded. The worst week of my life.

"So, you know how, at summer camp, you can just ball whoever you want, no strings, and it's forgiven? Just a summer camp thing? Girlfriends, boyfriends back home—none of it matters. It's an all-you-can-eat buffet."

Suffice to say, this had not been my experience at seventh grade Catechism Camp.

"Well, see, a film set is like that, too. A vacation from real life, from responsibility. Nobody's married on a film set. Things happen, especially between actors, right? Some people would say it's helpful, even necessary, for the creative . . . uh, atmosphere . . . to have a certain energy on set. I just need you to tell her that."

We stared at each other. If I understood him correctly, Ronnie Tower wanted me to tell the Angel of Rome that it would help the creative atmosphere of this movie if she slept with him?

This was well beyond my ability in English, let alone Italian, a language in which I could randomly order a milkshake (*un frullato*) or ask about an insect bite (*punture d'insetti*) but couldn't figure out how to ask a group of boys to stop kicking a soccer ball against my wall. And the Berlitz *Italian for Travelers* phrase book I carried in my coat pocket was unlikely to have an entry for "Perhaps it would improve the film if you had sex with your American costar."

I had also, that very day, received a profound lesson in authenticity, the trueness of truth, as Monsignor Festa had put it. I should have stopped Ronnie Tower right there and corrected his misconceptions. I did not actually *know* Angelina. I was *not* in Rome studying *Italian.* I was there studying *Latin,* a language that hadn't been spoken in Italy in five hundred years, a language that you could no more use in 1993 Rome than you could use the Old English of *Beowulf* to buy a car in London.

But I didn't say these things.

I was too mesmerized by the brightness of that dining room, and by the beautiful people in it. By her. And even though I knew it had been lit by a film crew—*that the vision I'd had wasn't even real*—this fact did not dull my hunger, my desire to be *inside* that room.

Instead, in the moment I could've cleared everything up, I stood staring into the luminous dining room, at the ethereal Angelina Amadio, sitting across from a younger woman, surrounded by makeup and hair people and a sound guy with a boom microphone.

"Damn," Ronnie Tower said. "Isn't she beautiful?"

"Oh yes," I said.

6

Angelina Amadio was not the most successful Italian actress of her time, nor was she the most famous. And aside from a single memorable performance—at least to me—she never made the transition to American movies. Yet everyone knew of her, born as she was to a famous filmmaker, Orenzio Amadio, a peer of Fellini's and Visconti's, in that golden age of Italian cinema from which she, too, looked like she belonged.

Angelina had started as a model in the 1970s, but from the beginning there was something incongruous about her, an elegance that seemed ill-suited to the brutish commerce of advertising. And when a popular ad portrayed her as a statue with wings (in very tight designer blue jeans), the Angel of Rome was born, a nickname which became, over time, less and less complimentary.

After all, what is an angel but a kind of ghost, untouchable, out of place and time?

This aloof quality carried over to her acting, too, in which she seemed mildly dubious of the lines she read. This was not entirely her fault. The daring, artistic Italian filmmakers of the 1960s had largely given way to the antic comedies and incoherent action films of the '70s and '80s. Her career had a whiff of tragedy: here was a generational beauty and talent, which, by the time I met her, had begun to fade without a truly meaningful role.

I knew about Angelina Amadio because of the one American film she'd made, a decade earlier, the underrated (in my book at least) cult horror classic, *A Feeding*.

American cinema had also fallen into artistic disrepair then, the '70s auteurs pushed aside for *Jaws* and *Star Wars* blockbusters and sequels. The indie-film boom of the 1990s was years away, and so, in the States, too, Angelina was stuck between golden ages.

Finally, in 1983, she got her Hollywood break in what was supposed to be a sexy, sophisticated thriller. *A Feeding* is about a group of mysterious jet-setting Europeans who move into an old mansion in Los Angeles and begin seducing, and killing, as many B- and C-list actors as one film could reasonably cast.

She is the first European we see in the film. Two men are in a Sunset Boulevard nightclub when they notice her sitting alone at the bar in her blown-out 1980s hair and a dress so small you'd be forgiven for mistaking it for a beauty pageant sash.

Kris Kristofferson plays one of the men at the bar and he flips a coin with his buddy to see who gets to talk to her. In the first sign of trouble, the less famous actor wins. The actor saunters over, asks if he can buy her a drink and she says, in heavily accented English, "This would make me happy."

They leave the bar together and go to a decrepit Beverly Hills mansion, where she leads the man into a candle-lit bedroom, no furniture other than a bed, the ominous breeze from an open window fluttering the white bedsheets.

Angelina immediately steps out of her tiny dress. And she is completely, magnificently, fully frontally, nude.

I have to admit, this is one reason *A Feeding* had such an outsized impact on me, and the reason I recognized the Angel of Rome immediately.

She was the first woman I ever saw naked.

I was sixteen at the time and still considering becoming a priest, so the effect of Angelina Amadio's body was profound. I can't say that it was an either-or proposition (a lifetime of ascetic, celibate contemplation vs. *that*) but it did put the choice in stark relief. Here were some other mysteries I wouldn't mind contemplating: Human beauty. Love. Sex.

"Take off your clothes. Get under the sheet," Angelina tells the man. "Close your eyes."

The man does as she says. But when he opens his eyes, he is surrounded by a dozen naked people, men and women, and as he screams, they leap onto the bed and tear into him like a pack of coyotes—swarming, ripping, biting.

And on screen, the title credits announce: A FEEDING.

I saw *A Feeding* because of that same girl, Clarissa Mills, who, in A.P. English, regaled me with stories of the wild midnight movies at the arthouse Dundee Theater in Omaha: *Eraserhead, Repo Man,* and the raucous *Rocky Horror Picture Show.*

"What do you mean you throw toast?" I asked Clarissa.

"Everyone dresses up in garters and vampire clothes," she said. "We yell at the screen, júmp up and down, do the Time Warp, and when Frank-N-Furter proposes a toast . . . we throw toast."

"Do you bring the toast?"

"Well, yeah, Rigel, it's a movie theater, they sell popcorn, not toast."

I couldn't imagine asking my mom if I could go to a Midnight Movie at the Dundee. ("I'll need to toast some bread, and oh, can I borrow your garters? Also, what are garters?")

Then, one day that summer, Mom got a call from her sister in Iowa City. Her stepfather, my surly Grandpa Dave, had suffered a stroke. He was okay, but Mom needed to go spend the weekend with her mother. I pleaded to stay behind and eventually Mom relented and left me home alone for the weekend.

Saturday night, I paced around until almost midnight. I didn't put on a cape or garters or makeup. I did, however, toast two slices of bread and put them in my pockets, just in case. And I walked alone to the Dundee Theater.

But that Saturday night, they weren't showing *The Rocky Horror Picture Show*. I didn't see Clarissa in line, or any of the cool kids from my school. Just two dozen or so night owls there to watch a different campy horror film, one that arthouse theaters hoped to turn into an interactive experience like *Rocky Horror*—the five-year-old box office bomb, *A Feeding*.

And as Kris Kristofferson spent the next two hours investigating what happened to his buddy and getting closer to this cult of vampirish Eurotrash, I watched the audience laugh and repeat the schlocky dialogue, taking special glee in mocking the visitors' heavy accents.

"*Thees would-a-make-a-me-appy!*" they yelled when Angelina accepted the drink from the man she was about to devour. A minute later: "*Take off-a-you clothes! Get under the shit!*"

And so on.

For almost two hours.

No wonder Angelina never spoke English again.

Meanwhile, I was captivated, not so much by the movie, which was indeed campy and overwrought, but by her. Every time Angelina appeared—which wasn't often—it was as if the rest of the characters ceased to exist. There was only her. Beautiful yes, but more than that, she had a presence that I still can't quite explain.

She is off-screen for most of the film, but toward the end, after dozens of people have been seduced and eaten, Angelina reappears at the same Sunset bar, looking for Kris Kristofferson. When he confronts her, she leans in and kisses him. "Please trust me," she says. ("*Please-a-thrust-me!*" the audience yelled, standing and thrusting their pelvises.)

Then Angelina agrees to take him to the place where his friend died. It seems she has grown tired of feeding on humans. ("*I no-like-a-eata-the-flesh!*" the people yelled.) And more than that, she has decided immortality is wrong.

"Everyone I love . . . is-a-no more," she says, one of the few lines that nobody mocked. I was moved, watching in the theater, the dry toast catching in my throat.

At the end of the movie, there is an epic fight, and the leader of the Eurotrash monsters is about to kill Kris Kristofferson when Angelina douses him with gasoline and sets him on fire. (Inexplicably, she does this while topless, a plot hole a certain sixteen-year-old Nebraska film critic was willing to accept without reservation.)

As the mansion burns around them, Kris Kristofferson flees with Angelina. But on the porch, she suddenly stops. It is almost dawn. She cannot leave the grounds of the mansion. He must go without her. She pulls a shawl around her shoulders, as, surrounded by smoke and flames, the sun rises behind her. Kristofferson has no choice but to leave. At the gate, he turns back to Angelina. But she has become an old woman.

She holds up one hand, exactly like she did to me at the restaurant. Not a wave goodbye, exactly, but an acknowledgment of something else. Without uttering a word, her eyes say, *Go.*

I was so moved by this that I would see *A Feeding* two more times. And I would research the actress who so dazzled me in this schlocky movie.

But that first night, with everyone around me laughing and

yelling at the screen, my hand went to my chest as I watched the once-luminous Angel of Rome dissolve into a pile of dust.

7

"Wow, great death scene," said Ronnie Tower that night, when I explained *A Feeding* to him.

His real name was not Ronnie Tower, of course. His stage name was Sam Burke, which he'd chosen because his real name, Sheldon Budenholzer, didn't exactly sound like a TV star. After the network canceled *Tower and Bridges,* Ronnie's agent had thought a European job could open a back door into American films, "like Clint Eastwood," he said. "Instead, I show up here and it's just like *our* shitty movies, but in a language I don't understand." He didn't know Angelina, or any of his Italian costars.

The film crew had wrapped for the night and Ronnie dragged me to a bar halfway up the Janiculum Hill, the door opening into a cave-like space carved into the hillside. Two men in tracksuits were playing a spirited game of foosball next to us, a miniature version of the soccer ball slamming against my apartment wall.

Bam! Bam! I flinched every time the foosball blasted against the tabletop.

"You seem jumpy," said Ronnie Tower. He looked down at the remnants of a plate of bread, salami and olives between us. "Also hungry."

I looked down, too. Ronnie still had his first piece of bread in his hand, but I had eaten the rest, all the salami and olives and the balance of the loaf. "Sorry," I said.

He asked me a few questions about myself. I gave him the

basics—Nebraska, Catholic school, English major, Mom wanting me to be a priest.

"You. A priest?" He looked dubious. "Yeah, I don't see it."

"No," I admitted. "I want to be a writer."

He made a face as if that wasn't much better. "What's your dad think?"

I explained that I never knew my dad, that my mother got weepy whenever I asked about him, so I never did. Then I told Ronnie Tower something I hadn't told anyone. Five months earlier, not long after I'd seen Clarissa in the mall, Mom and I had gone to the funeral of a man named Charles Weston, a secular deacon I remembered from church events.

Charles had been the administrator of our diocese and had hired my mom, twenty-some years earlier. He had six children, two dozen grandchildren, and was one of the pillars of our community. Everyone in our parish knew the Westons, the boys star athletes, the girls cheerleaders and straight-A students. There was a Weston a year ahead of me, Charles's granddaughter Bethany, who had been student body president and gotten a full ride to Notre Dame.

They filled the front four pews of the church, the Westons, as if they were an advertisement for *be fruitful and multiply*. Mom sat silently during the service, and she said nothing afterward. We didn't go to the reception. Then, a week after the funeral, the man's oldest son, David, showed up at our house. He was my mother's age and I figured they must be friends, but she left me alone in the living room with him.

David asked me a few questions, what I was studying, what I might do after college. Then he handed me an envelope. Inside was a check for two thousand dollars, some of which I would later use to buy my leather coat. He explained that he was the executor of his father's estate, and that Charles had stipulated in his will that I receive this amount for my future education.

"And that was it," I told Ronnie Tower. "Charles Weston was my father."

"Jesus," Ronnie said.

That's when the bartender came over, a man in black Elvis Costello glasses. He and Ronnie Tower had gotten into a rousing discussion of vodkas when we first came in, and the bartender had promised a rare Finnish bottle in back, "very special, very good."

He set two glasses on our table, ice cubes shimmering in three fingers of clear booze.

Ronnie toasted me. "To shitty stories." Then he drained his drink in a single swallow. He made a face and turned to the bartender. "This is Seagram's. I don't know who you're trying to fool with this shit, but it's well vodka."

The bartender began to object but Ronnie turned to me. "Tell him, Nebraska. Tell this ingrate I'm not paying for horse piss."

This, apparently, was to be my first assignment as Ronnie Tower's fake Italian translator, but I was pretty sure I didn't know how to say *horse piss* in any language other than English.

Thankfully, the bartender was fluent in angry customer.

"I bring you the bottle!" he said. "I show you!"

"Come on, pal," Ronnie Tower said. "What's that gonna prove? You could have been in the back filling fancy decanters from a plastic Seagram's handle."

The bartender began objecting again, but Ronnie lowered his voice. "Look, pal. I *majored* in vodka. I could identify every pour you have back there."

The next thing I knew, Ronnie Tower and I were at the bar, with twelve neat shots of vodka spread out in front of us, six each, the bartender leaning back, arms folded while everyone in the place, including the track-jacketed foosball players, watched us intently.

Ronnie nodded at me, and we picked up the first glass. I sipped it: fire in my throat. Ronnie drained the glass, held it in his mouth, swirled it, swallowed it, set the glass down and looked at me. "You getting notes of Russian toenails, Nebraska?"

I can't overstate what a good Catholic kid I'd been to that point: Sunday Mass, daily prayer and religion classes at St. Cecilia's Elementary and St. Pius X High School, reconciliation, first communion, confirmation—I had been devoted in body, if not always in spirit.

In college, I did drink a little with some friends who had their own apartment, but it was mostly Stroh's beer, whose taste and color made me wish I could skip the middleman and dump it straight in the toilet.

In other words, these vodkas were, like the grad-level Latin class I was failing, well beyond me. And yet I found myself eagerly reaching for the second glass. This was what I would come to think of as "the Ronnie Tower Effect," an acceleration of time and event until everything moved too fast and spun out of control. Like hanging out with a typhoon.

And, honestly, I liked it.

Eventually, sitting at the bar that night drinking vodka, I remembered my vow of truer truth and I came clean with Ronnie. I told him I didn't really *know* Angelina, just her one American movie. And that maybe he'd misheard me, but I was actually studying Latin, not Italian.

"Oh," he said, "but you speak Italian?"

"I mean, sure, I speak some."

He put an arm around my shoulder. "Well, that's still more than me, isn't it?"

Then I told him about applying for this scholarship because of Clarissa, and how it turned out she was studying in Florence, not Rome, and how I'd been caught up in a stupid fantasy—showing my old high school classmates that I'd become somebody. I told him about being broke and hungry, and how, right before I met him, I was on my way to sell my coat to buy a plane ticket home.

He looked me over. "It's kind of big on you anyway," he said.

Throughout my long confession, we drank vodka. And while I can't recall if Ronnie made good on identifying *every* pour, I have a vague memory of him yelling, "Stolichnaya!" and "Absolut!" and people in the bar applauding and slapping us on the back. And that he kept having me bless people, as if I were a priest. And that I did it because, by then, I was, as one might've said in Latin: *ebrius.*

Drunk! Oh no! I had class in the morning. I couldn't disappoint Monsignor again. And I . . . I . . . I . . . I sat up and opened my eyes. Where was I?

The backseat of a small sedan. In the front, behind the wheel, was the bartender. Next to him, Ronnie Tower turned and smiled. "Oh good, Nebraska, you're alive." We were parked under a streetlight in a part of the city I had never seen before— wide streets, lighted signs, newer cars. The bartender got out and approached a woman sitting in a kitchen chair on the sidewalk, wearing a miniskirt and high heels, looking emphatically bored.

Without looking back at me, Ronnie Tower said, "I don't suppose you know how to say blow job in Italian."

In the backseat, I pulled out the Berlitz *Italian for Travelers* guidebook from my coat pocket. There was no entry between blow dryer (*asciugacapelli*) and blueberry (*mirtillo*)—neither of which would've been particularly helpful.

Thankfully, the bartender came back to the car and said he couldn't come to terms with the woman. I took that opportunity to beg out, explaining that I had class in the morning. Ronnie said that he should get some rest, too, and had the bartender drive me back to my apartment. I somehow made my way inside and collapsed into bed, where I woke the next morning with a feeling that was very much like soccer hooligans pounding a ball against my cerebellum.

I still remember the last thing Ronnie Tower said to me that night. He stood and opened the car door and when I climbed out of the backseat, he grabbed my arm and steadied me.

"Hey, Nebraska," he said. "Remember. Nobody gets to choose who their parents are. We do, however, get to pick who *we* are."

8

Then: Latin.

I stumbled from my flat, hungover, conjugating verbs as I walked (*habet, habemus, habetis, habent*). It was a cool morning, and I pulled my coat tighter around me.

Back in Omaha, I had pictured "studying at the Vatican" as a solemn, monastic experience in a marble-pillared palace guarded by red-plumed Swiss Guard. What I found instead was a kind of papal community college, Monsignor Festa's class on the second floor of a nondescript 1950s industrial building.

This was the classroom I arrived outside that morning, bracing myself for the monsignor's deep disapproval. The way he'd looked at me when I confessed having only two years of Latin had cut me to the bone. How would he respond now to me showing up late and possibly still drunk? Call me out in front of my fellow classmates? Expel me from the program for fraud?

Through the door, I could hear Monsignor's voice but couldn't make out what he was saying.

I took a deep breath, turned the handle and went inside.

Every head turned except his. The monsignor was standing in front of the class, facing the other eleven students. Finally, he turned his whole body to take in the twelfth, his own lying Judas, standing there shaking, reeking of booze.

"*Discipule* Rigel," he said. "*Cur sero?*"

Why was I late? *Vodkus?* Was that a word? I scoured my limited Latin vocabulary, but I had no translation for: *Last night I stumbled into a movie set and got drunk with an aging TV star.*

I looked over the other students. They were mostly in their late twenties and thirties, from all over the world, four priests in various stages of training, a nun, and the rest scholars, teachers and grad students.

"Um," I said. "Well, uh." My mouth was a desert. And still Monsignor Festa stared, content to let me twist in the wind until I came up with an explanation. "*Sero veni,*" I muttered, confirming what he'd just said: I was late.

"*Res ipsa loquitur,*" he said, and the class responded with a laugh. *This speaks for itself.* Finally, Monsignor flipped me a handout with a wave of dismissal that was as painful as my headache. I took the pages and slid miserably into an open desk, and the class resumed its millennium-old banter.

When you have a hangover, Latin hurts. Next to me, Nicholas Loughton, the impending author, was holding forth about the embellishments of the Silver Age in *libro mihi scribendo*—the book he was writing, when I drifted for a moment, picturing Angelina Amadio's hand on that window and—

"*Discipule* Rigel?" Monsignor Festa was staring at me. "*Habesne opinionem?*"

I started awake. I looked around. Did I have an opinion? I had clearly missed something. The room was spinning, the others staring at me. He had never called on me before. "Um," I said.

"Yes," Monsignor Festa said in English. "I believe you said that earlier."

Sweat broke out on my brow and my stomach churned. The only Latin word that popped into my head: *vomitus.*

And that's when the door opened, and my salvation arrived—in the most unlikely of forms. A woman I recognized as one of the school secretaries walked into the room, followed by Ronnie Tower.

"Please forgive the interruption, Father," the woman said in Italian. "This man needs to see one of your students."

Ronnie bowed extravagantly before Monsignor Festa. "Orry-say, ather-fay. Emergency-ay."

Then he turned and winked at me. "Pig Latin, get it, Nebraska? Hey, she's in the makeup trailer. Come on! It's the perfect time."

I opened my mouth to speak, but had no idea what to say, or what language to say it in. My mind was vodka-stewed mush, and standing there, waiting for an answer, was the tall, hunched, eternally disappointed monsignor. He looked from Ronnie to me and back again.

Then a noise escaped his mouth, a high squeak that I'd never heard from him before—was that ... laughter? He clapped his hands and said, "Ronnie Tower?" Then he made the laughing noise again and said, "Here's trouble!"

Next to me, Nicholas Loughton, used to translating every word out of our instructor's mouth, muttered to himself, "*Hic est tribulatio.*"

Nothing I could do but nod in agreement.

9

Apparently, while working for the Archdiocese in Indianapolis, *Tower and Bridges* had been the monsignor's favorite television show. But he'd left America after season four and was desperate to find out what happened after that.

"What happened? Well—" Ronnie scratched his head. "More of the same, I guess. I mean it was a procedural, so we just kept solving crimes and kicking ass. There *was* a nice two-parter about a smuggling ring, in which I fell for one of the smugglers and had to arrest her anyway. But we lost our lead-in in '87 and our ratings just started going in the shitter. And then they moved us to ten p.m. on Saturdays, which, I mean—"

Monsignor nodded solemnly. Ah yes, 10:00 p.m. on Saturdays. No need to say more.

"Look, Padre," Ronnie said, "Jack here is helping me out with something very important, would it be okay if I borrowed him for an hour or two?"

Monsignor regarded me with new eyes. "Of course," he said. Then he motioned with his hand for me to hurry it up—*please*, his eyes seemed to say, *don't keep the detective waiting.*

I grabbed my things and we started for the door. We were almost out of the room when Monsignor said, "*Discipule* Rigel."

I turned.

"*De omnibus dubitandum.*"

"Be suspicious of everything," Nicholas Loughton translated.

"I *know* that," I said, although of course I hadn't. But now I wondered: Did the monsignor think I was actually helping Ronnie with some kind of case?

We hurried down the stairs, the Ronnie Tower Effect in full bloom—things moving faster than I could comprehend—and in the cab back to Trastevere, all I could think to ask was how he'd found me.

"You don't play a detective for six years without picking up a few things," he said. Then he shrugged. "Plus, you told me you had class at the Vatican, so it wasn't that hard."

"And you still want me to translate for you? After everything I told you?"

"Sure. I believe in you, Nebraska," he said. "I saw you last night. You speak enough Italian for this. Besides, she's gonna love you. You're practically a genius, and almost a priest. Whatever you say, I promise, it's gonna sound better coming from you than from me."

The cab dropped us off a block from the restaurant where they had been filming the day before. Three big white trailers were set up in the street, and Ronnie pushed me toward the center one, where Angelina Amadio was apparently having her hair and makeup done.

At the bottom of the stairs, I paused.

"You can do this," he said. "Just go in there, tell her I'm sorry, and the rest of what I told you."

"About summer camp."

"Right. And amnesty. Don't worry. She'll get it. It's not her first rodeo."

I imagined, actually, she had *never* been to a rodeo. But still, I went up the stairs, Ronnie Tower nodding encouragingly on the street behind me. He pointed and winked: you got this. I gripped the door, opened it, and went in.

Before me was a narrow room, brighter even than the restaurant had been, awash in LEDs and vanity bulbs, such harsh lights apparently required by makeup artists. There were three swiveling chairs facing a huge mirror, in front of a counter covered with brushes and eye pencils, curling irons and beauty products.

And there, in the middle chair, facing the large mirror, her back to me, sat Angelina Amadio. She was in a white cloth robe, her long black hair pulled up and pinned back, while a woman crouched in front of her with a pencil, tracing her lips. There was something almost violent about it: the light, the beauty tools, the intimacy. It was as if I had walked in on a surgery.

She caught my reflection in the bright mirror. Her eyes were striking, the famous ghostly blue irises hovering beneath those black brows, the combination communicating a worldly expectation. *Okay*, her eyes said: *make me believe*.

I cleared my throat and began: "*Uh, Signora Amadio.*" I looked down at the notes I had made in my Moleskine journal. And then I launched into my short speech, in broken Italian, with phrases I'd lifted directly from the Berlitz *Italian for Travelers* book (summer camp: *campo estivo*), that would've sounded to Angelina something like this:

Good day. I am called Jack Rigel. I am sorry and my Italian is very bad. I am the boy yesterday that you see in a restaurant. I am the fan of your movies. A Feeding I see in United States is very good. I am study Latin at Vatican and translate for Ronnie Tower, (I mean) Sam Burke. He ask me say he is very sorry. He ask me say cinema is similar to summer camp. He ask me say is very good for actors to go on date. Would you like to go on date with Sam Burke? Would you like to have dinner with Sam Burke? I know a good restaurant. Are you free this evening? Would you like to have a drink with Sam Burke? Would you like to go for a drive? Would you like to go dancing? I know a good discotheque.

Most of these lines I had copied directly from *Italian for Travelers,* under the section marked *Appuntamento*—Dating. I didn't really know a good discotheque, or a bad one for that matter, but I had memorized the whole section in case I needed it, and it just sort of came out in a big blob of stupid Cyrano de Bergerac.

The makeup artist had paused her work and was staring at me, too, now, her pencil still poised in the corner of Angelina's mouth.

And still Angelina watched me, her own eyes inscrutable, connected to mine in the bright, bulb-lit mirror of the hair and makeup trailer. Her lips remained slightly parted, perhaps so as not to disrupt the work of the makeup artist.

Had my rant made so little sense that she couldn't even manage an answer? Was she offended? Angry? Confused? Should I confess that I didn't really know a good discotheque?

Finally, she pointed to the counter. The makeup artist handed her a pen and a notepad and the Angel of Rome scratched something on it, ripped the page from the pad, and handed it to the makeup artist, who handed it to me.

Vieni a cena domani alle 19:00, she wrote. *Come to dinner tomorrow at 7:00 p.m.* She also had written an address. I muttered, "*Grazie, Signora,*" and backed out of the bright trailer, a last look at those haunting eyes, which took me in once more in the harsh glow of the lighted mirror.

10

Outside, Ronnie Tower was nowhere to be found. I descended the trailer steps, and looked up the street one way, then the other. I stood in front of the bank of trailers. Where was he? Had he gotten cold feet and ditched me?

I stood there a few minutes, watching members of the crew move past with various lights and other equipment, and was just about to leave when Ronnie and another man emerged from the small coffee tent at the end of the street.

The other man was speaking English with an Italian accent: "It's not the first time I've done revisions on set obviously, but this is outrageous."

"No, I hear you loud and clear," Ronnie Tower said. "What I'm saying is that maybe it's also an opportunity, you know?" Then he saw me. "Ah, there he is." Then, to me: "Jack, hey, I was just talking about you."

He gestured to his companion, who was in his thirties, thinning brown hair and a thick beard, round glasses and a warm smile. He wore a rumpled sweater and was carrying a bundle of pages. "This is Don Macaroni," Ronnie said. "He's a screenwriter, like you."

Like me?

The man thrust out his hand. "I am Domenico Macrino."

We shook hands. "Jack Rigel," I said.

"But he's so young!" Domenico said to Ronnie Tower.

"I told you. This is Hollywood now! The kids have taken over. I go to these meetings sometimes and I think, *Did your parents drop you off?*"

Domenico laughed. "It is good to meet you. I am a big fan of *A Few Good Men*. And *My Cousin Vinny*."

I looked at Ronnie Tower, who was smiling as if this somehow made sense. "Yeah, I was just telling Don here how you've been doing script doctoring back in the States, under the radar." He grabbed Domenico's arm. "See that? It's how you can tell the kid's a pro. Acts like it's nothing."

Then he turned back to me: "Don here has his pencil caught in a ringer. And I said you might be willing to help."

Domenico shook his head. "I'm the fourth writer on this piece of shit. You can't even imagine what it was like before I got my hands on it. And now, a week into shooting, the director wants the whole third act rewritten, wants me to cut every scene after the wedding dinner. He's way behind schedule, and he wants to lose pages."

Ronnie shook his head. "It's the same bullshit everywhere, am I right, Jack? Run out of money and it's always the art that suffers. Hey, don't worry, Don, this is the kind of thing Jack deals with every day."

Ronnie took the script from Domenico and handed it to me.

I stared at Ronnie blankly. What was he possibly thinking?

"I told him you'd take a look, see if you have any ideas, and while you're in there, maybe take a look at my character, too, sharpen him a little. I mean, if Don doesn't mind."

Domenico laughed. "If you can figure out how to cut twelve minutes off the end of fiasco and still have it make sense? Not at all." And with that, he patted me on the chest. "And who knows, maybe we could work on something in the States together one day. I have some ideas."

11

Domenico went to meet with the director and I was left alone with Ronnie Tower again. I held up the script. "I can't do this! I have no idea how to write a movie."

Ronnie shrugged. "Well, lucky for you, nobody does. Look, I'll help you. And we're not *writing* it. We just need to suggest a few cuts at the end and beef up my part. That's all."

"I don't even know what the movie's about!"

"Well, you're going to have to read it obviously."

I looked down at the title page. *Ciao, Bandito.* "Hello, Gangster?"

"It's a comedy," Ronnie said. "A remake, I think. See, there's this mafioso and his daughter is marrying the nephew of a different crime boss, a *Romeo and Juliet* kind of thing, and both families come to Rome for the big wedding party and there are a bunch of misunderstandings. I play an American cousin who crashes the wedding from California, where I work as a cowboy."

"A cowboy?"

"Well, like on a dude ranch, I guess. I don't really know. Anyway, I show up, like halfway through the movie and say a bunch of stupid things in English and then I fall for the bride and mess everything up and the one guy has to talk the other guy out of killing me, but the hit man's already there, and there's this wedding feast where all the misunderstandings come to a head, a bunch of yelling and . . . well, you can imagine the rest."

I could not, for the life of me, imagine the rest.

"I'm like the fourth lead, so I just need you to sharpen my lines. Give me something interesting to do. As it is now, I just say shit like 'Y'all don't have a keg-a-beer at this wedding?' And then at the end I chase a guy on a horse." He shrugged as if this were obvious.

"But I have zero experience," I said. "This is totally beyond me!"

"Calm down, Nebraska. It's not a big deal. They're gonna loop whatever I say anyway. They dub everything into Italian here. So don't sweat it. Just find something interesting for me to say and we'll suggest it to Don Macaroni."

"He's not going to listen to me."

"He probably will, actually," Ronnie said. "I might've implied that your dad is an executive at Sony."

I was so stunned by all of this that I'd forgotten the other slip of paper I was holding. That's when Ronnie reached over and took it from me. "What's this?"

"Angelina's address," I said. I explained that it had gone well in the trailer, that I'd apologized to her, said the thing about summer camp, and then asked her out.

"Whoa," he said. "What do you mean you asked her out?"

"For you."

"What are you talking about?"

"You said that's what happens on film sets. All-you-can-eat buffet? Summer camp?"

"What's that have to do with asking Angelina out?"

"Well, what did you want me to say?"

He rubbed his jaw, and then laughed. "Remember the young

woman sitting across from Angelina in the restaurant? The one I said was beautiful?"

"I thought you were talking about Angelina."

"No, Angelina's niece, Gianna! She plays her daughter in the film. And I kissed her. The first night. We were having drinks at the bar, and Angelina came outside and caught me kissing Gianna. That's what you were supposed to apologize for." Then Ronnie laughed. "Damn, Nebraska, I know I told you that. In the bar last night."

"I was drunk!"

"Yeah, you were." He looked at the makeup trailer. "I can't believe you asked her out." Then his face changed. "And she was . . . interested?"

I nodded at the paper in his hand. "Seems like it."

"Huh." He stared at the page. "How old do you think she is?"

"I don't know," I said. "Mid- to late-forties? Around your age."

Ronnie held his hands out, as if saying, *Exactly.*

Then he looked down at the paper again. "Huh," he repeated. "Well, I guess what's done is done." I wondered then if even Sam Burke didn't sometimes underestimate the Ronnie Tower Effect. "Well, this just got more interesting, didn't it?" He laughed and slapped the screenplay in my other hand. "Let's just hope you're a better screenwriter than you are a translator."

12

The monsignor sat on a stool in front of the class, hunched over the pages in his lap, the rest of us hanging, as always, on his every word.

I sat in the front row, and looked around at the class, people rubbing their jaws and staring at the ceiling. "*Faber est suae quisque fortunae,*" the monsignor said, the students around me nodding as they contemplated the idea of man as the architect of his own fate.

"Oh, I know!" The monsignor looked up suddenly. "What if, when the cowboy shows up for the wedding, he has been through something deeply personal? Such a thing might explain his strange behavior."

People nodded and hummed. "Mmm-hmm." And "Right."

"Yes," volunteered an American art restorer named Louise. "Maybe his wife died in a car accident. And he's grieving."

Another student, an Italian nun named Sister Antonia, shook her head. "It's a comedy. I believe this would change the tone quite drastically."

Monsignor said, "Good point, Sister."

How had this happened? How had *Hello, Gangster* become our class project?

I'd showed up early, ready to apologize for the disruption the day before and to try getting back in the monsignor's good graces, when, somehow, in relating how I came to be Ronnie Tower's translator, I explained that now he needed me to cut twelve pages from his movie, while simultaneously improving his part.

Monsignor asked how I intended to do this. I admitted that I had no idea. Then he said, "May I see," and I pulled the script out of my backpack and handed it to him. He flipped through the pages, nodding and reading lines aloud. As the rest of the class filed in, he asked if he could make copies.

"I guess so," I said, and the next thing I knew our Latin class had turned into the most unlikely of TV writers rooms.

The monsignor split us into two groups. He put Nicholas Loughton in charge of one group, assigned with finding ways to cut twelve pages from the end, and he took the rest of us himself. We were the group charged with making sense of Ronnie's cowboy character.

"Perhaps you *don't* explain his behavior," said Louise. "After all, isn't ambiguity for a writer like the painter's brushstrokes. The very texture of a piece."

Monsignor nodded. "Yes. Very good."

Other ideas flowed. Perhaps the cowboy had cancer. Also not funny, said Sister Antonia, who had somehow become our arbiter of comedy. Maybe the dude ranch was closing, someone said, and he was losing his cowboy job.

"Or maybe he's not a cowboy at all."

Everyone looked at me. I felt my face flush.

"*Perge!*" said Monsignor. Keep going.

"Well." I sat up and cleared my throat. "I mean, he's a cousin from America, right? So maybe he wants them to think he's a big deal there. So he randomly chooses this thing that fits their expectations, that sounds the most American. A cowboy. But really, he's not a big success in America at all. He's struggling. At the rehearsal dinner, after the bride shoots him down, maybe he admits to her he made it all up. Bought boots and a hat at the mall before he left. He's, like, a parking valet at a restaurant or something. He just wanted to impress his family back in Italy and now he's stuck in this lie."

From the group assigned to trim twelve pages from the ending, Nicholas Loughton chimed in. "Then we could cut the scene with the horse. That's four pages."

"But we would lose the antic chase sequence," said Sister Antonia, whose negativity, frankly, was starting to annoy everyone. "That's the climax of the cowboy's arc."

"No," I said. "We don't *lose* the chase scene, we just cut it back. Do the whole thing like he *is* a cowboy chasing someone on a horse . . . but instead of the long setup where we show the stables and he runs into them and saddles the horse, we just have him jump on a bicycle, from behind, the way old cowboys sometimes jumped on horses. Then he chases the hit man, leaps off the bike and tackles him. We turn four pages into one."

"That's funny," said Sister Antonia.

"*Animus risu novatur,*" said Monsignor.

"The spirit is renewed with laughter," said Nicholas Loughton.

"More *refreshed* than *renewed*," said Monsignor, "but yes, I think Cicero would approve."

By the end of the three-hour class, we had somehow managed to cut twelve pages and still give Ronnie Tower a moving speech about how he'd tried to impress his Italian relatives. And the new chase scene was half as many pages and twice as funny. Even that hard-ass Sister Antonia approved of the changes. Then Monsignor assigned everyone a role, and he announced that we would be doing a table reading of the script the very next day. Extra points for anyone who learned their lines in Latin.

13

When I got back to my apartment that afternoon, Ronnie Tower was waiting for me, leaning against the wall of the old automotive shop, finishing a cigarette. "I smoke when I'm nervous," he said, and dropped it, grinding it out with the toe of his boot. "Hey, I need to talk to you, Nebraska."

"I wanted to talk to you, too," I said. "You're not going to believe this, but I think we actually improved your script."

Sister Antonia had compiled the best of our notes onto a single copy, cuts in red, new dialogue in black. The monsignor had carefully signed it in his large elaborate hand: "Submitted this day with the greatest honor and humility, Mgr Arturo Giacomo Edoardo Festa, Secretariat of State, Vatican, Rome, *Societas Iesu*: Society of Jesus. *Docendo Discimus*."

He translated the last bit for me: "By teaching we learn." I imagined, for a moment, this strange document somehow making its way into the official archives of papal bulls—but then Monsignor Festa handed me the script and held out his pen. "You should sign it, too." And so, I did, beneath his florid signature, in my tiny elementary-school penmanship: "Jack Rigel, Oct. 11, 1993."

And now I handed Ronnie the script, but he barely looked at it as he followed me inside the old garage. Something else was on his mind. He glanced around the hallway as I opened the door of my cold, dark room. With both of us inside, there was nowhere to stand so I sat on the bed. He leaned against my writing table and looked around.

"This is where you live?"

"Yeah."

"Yikes." He bent over the typewriter. There was a page in it and two pages stacked next to it, the sum of my creativity since I'd arrived in Rome. He picked up the pages and thumbed through them without seeming to register that there were words on them.

"It's not finished," I said. "And it's . . . kind of personal."

He set the pages down, reached in his coat pocket and emerged with a familiar slip of paper, which he handed to me. Angelina's address.

"You go," he said. "Tell her I can't make it."

"Why?"

"I had them bring me a VCR last night. And I watched a couple of her movies."

"Angelina's?"

He nodded. "She's the real thing."

"Yes," I said. "I think so."

"Yeah, I'm not going over there."

"Why? I don't understand."

Just then, a soccer ball pounded against the metal door outside my apartment and Ronnie jumped. I had never seen him like this. "What the hell was that?"

"These kids play soccer in the piazza. Happens a lot."

"Right," he said. "Because this place isn't shitty enough." He chewed the inside of his cheek. "Anyway, you can just go in my place."

I looked back at the address. "And say what?"

"I don't know. Make my apologies. Tell her I'm busy." Then another blast of the soccer ball. *Bam!* Ronnie jumped again. "Christ, how do you put up with that?"

"I've talked to them," I said. "They don't listen."

Bam! The loudest one yet, and Ronnie bolted out the door of my apartment. I followed him, down the hall and outside, where he stood on my single-step stoop, glaring at the kids, arms crossed. They ignored him, of course, and kept playing. There were four boys, the oldest thirteen or fourteen, all of them in baggy shorts and skate shoes.

Hoping to avoid trouble, I decided I should give it one more try. "*Uh, scusate,*" I called to the boys. "*State calmi, per favore?*"

They barely glanced up, offering their usual profanities: "*Vai a farti fottere, a cojone!*" and "*Alla pecorina!*"

Ronnie looked over at me.

"I think they're saying we should go have sex with ourselves," I said, "in, uh, the manner of sheep."

Ronnie gave a small nod, as if he appreciated their profane creativity. Then he started toward the boys, hands in his pockets. He looked calm, but I was worried. He wasn't going to fight with children, was he? And if he did, should I help?

He walked right into the center of their game, like a coach intent on correcting their form. The boys paused. In the center, Ronnie looked around, from slack face to slack face. The tallest of the boys barely came to his shoulder, and still, somehow, I was afraid for him. Finally, he held out his hands. "What do you call that," he asked. "*Futbol?*"

Surprisingly, one of the boys kicked the ball to him.

Ronnie picked it up. Turned it over in his hands. He looked at the boys again, one by one, then said, "Here's trouble," and dropped it onto his foot and booted it, his leg coming up nearly as high as his head. The faces of the soccer hooligans rose in shock and appreciation as they watched the ball sail over the nearest building and disappear.

"Chico State University, 1967, Division II all-section punter," he said. Then he added, "Don't ever mess with a *real* football player, boys." And with that, Ronnie Tower walked off.

14

Later that evening, I crossed the Tiber alone and walked through the Roman Centro, up the Spanish Steps and the Pincian Hill into the huge Villa Borghese Park. It was a warm evening, and the streets were crowded with people out strolling. Angelina's house was just off the tree-lined via Veneto, in Rione Ludovisi, a neighborhood of luxury hotels and restaurants with outdoor tables filled with tan men in loafers and bejeweled women with leashed-up little dogs.

As I walked, I practiced my Berlitz small talk (*Che bella casa! Mi piace molto il paesaggio.* Nice house. I like the landscaping.) before turning the corner onto Angelina's street.

The buildings here were less grand than the palaces and museums on via Veneto, but still beautiful, in classic Roman colors: coral, copper-red, marble white, with small groves of trees and classic-looking sculptures matter-of-factly adorning the gardens. Angelina's villa was the largest, taking up half a block, a broad, three-story stone house built around a courtyard whose gate was propped open so that I could see a small blue convertible parked at an angle inside.

Should I go into the courtyard? Immediately begin complimenting the landscaping? Or knock on the big ornate front door and remark on the *bella casa*? And if I did go to the front door, should I ring the bell or swing the big door knocker?

I suddenly found myself stricken with insecurity. What was I even doing here? I wasn't inside yet and I was already frozen. Who was I? Ronnie's translator? His apologist? A Latin student? A priest? For god's sake, a script doctor?

Standing outside her lavish home, my thin confidence gave out entirely, once and for all, and I felt a great fatigue come over me, weary from all the pretending I had been doing. *Truer than truth*? I felt like nothing, a blank piece of paper, one that a breeze might pick up and blow away. And maybe that would be for the best. At that moment, I could not imagine a soul in the world would miss Jack Rigel—new version or old.

"Were you planning to stand there all evening, or would you like to come in?" The voice was Italian, but with just the slightest hint of a British accent.

Startled, I looked up at the front door to the house. And like Venus out of the sea, Angelina Amadio emerged wearing a pair of silky blue pants, sandals, and a white top, her luscious dark hair piled on top of her head.

She was, as always, beautiful. But I realized this was the first time I had ever seen her in normal light, not behind glass, on a movie screen, or in a makeup trailer mirror. I suppose you could say it was the first time I'd seen her as a human being. Afterward, I would think about that, as well as that word, *beautiful*, how arbitrary the collection of attributes it entails: a certain bone structure, the contrast of eyes and hair, a quality of skin.

But in that moment, it wasn't her looks that stunned me. It was that she'd addressed me in pitch-perfect English.

"Are you all right, love?" She came down the steps and walked toward me. "You look as if you've seen a ghost. Would you like a glass of water?"

I had planned to arrive and give Angelina my clear-up-this-misunderstanding speech in my usual choppy Italian—"*Buona sera, Signora Amadio. Sono molto dispiaciuto per l'equivoco che ho causato ieri.*"

But hearing her speak English had frozen me again.

Was I now expected to explain all of this in English? That Ronnie wasn't coming? That his affections had been aimed, not at her, but at her *niece*? I had counted on my bad Italian to at least go halfway in explaining the misunderstanding. But now, in a language that I actually spoke fluently, English, I had nowhere to hide.

As I mulled this, the Angel of Rome strode easily toward me, a warm smile on her face, her movements as smooth as if she were skating across a pond. "You're rather a skittish creature," she said, "aren't you?"

"I—I'm sorry," I said. "I didn't expect you to speak English." Then I caught myself. "So well, I mean."

"Ah, yes," she said. "The young man who saw *A Feeding*." She shook her head. "Isn't that the way of the world? You make one awful vampire movie and the world expects you to be a moron."

"No, no," I said. "You were amazing in it. The best part."

"Thank you." Angelina smiled. "Though it's rather like being told you were the best part of a plane crash."

Then she explained that the director of that movie had told her to lean on her accent even harder, since the vampires' foreignness was meant to be part of their mystery. "In the meantime," she said, "I only realized later that the script, besides being awful, was an Italian speaker's minefield. Hard *h*'s and stacked consonants, long *e*'s and sibilant *s*'s. It was as if someone wrote an entire script whose sole purpose was to make an Italian sound insane. 'Theese make-a-me-appy! Get under the shit!'"

She said she was so horrified after seeing the final cut of *A Feeding* that she immediately signed up to study English in London, so that she would be ready the next time Hollywood came calling. "But alas," she added, "there was to be no second call. And by then, I was a joke in America."

But she didn't say this with sadness, exactly, or with what I would even call regret, but rather, a kind of bemusement, as if it had happened to someone else. Sometimes, she said, it even paid off to have people believe that she couldn't speak English, to withhold that part of herself. "It simplifies things," she said. "Like with your friend, the American TV star."

I explained that Ronnie wasn't coming.

"Oh," she said. "I hadn't expected him to. The invitation was for you."

My face must've given away my shock. She hummed a little laugh, took my arm and gestured to the house. "Mr. Rigel, please, won't you come inside?"

15

She showed me around the main floor of her grand house rather quickly and dismissively, as if it were all a bit embarrassing. Here a simple Borghese vase, there a minor Caravaggio, over there, a Modigliani portrait. Beautiful frescoes adorned the ceilings, and books and pottery sat on every shelf and surface. If I had expected the trappings of a film star—movie posters and crystal chandeliers—what I found instead was like the home of a retired professor, a bit like Rome itself: two thousand years of culture and art existing side by side.

The house was a large, hollow rectangle, with a courtyard and gardens in the middle, which is where we ended up, beneath a squat lemon tree, sitting on wrought iron chairs with glasses of iced Venetian spritz she poured us from an outdoor bar, garnished with a fresh lemon she picked and sliced right there.

Between us and the little blue convertible in the car turnaround was a weathered sculpture of what appeared to be a toga-clad Roman addressing the Senate, his broken finger raised as if in debate.

She saw me looking at the statue. "I had it appraised after my father died. Turns out it's a copy, at least four hundred years newer than Papa believed it was. But still, it reminds me of him." She caught herself. "Not that Papa was a copy. He was nothing if not original. But I always used to say that his generation was made of marble, and mine, of plastic."

Then she smiled wistfully, and asked several questions about me, where I was from, and how I came to be in Rome working as the curiously inept translator for an American TV star. So I told her about the Knights of Columbus scholarship and my mother wanting me to be a priest ("You, a priest," she said, "I'm afraid I don't see it.") and about Ronnie, er, Sam Burke, misunderstanding my studying Latin for studying Italian.

She laughed at this and clapped her hands. "Latin! Oh, how I would love to take a class in Latin. To study the taproot of all of this." She waved her hand around at the courtyard, at the art around us. "You must feel so fortunate."

I blushed. Did I? Feel fortunate? I felt rather embarrassed in fact, seeing my opportunity through her eyes, and realizing I was wasting it feeling sorry for myself. I imagined what the starstruck film and TV buff Monsignor Festa would think if, unannounced,

I should happen to bring the Angel of Rome to class one day. I pictured the man's head exploding.

"I wish I had known about languages when I was your age," she said, "when I had more capacity for learning. Instead, I wasted the years when my mind was its hungriest making my body look famished for the cameras."

I was surprised at how easy she was to talk to, and how forthcoming she was about herself. She told me this was to be her final movie, and when I reacted with surprise, she confided that she'd always promised herself she would only act as long as the possibility existed for a great role.

"I was just explaining this to my very impatient niece," she said. "I told her that during my acting years, I was always waiting for the perfect part. Something complex and human. Of course, it never came. Instead, I was offered the detective's love interest. The other woman. The vampire in Los Angeles.

"Then, perhaps two years ago, I was in the makeup chair—like the one you saw me in yesterday—watching my face being made up for the thousandth time, and I thought: *Wait*. What if *I* am the role I've been waiting for? Oh, I cannot tell you the excitement that came over me then. The sense of wonder. Of all that I might do. Why wait for the opportunity to act interesting for other people, when I could act for myself?"

She stared off, past the statue in her courtyard, and hummed another laugh. "I always said that I would quit acting when they began offering me the mother roles. That's the beginning of the end for an actress. I was lucky to have made it well into my forties without playing a mom, but look, here I am, playing the mother of the bride." She clapped her hands and showed them like a magician. "*Sei finita. Ciao Bandita.*"

Goodbye bandit.

"So, what now?" I asked.

A deep breath and a smile. "Oh my," she said, "so many things! I honestly don't know where to start! I am going to learn to paint, to write, to travel without purpose, to wake up each day and decide what I want to do." She laughed. "To eat like a human being, and let my hair go gray. Who knows, maybe I'll take Latin."

She reached out then and squeezed my forearm. "I have this fantasy."

And even though I knew this wasn't what she meant, I must admit that my breath left my body when Angelina Amadio put her hand on my arm, leaned forward and said she had a fantasy.

She sat back in her chair. "I wake up. I put on shoes. I walk down the stairs. I go out into the street. It's quiet, no one is about. I look both ways. And in that moment, I can do anything. I can go right. Or I can go left. Up a hill or down. To the ocean or to the country. And I don't know what I will do." She laughed. "And that's it. That's the whole fantasy. That I might go left. Or I might go right."

I could see it then, someone like her, who had spent her whole life feeling watched, anticipated, expected to be something, longing for the freedom of such a simple choice. "That's lovely," I said.

She shrugged. "You are easy to talk to, Jack. I see after all why your mother thinks you'd make a good priest."

By now I had forgotten all about Ronnie Tower, or how I got there. I just wanted to sit all evening in that courtyard, beneath a lemon tree, sipping this drink and talking with the Angel of Rome. But at that moment, one of the doors to the courtyard was flung open, and a young woman appeared, tall and thin, in a multicolored skirt that trailed her as she hurried outside.

I recognized her immediately, of course: Angelina's niece Gianna, the girl who had been sitting across from her in the restaurant two days earlier, and the one Ronnie Tower had *actually* wanted to have summer-camp amnesty sex with.

Angelina rose. "Gianna. Good, I want you to meet someone. This is Jack Rigel. He is a translator and a Latin scholar from America."

It sounded so impressive hearing it in her voice.

"Jack," she said, "this is Gianna, my niece, and quite the budding actress. Although I have been encouraging her to go to university next year instead."

Her niece sighed at Angelina's not-so-subtle dig, her eyes barely passing over me. "Hello. Nice to meet you."

If Angelina had just a hint of British schooling in her accent, Gianna could have been mistaken for a Londoner, which made sense, I would find out later, since she had spent the last four years at a British boarding school. "*Zia,* I am going out."

Angelina seemed surprised. "Right now?"

"Yes." Gianna walked toward the blue sports car. "I told you that, remember?"

"I assumed that was after dinner. You're not going to meet Mr. Burke, I hope."

"Who?" she said.

For the first time, Angelina seemed irked. "Sam Burke? The esteemed American television actor? The man whose mouth you were sticking your tongue into the other night?"

Gianna smirked as if this were hilarious. "You're going to have to be more specific." Then she looked at me and made a can-you-believe-it face. "It was a party, *Zia*! I was drunk. I probably kissed five people that night. But you know that nothing happened. I came home with you, for god's sake."

"Right," Angelina said, "that's why I thought you might like to get to know Jack here. I thought it would be good to meet someone your own age. Someone who does more than go dance in clubs and do coke all night."

I was quiet during this testy exchange but already my thoughts were racing: 1. Angelina had invited me over to meet her niece? B. Poor Ronnie Tower. This girl didn't even know who he was. And 3. On the bright side, I did finally know where he might score some cocaine.

"Oh my god!" Gianna said, her voice now sounding less British boarding school than indignant American teen. "Are you trying to set me *up*?" Then she looked at me, really for the first time. "With him?"

Before I could say a word—not that I would've known what to say—they were yelling at each other, some English, some Italian, my eyes going back and forth like it was a tennis match:

"I can't believe you!"

"Gianna, I told my brother I'd watch out for you!"

"Leave my father out of this!"

"Do you want him knowing that you're out all night!"

"You never wanted me to be in this film!"

"I didn't want you making the mistakes I made!"

"You can't stand anyone else getting any attention!"

"That's not at all true!"

"There's no room for anyone to be a star but *you*!"

"Have you even heard a word I've said?"

Back and forth it went like this, as I sank into my leather coat.

And if there is one thing I can say for my employer and good friend, Ronnie Tower, it's this: the man knew how to make an entrance.

"Bwon-Jerno, ladies!" he called out just then, as he stepped into the courtyard alongside the blue sports car. He was wearing a suit jacket over an open shirt and what looked like a cravat, or an ascot. And he was carrying a large bouquet of flowers.

"Here's trouble," I muttered to myself.

16

"Good," Ronnie Tower said to me, "you're here."

"Oh, hey," I said, "I was just about to explain——"

"No," he interrupted me. "Listen, I was an idiot. I was scared, stupid. Just help me do this now. I'll talk, you translate."

Then he turned to Angelina's niece and spoke to her across the blue car. "Gianna. First, let me say, you are a beautiful girl. But it was wrong for me to kiss you the other night. It was, as we say in America, not appropriate."

He looked at me, and even though everyone spoke English in that courtyard, I felt obliged to translate. This was the Ronnie Tower Effect: if the man said you were a translator, you were a translator. "*Uh, sei bella, et in America, baciare e brutto,*" I said. You are beautiful and in America, kissing is ugly.

I glanced over at Angelina, who had a befuddled look on her face.

"You should not worry though," Ronnie continued to Gianna. "You are young, and you will find someone, hopefully someone closer to your own age." He turned to me, and I said to Gianna, in Italian, something like, "No be sad. Is good get old."

"And while I know the pain of heartache will be difficult for you," Ronnie said, "one day, perhaps many years from now, you will see that this was the right thing."

"In years, the heart pain is good," I said in Italian.

"Oh, for Christ's sake," Gianna said. "Idiots, the lot of you." She climbed in the car, started it, and zipped off.

The rest of us watched the convertible pull up to the open court-yard gate, wink its taillights and disappear around the corner.

"She'll be okay," Ronnie said. "It was hard, but it needed to be done."

Then he turned to Angelina. "And to you, my dear Ms. Ama-dio, I owe the deepest of apologies. As you can surely see by now, I am not a sophisticated man, but even I know when I have met someone remarkable."

I have no idea what I said to approximate this part of Ronnie's speech. I just tried to make noises that sounded vaguely Italian.

"I was up all night," Ronnie said, "watching some of your films. You are wonderful. And honestly, I got intimidated. I will be fifty years old in a couple of weeks. And what do I have to show for it? A bungalow in Malibu? A TV show that isn't even on the air anymore?"

He looked at me. I muttered a few words in Italian: house, pencil, automobile, and then nodded for him to continue.

"I was scared," he said to me, "but that's no way to live." Then, a deep breath and he turned back to Angelina. "Jack here tells me that he asked you out on my behalf. Well, I would be honored if you would consider that invitation again, this time from me."

I did my best to translate this part. And when I was done, Angelina looked from me to Ronnie and back. Then she stood. She turned to me, and said, formally, in Italian:

"Mr. Rigel, would you please tell Mr. Tower that I will give some thought to his request. And when we have finished this movie, he may call upon me again. At that time, if he and I have gotten along well, and assuming his translator has finally found the name of a good discotheque, I may take him up on it."

17

Translation is the art of imprecision. You can never get it exactly right. And so, you do the best you can, with the knowledge that accuracy is less important than the feelings you're trying to convey.

Looking back over the years, I think it's been that way with writing, too. This is something I've come to realize in my career as a television writer, that *feeling* is what matters. Sure, the screenwriting books tell you there's a formula, three acts here, rising action there, resolution over there. In the meetings, you can see the nervous producers cling to these formulas like blind beggars hoping for salvation.

It's all bullshit. You're just trying to create feelings. It's what works on the page. On-screen. In life.

IT'S BEEN ALMOST thirty years since I went to Rome for the first time. And now I am landing at Fiumicino–Leonardo da Vinci Airport again, with Sela and our two boys. Ostensibly, this is a vacation. The cable TV show I've helped write for the last seven years, *Communion,* about a priest who sets out to help migrants but ends up becoming a drug runner, just filmed its final episode, and I promised Sela we would do something to celebrate my new-found freedom from the unending demands of the writers room.

I am blessed to have had the career I've had, although this middling TV show will probably be the pinnacle of it, at least as far as the world will know. Like most writers, maybe like most people, my actual screen credits reflect only a fraction of what I've worked on, and certainly not my best work. It's something people don't really get about Hollywood, how little of what we do actually gets made. It's been the hardest part of writing scripts the last twenty-five years; each one is like a small prayer, offered up to the most callous of gods.

I hope I don't sound cynical. I'm not. I love what I do, and I've always tried to carry myself with the bemused grace and good fortune of the great Angelina Amadio. I know how lucky I am to do something creative with my life, to do what I love.

Of course, I got no official credit on the first film that I worked on, the surprise 1994 Italian hit, *Ciao, Bandito*, released in America as *The Wedding Party*. But then again, neither did the stars of our Latin writers room, Monsignor Festa and that comic genius, Sister Antonia. Our work was done, like that of most script doctors, behind the scenes.

But Domenico Macrino thought the changes were brilliant, as did the director, and they used most of them. And when Domenico moved to America a few years later to work in the writers room of *The Sopranos,* he remembered my contributions, and was quick to connect me with industry professionals, as was my good friend and mentor Ronnie Tower.

By then, I had finished my time in Rome and was in film

school. But no matter what's happened since then, that year in Rome will always be the best of my life. Getting to know Angelina and working with Ronnie—who paid me so generously I survived until the Italian mail system delivered my next scholarship check—and devoting myself to Monsignor Festa's class and to the pure love of languages—which, in turn, made me a better writer—all of it was life-changing, even though I remained the worst Latin speaker in the class.

Feeling over precision. This is true not only of translation and film, but also of memory. And so, I finish my Rome story now, with no guarantee of accuracy, only that this is how it felt:

That evening in October of 1993, Ronnie Tower and I walked away from Angelina's villa straight to a pizzeria. "That went surprisingly well," he said.

We got a carafe of wine and a pizza and Ronnie told me he had another idea. I had been so helpful to him that he wanted to do a favor for me. Next weekend, he said, we could rent a car and driver and go to Florence, to the Georgetown campus, where we would drive around until we saw "Cassandra whatever-her-name-is."

"Clarissa Mills," I said. "But I don't think we need to do that. I mean, *I* know I'm in Rome. I know what I'm doing here. Maybe that's enough, huh?"

He thought about this for a while. Then he looked down and seemed to notice that he was wearing a scarf tied into a cravat. "A guy at the hotel did this for me." He took it off and considered it in his hand. "Hey," he said, "did I ever tell you how I got cast as Ronnie Tower?"

I said he hadn't.

"After college and Vietnam, I got on as a union carpenter, working for CBS, building sets. Another vet, an old Seabee, got me a job on the second-to-last season of *Gunsmoke* and one day my girlfriend and I got in a fight, and she kicked me out. I was sleeping in my car, and I came to work all dirty and unshaven. The director took one look at me and asked if I could ride a horse. 'Of course,' I said. I signed up for horseback riding classes that very day. Got an agent, changed my name, and before you know it, I'm in front of the cameras. One role led to another and a few years later, I'm an ass-kicking detective in Santa Monica."

"Here's trouble," I said.

He smiled and stared into his wineglass. "Here's my point, Nebraska. The night we met, you said something I've been thinking a lot about. You said you wanted to live authentically, to stop pretending you were someone else. I get that. But I don't think I agree with it.

"I mean, who are you if you can't make it up? Especially people like you and me. Are we just supposed to stay the shitheads our parents and high schools sent out into the world, the ones our classmates assumed would do nothing with our lives?"

He looked at the scarf in his hand again. "Not me. No way I'm going to be the loser my old man thought I was. And your dad! He didn't even know you. Two thousand dollars? Shit." He shook his head. "I mean, guys like you and me, Nebraska, what choice do we have *except* to invent ourselves? Over and over if we have to, until we get it right."

18

I have thought of that conversation every day for almost thirty years. And I remember it now as my family and I ride in a van toward Trastevere, where we will be staying for the next three days in an old convent converted into a hotel at the base of the Janiculum Hill. After that, I have promised my wife a real vacation, so we're taking the train to Naples, where a car will deliver us to a fancy hotel on the Amalfi Coast.

But first, we check into the old convent, and I get the air-conditioning to work, sign the boys into the WiFi and watch them disappear into handheld heaven.

I kiss Sela and grab my messenger bag. "Wish me luck," I say.

"You don't need luck," she says. "You're Jack Rigel."

Rome has changed, of course. It always does. This is the first time I've been here in more than a decade, and only the third time since my year at the Vatican.

Monsignor Festa died just a year after that. He probably had cancer while he was teaching our class, but I don't know if he knew it or not. I never saw Nicholas Loughton's book, but I have no doubt that it was eventually published. He didn't lack for ambition. As for the art restorer Louise, and our resident aesthete, Sister Antonia, I never saw them or any of the other students again. And me? I still speak both Latin *and* Italian like a six-year-old.

I look out the window as my cab winds along the beautiful via Veneto. It seems smaller and less grand than in my memories. When we turn and park in front of Angelina's villa, it, too, seems to have been shrunk by time.

I consider standing in front of the house until she notices me, like she did years ago, but instead I walk up to the door and ring the bell.

And with a wide smile, my own Angel of Rome answers the door. "Nebraska!" says Ronnie Tower. "What are you doing here?"

"How are you, Sam?"

"I'm excellent!" he says, his voice a gravelly remnant of that old Ronnie rumble. He turns and yells back into the house. "Angie. Jack's here! Did you know he was coming?"

Sam's turn in *Ciao, Bandito* led to a string of comedies in which he played a well-meaning but dim American. Italian audiences loved to watch Ronnie Tower look stupid. This led to his old cop show being syndicated in Italy, and to endorsements, and while he never quite made it back to the States, he had a nice second act in Italy.

Still, even less conceivable to me is how he managed to get Angelina to fall in love with him. I suppose he just imagined it, and it happened. Either that or it was the discotheque I eventually recommended.

And now Angelina comes down the stairs, in a white sundress, her gray hair cut short and spiky. Even in her seventies, she is striking. I have still never figured out that word *beautiful,* but pressed for a definition, I think I would simply offer up Angelina Amadio. True to her word, she never acted again after *Ciao, Bandito,* but she did write two books, a memoir about her father's era of Italian filmmakers, and an illustrated children's book about a caterpillar who befriends a cloud. I don't know if she ever mastered Latin, or learned to paint, but I would be surprised if she didn't.

"Jack," she says, and envelops me in her arms.

We settle in the courtyard with glasses of iced tea, a drink Angelina says Sam introduced to her. "You cannot believe how hard it is to get good iced tea in this country," he says, as Angelina slices up another lemon from that craggy old tree.

They ask about my kids, and I tell them the boys are great, twelve and ten.

"Sam's daughter has kids, a boy and a girl," Angelina says. "They visit every year."

"We have to rent a place on the coast," Sam says. "Turns out this is not the best house for grandkids. Break a vase with a football and you find out it's, like, a thousand years old."

"Two, dear," Angelina says, and reaches over to squeeze his hand.

"Two thousand, my bad." He smiles at me, then looks back at Angelina. "Did you know Jack was coming today?"

She squeezes his hand again and we small talk some more and Angelina tells me they're on season four of *Communion*. "It's very good," Angelina says, "quite suspenseful."

And that seems like a good lead-in to why I'm here. I explain that after finishing a successful TV show, a writer has a rare combination of juice and latitude. "So, I decided to write something different. A feature."

I reach in my bag and pull out the script, which I hand to Sam. He reads the title. "Hey!" and shows Angelina: "*Tower & Bridges*. By Jack Rigel."

"It's a two-hour movie," I say, "kind of a reboot, this time with women playing the detective roles. And the original Ronnie Tower is the police commissioner."

"You're kidding." Sam opens the script. "Nebraska! I don't know what to say."

"I got permission from CBS, which owns the series. Your pages are flagged, Sam."

"My pages?"

"You think there's someone else who could ever play Ronnie Tower?"

Sam laughs—a deep hoot—and I look over to see Angelina smiling widely as she watches him.

"There's something for you in there, too," I tell her. "It's not a big role, but I tried to make her complex and human. You told me once that it's what you were waiting for. Oh, and she's nobody's mother. She's just herself."

"Jack." Moved, Angelina puts her hand to her chest. "Thank you. I honestly can't imagine acting again, but it's wonderful that you thought of me."

"And," I say, "she keeps her shirt on the whole movie."

"Boo," says Sam.

Then he turns to Angelina. "You have to at least read it. How great would it be to work on something together?" Then, back to me. "She always says no, but you can sometimes convince her of things." He studies the title page again, as if it might have changed in the last minute. "Ha! I don't know what to say."

Now Angelina reaches across the table for my hand, and squeezes it.

We finish our drinks, and I tell them I should get back to my family. Angelina says she'll see me out.

At the end of the courtyard, I turn back and look once more at the great Ronnie Tower, leaning forward in one of the wrought iron chairs, a little grayer, maybe a little smaller, but still so big, still so . . . *himself.* He reads something from the script and laughs again, "Ha!"—a broad smile on his face as he flips the pages.

Outside, on the curb, Angelina takes both of my hands in hers. "Thank you so much for this."

"He seems good."

"The medication is helping," she says. "He gets confused in the afternoons, but for the most part—" She smiles and doesn't finish the thought.

"I'm so sorry," I say.

She smiles again and her voice levels into a tone that tells me there will be no pity allowed here. "We've been having the love-liest summer. And this thing you've done for him—for us—what an amazing gift, Jack."

"You know that it has very little chance of ever getting made."

"Of course," she says. "That's what makes it so generous. And for him? To wake up each day and discover that someone he cares so deeply for has written something just for him? What a won-derful tribute."

Angelina hugs me again, and we both hold on a second longer.

She steps back and takes me in with her eyes once more. She says—"*Vale, dilecte mi*"—Goodbye, my adored—in Latin. (Of course she has learned it.) And then Angelina Amadio turns and goes back to the house, pausing at the door to give me a small wave, as I think of her hand against the restaurant window all those years ago.

The door closes, and I walk back to my waiting car. But I'm not ready to go back to the hotel just yet. I ask the cabbie if he can just drive around a bit. "*Sì*," he says. "Where to?"

I look out at the street and I think: we can go left. Or right. Up the hill. Or down. "It doesn't matter."

The driver steers us onto via Veneto and I sit back as the cab navigates a gentle tree-lined curve. There are red geraniums in the median, and on the sidewalk a young couple—they can't be twenty—are holding hands, swinging their arms as they walk, laughing at something only they know. It just keeps happening, Rome—over and over, the city reinventing itself for each new generation. And us, too, I suppose, if we have the courage, and the people to show us the way.

Written in collaboration with Edoardo Ballerini

Before You Blow

THIS WAS THE SUMMER you spent at the river, the summer of your first beer, first job, first love—the summer of '83. The summer of Joey.

You met him at Geno's Fabulous Pizza at the end of your junior year of high school. Geno's was a fixture in the Gonzaga neighborhood: checkered tablecloths, candles in Chianti bottles, oregano-red sauce splattered on overcooked pasta. All the Catholic families in Spokane went there, yours included—the kids for pizza and spumoni, the parents for rigatoni and chilled Lambrusco. One night, your family was having dinner and the owner asked if you needed a summer job and the next thing you knew, you were busing tables. You were fast and could carry three water glasses in each hand. You felt like an adult. Then, in July, one of the waitresses broke her wrist and you got promoted. And immediately Joey began flirting with you through the kitchen pass-through window, as if, when you were a busser you had been too young to notice, but as a waitress, you were fair game.

You could feel his eyes on you every time you spun a ticket on the order wheel. "Lasagna, spaghetti with tips, small mushroom and sausage pizza."

"Got it, Jeans," he'd say.

The owner, Shirley, had recently allowed waitresses to dress more casually, instead of buying uniforms from the food service catalogue. So, while the older women wore their old poly pants and hip-pocket shirts, you got to wear jeans.

"Order up, Jeans," Joey would say, sliding a lasagna through the window.

He worked the pizza oven on Friday and Saturday nights and baked the comically big lasagnas, whose recipe, he claimed, was: "noodle, sauce, cheese; noodle, sauce, cheese; lather, rinse, repeat." You thought this was hilarious. But then, everything Joey did and said that summer was hilarious.

It felt like flirting, but you knew it could just be teasing. After all, he was at least four years older than you, an upper classman at Gonzaga University, and what college senior wants to date a high school kid? Then, one day you were counting tips and you felt someone over your shoulder. He smelled like shaving cream. You turned, and Joey smiled. "Hey, Jeans," he said. "Don't suppose I could get the phone number of that ass?"

Okay then.

It was to be love.

That night, he pulled you into the walk-in and kissed you.

Joey was twenty-two. He had a grown man's body: a series of squares all the way up to his block of brown hair. His eyes were green and arched, with a quality one might generously call mischievous. He was prelaw, and already applying to law schools.

"'Law school!'" your mother said, as if he'd just confided that he was a prince. "Well!" She looked at your dad. "Do you hear that, Mark? A lawyer."

Your parents and brother had come to the restaurant the weekend after Joey kissed you, the hostess seating them at a four-top in
your section. You'd explained to Joey that you weren't sure your
parents would approve of you going out with a college boy, so
he'd volunteered to bring two glasses of Chianti to the table and
introduce himself—an old-fashioned move meant to score points
with your dad.

There was small talk about Gonzaga (Joey: "It was important to me and my parents that I go to a Catholic school.") and
his career plans ("I hope to do more with the law than just
make money.") and finally, Joey gestured back at the kitchen
("Well, I'd better get back to work."). He shook your dad's
hand firmly. "It was a pleasure meeting you." Then he bowed
to your mother. "I certainly see where your daughter gets her
good looks. Those are some strong genes."

And with that he turned and winked, knowing what you
would hear: *Jeans*.

"A lawyer!" your mother said again after Joey had left. She
looked at your dad, who raised a single eyebrow of approval.

Later, you would wonder at the way your parents had reacted;
you almost felt *presented* to this college man, like maybe your dad
expected two cows and an acre of land in return. You would also
wonder, did they *know* any lawyers, so apparent was it that they
saw Joey as being in a higher class. Your father was an electrician,
your mother was . . . well, a mother. Your older brother Mike
wanted to be a motorcycle cop; that's what passed for ambition in
your family. It was the first time you really thought about a career
having anything to do with your station in life. Before, you always
thought of careers as simple job descriptions, like figurines in an

old PlaySkool town. This one's a fireman. That one's a teacher. It didn't occur to you that a certain profession might make you a more important person, a better human being.

"What made you want to be a lawyer?" you asked Joey that night.

He shrugged. "My dad's a lawyer. His dad's a lawyer. Dad's dad's dad. My first ancestor probably practiced cave-law."

Joey's roommate Patrick was also prelaw and was also from the Bay Area. For California Catholics like them in the 1980s, Gonzaga was a last-ditch safety school—get a minor-in-possession or flunk a class or two, and the parents might nix Santa Clara or San Francisco (don't even think about Stanford or Cal) and exile you to cold, sleepy Spokane. There, the transplanted Californians whined about the lack of nightlife and trudged monastically through the snow, hoods up on their parkas. As Patrick used to say, "I messed around and ended up here. At Fuck-up State."

It was shocking, the way Joey and Patrick talked about your hometown. Not that you thought Spokane, Washington, was anything special—but back then you had nothing to compare it to. You'd never lived anywhere else, had never really *been* anywhere else. So, the way they treated it—the dismissal, the condescension, the mockery, these were a revelation to you.

Spokane was indeed cold, and it was surely remote, and yes, its downtown was sleepy, but Joey and Patrick were anything but monastic. They ran around like Butch and Sundance, charming their way out of Ds from professors and DUIs from cops. They got drunk almost every night, sometimes with the Jesuits. They made impromptu road trips to Canada to buy cases of Kokanee and Labatt, because those beers had higher alcohol content. They bought pot from the girlfriend of an English prof and speed from a biker who lived down the street. They bought booze for your high school friends and let you invite them to parties.

You thought they were hilarious. Sexy. They had pet names for everything, a language all their own. They called Gonzaga *Gonzo U*, and they called each other Fitz (Patrick Fitzgerald) and Mac (Joseph McCune). They called you Jeans. They treated the city like a playground, or a college rental, with no respect for windows, walls, drapes, curbs, carpets, speed limits, property, daughters. To them, the word *Spokane* was a modifier that meant decadent fun. They didn't just get drunk, they got *Spodrunk* they peed off the Monroe Street Bridge. Joey was *Spohungover* the next day he puked in a neighbor's flowerbed. Patrick got *Spohorny* that night he asked out the twenty-five-year-old checker from Safeway, Harmony.

And that's how you ended up one night late that summer in Harmony's brown Ford Pinto, Patrick in the passenger seat, you and Joey pressed into the small backseat on either side of Harmony's kid, Morton. Morton was maybe two, a pacifier bobbing in and out of his mouth, no car seat to be seen.

"Morton?" you asked his mom. "Is that a family name?"

"It's a salt," Harmony said.

Everyone was drinking Schlitz, the cans with a big blue bull on them—because Patrick insisted malt liquor was *classier* than regular beer.

"You should call him Sporton," Joey said. "Like . . . Morton from Spokane."

"I feel like that would limit his options," Harmony said.

You drove around that way for a while, drinking beer and looking for something to do. Harmony asked what you did for a living. You didn't even consider telling her that you were still in high school. "I work with Joey," you said.

"At Geno's? I love the salad there. What kind of dressing is that?"

"Italian, I guess."

"Oh yeah, that makes sense," she said.

What could fill the hours between 5:00 p.m. and sunset on a summer day? You drove here, drove there, chattered inanely. You went to a thrift store and Patrick bought a trench coat. You got burgers and milkshakes. Sporton sucked on French fries, and everyone laughed. Someone suggested painting the graffitied railroad abutment, but you couldn't think of anything cool to paint.

Sporton sucked on his Binky until he fell asleep.

You'd been going out with Joey for three weeks by that time, and this was your second double date with Harmony and Patrick. You were surprised that Patrick would date a grocery store checker, especially one with a kid, and that's when you heard something that bothered you—Patrick telling another friend of theirs: "I like the lowered expectations of townies."

That night, with the sun going down, Harmony drove her Pinto along Upriver Drive, and parked near Boulder Beach. Dates often ended up at the river that summer, where you would wade and swim, fly from tire swings. That night, someone—Patrick, maybe—suggested skinny-dipping. You were nervous, but you didn't object, knowing that a vote would go three-to-one— Sporton abstaining as he slept against your side in the backseat.

You were nervous because you and Joey had been progressing steadily that summer with each make-out session—kissing (he did not *kiss* like a high school boy) to fondling (those big, meaty *adult* hands) to . . . well, you knew what was next.

You and a college boy were about to have sex.

Crazy thing, love.

Sometimes you just fall for a person. But sometimes you *decide* to love them. You set your reservations aside and you say, Okay, *this* is the boy I'm going to love, *this* is the boy I'm going to lose my virginity to—this summer, right now, right here on this blanket next to this cold river.

And when you decide that, well, he can do anything, say anything, and you will approve. He can say something like, *You should call him Sporton*, and you don't think, *What an idiot*. You think, *That's hilarious. We should have sex*.

Crazy thing, love.

In the back of Harmony's car, you turned once more and looked into Joey's wry, cocktail-olive eyes. Yes, you told yourself. Then he reached across the sleeping toddler and put a hand on your thigh. "What do you say, Jeans?"

YOU THINK ABOUT that moment now, thirty years later, at home in Spokane to visit your ailing father, sitting in traffic on Division Street, after you've happened to glance over and see, painted on a bus bench, those same green eyes, settled in a bloated, balding face.

Joseph J. McCune is now an attorney-at-law here in Spokane, a specialist in personal injury cases and DUIs who apparently attracts his clientele through bus bench advertising.

Coincidentally, or not, you also became a lawyer, graduating summa cum laude from Seattle University and in the top 10 percent of your law school class at the University of Washington. You should probably thank Joseph J. McCune for giving you the idea of becoming a lawyer. Or thank your parents for reacting the way they did when Joey said those words: *law* and *school,* because now you work in San Diego as a corporate lawyer, specializing in intellectual property rights. Most of your clients are tech companies.

And while you feel a bit guilty condescending, you can't quite help it. You have come to think of lawyers like Joseph J. Mc-Cune as "bottom feeders," Joey's singular contribution to *juris prudence* being the idea that one should not immediately consent to a Breathalyzer from police after one has crashed one's car into a Taco Bell.

CALL JOE BEFORE YOU BLOW! his bus bench advises.

"Mom!" snaps your daughter. "Would you go? The light changed, like, two days ago!"

Coincidentally, Amber is at the very age, seventeen, that you were the summer you met Joey. And she is not happy being back in sleepy Spokane, visiting her ancient grandfather, who keeps staring at her septum ring like . . . well, like there's a ring in his granddaughter's septum.

For the last year, you and your youngest have battled over nose rings, grades, curfews, and mostly, over this hunk of idiocy named Kyle, whom Amber calls "muh boo." When you suggest that perhaps her boo might not raid the refrigerator every twenty minutes, or that her boo might write his own damned term paper, Amber cries out in the endless song of her people: *When are you going to start treating me like an adult?*

"Mom! Go!"

Horns are honking behind you.

But you can't look away from this bus bench and from Joey's green eyes. "Do you want to know when you become an adult?" you finally ask your daughter.

"*What?*" Amber is horrified, the way she gets whenever you try to say something meaningful, or actually, whenever words of any kind come out of your mouth. "What are you saying? Seriously, Mom! Are you having a stroke?"

Finally, you look from the bus bench to your daughter and say, "You become an adult the first time you see through love." And then, with your daughter fuming and the light turning yellow, you drive away from Joey's green eyes forever.

THE FOUR OF you got out of the Pinto quietly, hoping to not wake little Morton. Doors latched gently, Harmony nodded and looked back, *still asleep,* and you carried blankets toward the shoreline, you and Joey veering off slightly from Patrick and Harmony.

You were shaking. "It's cold out here," you said.

"We don't have to go in," Joey said. "We can just lie down somewhere. I'll warm you up." You felt his hand on your waist. Even at dusk, you could sense those green eyes taking you in. You tried to muster courage. It's okay. You could do this. It's what adults did; they had sex. What, you were going to be a virgin forever? Stop shaking! It's Joey, hilarious Joey, who better to—

Then, in your peripheral vision: something you couldn't quite put together. You turned back. On the hill behind you, the Pinto was creeping forward slowly. Toward the river.

The parking brake—*had she set the parking brake?* Your mind worked over that single detail as if you could go back in time and set it yourself.

The car began moving faster, crunching over gravel.

"No, no, *no!*" Harmony yelled.

Then the car picked up speed and went over the bank, nose

first, three feet over the bluff and down into the river. It didn't make a big splash but dipped like a soft ice-cream cone in chocolate, then bobbed back up, and tilted upright—for just a moment you wondered if the car would float, or maybe settle in shallow water. But then, the front of the car began sinking, moving forward like someone easing down a hill.

The rest was a blur, as hard to completely remember as it is impossible to forget, a rush of adrenalized flashes: Running. Splashing. Screaming.

Of the four of you, it made sense you'd reach the car first. You'd grown up on that river. Four years of swimming lessons at Cannon Pool. Summer camp swims to Shark Island. You splashed over slippery rocks, current tugging at your clothes, Harmony screaming behind you, the car drifting, pointed down like a sinking ship, the hood going under, and river water at the windshield by the time you got to the passenger window, which Harmony had left half-open so she could hear if her baby cried.

Morton was in the backseat. Harmony had locked the door. The water was above your waist. You could just get your arms through the window, but you couldn't reach him. "Morton! C'mere!" Your feet moved along the rocks with the car, river at your chest now.

He was wide awake, chewing his pacifier as water swirled around his feet. He stared at you, and all was lost, until he suddenly crawled across the wet backseat and into your arms, otherwise—

You can't think of the otherwise. Even now.

You got his little head sideways through the open car window, scraping it on both sides—and only then did he start crying. The rest of his body slid through like a mocking version of birth itself.

You held him against your chest, both of your heads out of the water as you walked back toward shore.

You would end up having three of your own: Jerome, Erin and thankless Amber. But no child ever felt better against your body than that one. You moved slowly back toward shore, looking once more over your shoulder. The top of the car lurched forward, water rushing through that open window and then it went under, bubbles rising everywhere, the shape of the car on the surface of the water for just a moment, like dirt over a grave.

Harmony had reached you by then—"Oh my god! Morton!"— and even though she was shaking, you handed her child over. Patrick was at her side. "Holy shit! Thank you."

And only then did you look back to shore. It's not like you expected Joey to save the kid. But something about him, standing alone on the shore, clothes completely dry, told you everything you'd ever need to know.

Town & Country

MY FATHER'S GIRLFRIEND CAME home from the casino a day early and caught him having sex with the woman across the street.

"I thought you were going to be gone another day," my dad said by way of apology, or explanation, or perhaps just narration. His girlfriend, Ellen, had been away on her annual girls' weekend in Jackpot, but since these "girls" were all at least seventy, they were forced to cut the trip short when one of them had a heart attack playing keno at Cactus Pete's.

All of which is to say, my father and his girlfriend were not the age you'd expect for this kind of drama. Dad was seventy-three, but he'd lately begun exhibiting signs of dementia, one of which, I was surprised to find out, was this late-in-life promiscuity, an erosion of inhibitions. Dad literally could not remember to *not* screw the sixty-year-old lady across the street.

This wasn't the first time, either. To hear Ellen tell it, my father had devolved to the point that he had the impulse control of a teenager. He'd whistle at women on the street and proposition waitresses right in front of her. Ellen could be a little crass herself, and she didn't seem overly angry, or even that sad. "I'm just done with the son of a bitch," she said. The neighbor was the last straw. She told me she had no choice but to kick Dad out of her house, where he'd lived since my mother died fourteen years earlier.

As I backed Dad out of her driveway, Ellen stood, arms crossed, behind the screen door. Next to me, in the passenger seat, Dad squirmed under his seat belt like a kid. The backseat was filled with boxes of his clothes.

"I feel like she's slut-shaming me," Dad said.

"That's not what that means," I said.

I HAD KNOWN for some time that Dad was fading; it was one of the reasons I moved back to Boise from Portland three years earlier. Dad had begun forgetting names and places and said increasingly strange and inappropriate things. He seemed lost at times, disoriented, and was often unsure of the year, the season, the day—classic signs of dementia. But, for me, there was nothing as alarming as the day in 2016 when Dad told me he'd voted for Donald Trump for president, that he liked Trump's whole "make shit great again" thing. There were two reasons this worried me: (1) Dad was a lifelong Democrat, a third-generation union craftsman who had never voted Republican in his life. And (2) my father was not a moron.

"Dad, you said a month ago that Trump was a dangerous idiot."

"Yeah, but that woman he's running against, I don't like her."

That woman. Could he even remember Hillary Clinton's name? I pointed out how that woman had been secretary of state, a U.S. senator, and first lady for eight years. That Dad had twice voted for that woman's husband.

"But this email thing——" he said.

My dad didn't own a computer. He wouldn't know an email

from an emu. But this was what happened with him now——he would hear some phrase on TV (*Hillary's emails, slut shaming, Make America Great Again*) and it would rattle around in his brain until it became real.

"What *about* her emails?" I asked.

"Well." He paused for a moment. "I sure as hell don't want her sending any to *me*."

I HAVE MY dad's eyes. Or so I've been told. Ever since I was a kid. The long forehead, too, and the square jaw. When I was young this confused me: *How can two people have the same eyes?* As I got older, I realized what was strange was looking so much like a man with whom I had so little in common.

I am gay, an only child, a nonathletic, monogamous nonsmoker. At this point in my life, my idea of fun is a walk, a late dinner, and a glass of wine while I watch cooking competition shows with the boyfriend that I wish I still had.

Dad grew up rowdy, as he puts it, in "a different time," boozing and brawling from birth with his three rough brothers, smoking at thirteen, and, by sixteen, dropping out of high school. He joined the army at eighteen, was drummed out dishonorably at twenty, married at twenty-three, and worked the next forty years as a machinist at a tool-and-die——all while treating his body like a tavern ashtray. Even in his seventies, Dad was going through four packs of smokes and a fifth of bourbon a week. And then there were the indiscretions against my mom, "the occasional broad," as Dad put it.

"I was never a choirboy, Jay," he said over breakfast a few days after Ellen tossed him out and he moved in with me. I wondered if he remembered that I actually *was* a choirboy, a decent baritone in my high school choir and later at the University of Portland.

"And I wasn't always loyal to your mother," Dad said.

"I'd rather not talk about this," I said.

"I'm just saying—"

"Dad, I know what you're saying—"

"I was quite the cocksman in my day."

"Okay." I pushed my cereal away.

"Damn right," Dad said.

I could still see my father under this molting old man shell—his sturdy jaw beneath the whiskery jowls, the roping arms, the black pompadour beneath the thinning gray, the bar-fight danger he carried into his fifties and sixties.

And if Dad's profane candor was new, my father embarrassing me certainly wasn't. When I was growing up, Dad was the guy smoking in his car outside high school, the guy saying inappropriate things about my teachers. ("Quite a rack on that Mrs. Kennedy.") He came to choir concerts with a cocktail he mixed himself. Not a beer. A thermos full of R&R and Pepsi.

For years, I had pushed both of my parents to get healthier. I eventually convinced Mom to quit smoking, but it was too late, and her end was excruciating, as she suffocated from emphysema.

If initially she had been heartbroken by what she called my "lifestyle," Mom and I eventually made our peace and she came to see me as the same conscientious, straight-A student I'd always been—well, minus the straight part. Her early death (I was only twenty-five) hit me harder as time went on, and after a year or two I realized what I'd lost: the one person whose hopes for me were as profound as my own. It was around this time that I began pleading with Dad to change his lifestyle. "I don't want to lose you, too," I told him, a confession that clearly made him uncomfortable. "You need to start taking care of yourself."

"Oh, I'm taking care of myself," he said. Then he winked and took a long drag of a Carlton.

And now, fourteen years of booze and cigarettes later, here he was, moving into a bedroom in my apartment—just as I'd once lived in a bedroom in his house. My most recent and most serious boyfriend, Levi, had moved out of my place a year earlier, so I put Dad in the spare room we'd used for Levi's home office.

There were still indentations from Levi's big desk in the back bedroom. We'd found this antique executive desk at a thrift store, and Levi had fallen inexplicably in love with it. It was a desk for a mining magnate, not a work-from-home freelance writer. But Levi just had to have it, and the carpet was still dented where that behemoth had once sat.

"Absolutely no smoking in here, understand?" I said to Dad. "I'll never get that smell out of the carpet. Go out to the landing if you need a cigarette."

"Got it," he said.

Two minutes later I smelled smoke.

I threw open the bedroom door. Dad was lying on the bed in his underwear, reading from his old collection of classic *Hustler* magazines, one eye closed against the curling smoke of his cigarette. "A little privacy?" he said.

EVERY GAY KID must remember the day he came out to his parents. Mine was fairly late—sophomore year of college. But I was late admitting it to myself, too. I grew up in suburban Boise and went to a conservative high school filled with Mormons and

Catholics—I don't think I realized that I *could* be gay. I know that sounds crazy or deluded or repressed, but it's strange how you can just close off part of yourself if you sense that it's un-accepted. So, all through high school, I maintained a series of relationships with girls that lasted three or four months. But at some point between first kiss and taking off clothes I always managed to engineer a heartfelt breakup. Then I'd mope around my room, missing Christy, mourning Courtney. These tended to be choir and drama girls—not the leads or soloists, but pleasant wallflowers with some basic adolescent affliction (lank hair, bad skin). My mother had tried for years to have more kids—she had miscarriages before and after me—and so whenever I brought home a girl, I could see on her face the desire for grandchildren. As for Dad, it was a chance to run through his old up-down-up fe-male inventory: legs-butt-boobs-face, face-boobs-butt-legs. Then he'd give me a look from his recliner that said: *Not bad.*

These high school girlfriends and I did a lot of talking on the phone, posing for dance pictures, kissing in cars. But I was two seconds into my first kiss with a boy in my dorm, accompanied, a few days later, by my first hand job, when I knew this felt differ-ent. Oh. Right. I see.

I spent the requisite semester of freshman year trying to con-vince people, myself mostly, that I was bisexual (perhaps I would only *half*-disappoint my parents), but that line of defense fell away early in my sophomore year, when I met Phillip, who lived on another floor of my dorm.

Phillip was the most out person I'd ever met, a master of the hip-tilt-snarky-comment-Broadway-musical affect that I felt would be required of me at some point to even get into a gay bar. It was like he had taken some class that I'd missed. I started to see him as a kind of queer mentor and one day I asked his advice: How should I go about telling my old army dad and housewife mom about my new self?

"First of all, don't say it's 'new' or they'll think it's a phase and put you in conversion therapy," Phillip said. "They have to know that this is just who you are. Who you've always been. Don't apologize, or make excuses, or act like you didn't mean it. Just walk in and say, 'Mom? Dad? Turns out I like dudes.'"

"You didn't do that——"

"Of course I didn't do that! I was eleven!"

"You came out at eleven?"

"My parents knew before I did anyway," Phillip said. "They were like, 'Yep, more Mini-Wheats, Nancy?'"

I felt so emboldened by Phillip's story that I wondered if maybe my parents suspected, too. I called Mom and said I'd be home for the weekend and needed to talk. No one in my little family had ever scheduled a talk before, and she was suspicious. It was a seven-hour drive from Portland to Boise, and I had second thoughts the whole way, third thoughts parking in front of the house, fourth opening the front door to our rancher, and fifth when I saw the backs of their heads in the living room.

It was early evening, just after dinner. Mom and Dad were on their reclining sofa watching *Wheel of Fortune*. They were drinking whiskey sodas, the smoke from their cigarettes mingling in the air above the ashtray they shared. This was the most romantic thing I'd ever seen my parents do.

They glanced over at me in unison.

"You got someone pregnant," my mother said. In her voice I heard equal parts worry and hope.

"No, Mom," I said. "I'm gay."

"Oh." Mom stared at me for a few seconds. "Oh!" she said again. Then she burst into tears and left the room.

I couldn't read Dad's face at all. He took another drag of his cigarette and turned back to the TV. Finally, he said, "But you haven't done anything about it, right?" He seemed to think that as long as I hadn't, say, waxed my chest or blown anybody, it wouldn't be official, and I could still change my mind.

Mom came back into the room then. She had composed herself and put on makeup. My mother had beautiful, porcelain skin, even as a lifetime smoker, but she was insecure about her fair coloring. "It's good that you got your father's skin and not this wet paste," she'd always say. Freshly blushed, she sat down next to me on the love seat and took my hand.

She apologized and said she hadn't cried because I was gay. She said, above all, she wanted me to be happy. The reason she'd cried was the sudden realization that she would never be a grand-mother.

"But, Mom," I said, "gay people can have kids, too."

"Oh," she said. And then she burst into tears again. "I'm sorry. I guess that doesn't make me feel better."

But, as I say, we made our peace after that. Which I'm glad for, because five years later, she was gone. And then it was just Dad and me.

AFTER ELLEN THREW him out, Dad lived with me for about three months. It was even harder than I'd imagined—living with his terrible habits and his fading memory. Eventually I got him to confine his smoking to his room, and I did my best to keep the other disasters at bay.

Most days when I got home from work, Dad was already drunk—and we'd spend the rest of the night arguing over what to watch on TV—or he was gone, and I'd have to tour the neighborhood bars looking for him. He'd lost his driver's license two years earlier, after his third DUI (when he also totaled his car), so he always ventured out on foot. There were five bars within a mile of my apartment, but sometimes he just kept walking, looking for a specific tavern from his youth. I put my business card in his wallet, and bartenders would call when Dad had worn out his welcome. Once, I got a phone call from a massage therapist saying that Dad had come in and asked about getting a happy ending.

When Levi and I moved back to Boise three years earlier, I had taken a job as a graphic designer for the state of Idaho, making brochures for various state agencies, so now I at least had the flexibility to leave work early to pick Dad up. I'd lecture him on the way home about urinating outside or shoplifting porno mags. I've heard people describe caring for their parents as a kind of reverse parenthood, but I had no idea. I had to cook for him, clothe him, clean up after him.

It was like living with a horny, alcoholic toddler. At the same time, his memory seemed to be leaking out even faster. He forgot basic details and was easily confused in conversations. "Why don't you ever have any girlfriends over?" he asked me one day.

"Dad, I'm gay."

He laughed like I'd just told a great joke.

Another time I said something about Mom, and I could see by the way he stared at me that he was remembering that his dead wife had also been my mother. On Valentine's Day, I asked if he wanted to bring flowers to Ellen, to see if she might forgive him and take him back.

"Your mom?"

"No, Dad. Ellen. Mom's name was Marjorie."

"Marjorie," he repeated, as if he'd been trying to remember that fact.

"That's right. And your girlfriend's name was Ellen. Until she threw you out."

"Marjorie threw me out?"

"No, Dad," I said, speaking more slowly. "Marjorie was Mom's name. She died fourteen years ago. You moved in with Ellen a few months after that." I didn't mention how, at the time, I had been uncomfortably aware of how quickly Dad took up with Ellen and had suspected some romantic overlap. "Ellen threw you out because you slept with the lady across the street, remember?"

Dad smiled like he was hearing this story for the first time. "I always was quite the cocksman."

"Yes, so I've heard."

Another time, when I went into a bar near my apartment to pick him up, he raised his glass as I approached. "Another one of these," he said. I could see he had no idea who I was.

"Dad? I'm not the bartender. It's Jay. Your son."

He stared at me. He was quiet a moment. Then: "Why don't you ever bring girlfriends home?"

So. This was to be our Sisyphean hell—me coming out to my fading father every day for the rest of his life.

"YOU CAN'T KEEP taking care of him like this," Levi said on the phone one day. Levi and I still talked once a week or so—which was great, although I feared I was hanging on to something that was clearly over, like a spoiled grandkid selfishly keeping Nana on life support.

"I can't just throw him out," I said.

Levi didn't say anything. Technically, I had thrown Levi out a year earlier.

The trouble had started over my infatuation with a guy at work. It got serious rather quickly and I eventually asked Levi for some time apart to think about what I wanted. He wasn't nearly as upset as I'd imagined he'd be. In fact, he said he'd suspected this was coming and had a place picked out in Portland. I was flummoxed. "How could you know this was coming when I didn't?"

"You always call yourself a serial monogamist," Levi said. "But what you really do is trade people in when they get too close." He didn't need to remind me of my past: a series of one- and two-year relationships, or that when he and I had gotten together, I had broken up with my boyfriend Aaron to date him.

"I don't think that's fair," I said, as he measured his ridiculous, giant desk for the movers.

He turned. "I say this with love, Jay. But ask yourself this— how much have you really changed since you were running away from those high school girlfriends before they could figure out who you really are?"

That was ridiculous, I told him. I wasn't closeted anymore. But his words stung. And they felt true in some way that I could see, but not understand.

At work I tried the new guy for a while, but Levi's words haunted me, and I found out pretty quickly the limits of falling for someone simply because of a CrossFit chest. (Just shy of three weeks, it turns out.) By then, Levi and his big desk were back in Portland.

And I hadn't dated anyone seriously since.

"But look at you now," Levi said, "living with a sophisticated older gentleman."

"Yes," I said. "And apparently quite the cocksman."

"How does he like *Chopped?*" Levi asked.

"He says, 'Why are we watching people cook food we can't eat?'"

"It's a good point," Levi said. "So, what are you going to do now?"

I said I didn't know.

It was probably a week after this conversation that the state police called me at work. "Jay Curtis? We have your father." The trooper said that Dad had wandered nearly four miles from my apartment and was walking up a freeway on-ramp, headed north. He was drunk. When the trooper questioned Dad, he told them he was headed to the old mining town of Wallace, to find "the whore who popped my cherry." This had happened in 1963.

IT'S ONE OF the hardest decisions you can make, putting a parent in a nursing home. We started visiting places—Something Garden and Whatever Glen—but each place seemed worse than the last. Dad was fading mentally, but his body still seemed reasonably healthy, and I couldn't imagine putting him in one of these places, with their long, sad corridors lined with palsied people looking up desperately from wheelchairs, the depressing activity room airing some old black-and-white movie, the hacks, coughs and cries coming from behind closed doors, the antiseptic whiff of all those cleaners, none of which could cover the deeper smells of urine and death.

The less restrictive assisted living and transitional retirement homes didn't have a spot for Dad, because of his dementia. They recommended memory care—secure facilities that tried to hide their locked-down, institutional nature with bright paint and children's toys. But when we visited these kinder-prisons, with their bolted doors, their suspiciously patient, ass-wiping staff, and all those vacant faces staring off into nothingness, I felt bereft. Worst of all, there was no one I could talk to about any of this. I had never really missed the siblings I didn't have—but I felt a great loneliness in this decision. Dad was stone quiet during the tours, and the minute we left, he seemed to have no memory of what we'd just seen. Still, I wanted his input. As much as he'd drunk and smoked and screwed his way through life, I still valued his opinion on practical things. Don't ever buy a car on time. Get a fifteen-year mortgage if you can afford it. Don't get caught up in gossip at work. Even drunk, Dad had been a decent source of that rare commodity: common sense. And after all, this was his life we were talking about.

"What do you think, Dad?" I asked as we left the Something Eden adult care center, where the director had talked to Dad like he was a four-year-old.

"I think Marjorie lives over there." Dad pointed to an empty field.

At one point, I had asked the director if there was a place in this facility where Dad could go to smoke. Or if he could have a cocktail now and then.

As with all the nursing homes and dementia care units where I'd asked those questions, the director sputtered and said he didn't think that was possible.

But these were the only things that still gave Dad any joy: A smoke. A mixed drink. "Not even one cigarette?" I asked. "Or a nightcap before bed?"

He looked at me like I was crazy. "Legally, we could never allow that."

Then, as we were leaving one of the memory care units—Something Manor—a janitor sidled up to us. I'd seen him mopping outside the office. He grabbed Dad by the arm. He was short and bald, with a ruddy nose. His eyes went in different directions.

"There is a place," he said, his voice a Gollumy rasp. "Town & Country. Up north. My sister is there." He repeated it for emphasis. "Town. And Country!" Then he pointed to his temple, blinked twice, and scurried away with his mop.

IT TOOK ME a week to find the Town & Country Senior Inn. This was partly because it was nearly four hundred miles away and partly because, as the director said over the phone, it was not technically a licensed elder care facility.

"Wait, which part are you technically not," I asked, "an elder care facility or licensed?"

"You really have to come and see for yourself," he said, and when I described my father, he said, "Oh, you're definitely going to want to come."

So, one Saturday I threw Dad in the car and we drove seven hours north on twisty Highway 95, straight up the long spine of Idaho.

The Town & Country, it turned out, was an actual motor inn, built in the 1950s on an unincorporated stretch near a stain of a town called Stateline. The building had been updated when it was turned into this "senior residential hotel," but it was basically the same sprawling, seedy one-story motel it had always been. There was a carport fronting the lobby and, behind that, a chophouse lounge with no windows, a small stage, and smoke-stained carpeting halfway up the walls. The staff at the Town & Country were dressed not like orderlies or nurses, but like employees of a 1960s hotel: women in waitress dresses, men in high-collared blue jackets and gendarme hats. The grounds (if you could call a gravel parking lot that) were dotted with old people wandering around behind tall fences, being steered back to their rooms by men dressed as bellmen and porters.

The director of the Town & Country was named Skip. He was three shades of gray stacked one on top of the other and looked like he might be checking into the hotel himself soon. He said he'd started this place for his own parents, who had run a saloon in one of these old Idaho mining towns. "They really weren't cut out for the kind of place where Grammy does art projects," he said.

The Town & Country had a simple, respectful ethos: The elderly folks were not decrepit patients but "hotel guests" checked into one of the forty guest rooms. A few of those rooms were reserved for couples, but most of the guests were single, divorced, widows, or widowers. They could do whatever they wanted in their rooms—smoke, drink, screw, watch TV—but, in a nod to nostalgia, the TVs had only four channels and the phones were rotary dial. (One necessary concession had been to put in a state-of-the-art sprinkler system and nonflammable bedding. "We do tend to get a few snoozing smokers," Skip admitted.)

A continental breakfast was served each morning in the old hotel lobby from 5:00 a.m. to noon, although if the guests became sick or nonambulatory, the food could be delivered to them "for a room service fee." Anything extra at the Town & Country would be tacked onto the bill, just like at a hotel. Laundry, meds, a haircut—all could be arranged "for a fee." There was no group therapy, no activity rooms, no sing-alongs, no crafts projects. There were only two things on the calendar every day: continental breakfast and, beginning at 3:30, dinner and happy hour. "This is what we are most proud of," Skip said, and with a flourish he produced a thick dinner menu and handed it to my dad.

The food was straight out of my childhood: roast and potatoes, pork chops and applesauce, French dip, Monte Cristo. And the prices! You could have London broil and a baked potato for $4. You could have goulash or spaghetti and meatballs for $2.50.

Skip saw my smile. "Yeah. The prices make them really happy. The real price, the price you'll get on your monthly bill, is approximately four to five times that."

The bar menu was just as amazing. A screwdriver for $2. A Tom Collins for $2.50. Beer for 75 cents.

"Our beers are six ounces, and we make really weak cocktails," Skip said. "We can also break up medication and serve it in nonalcoholic drinks, basically soda or tonic water. They don't mind taking their Coumadin when it comes in a martini glass. We have a light-jazz combo that plays standards three nights a week—quietly—and two nights we have classic country. No music Sundays and Mondays. Lights out at eight, nine on weekends."

I looked over. Dad was staring at the menu like it was a time travel portal. "My dad has been having this other issue," I said. "His, uh, libido."

Skip nodded, then chose his words carefully. "The dominant

model for elder care focuses, of course, on longevity and health. But this can be at the cost of what I would call personal choice. At the Town & Country, we want to preserve personal choice."

"Which means—"

He smiled, and I saw a black eyetooth. "We go through a lot of penicillin."

It was unbelievable, like a Rat Pack nursing home. "I have to ask, is this all"—I looked over at Dad, still intently reading the menu—"legal?"

"Oh yes. Well, it is here." Skip didn't seem offended. "We picked the county in Idaho with the fewest restrictions. I'm sure if you've done your research, you'll see that we faced some hurdles early on. Regulatory issues, a few fines, back when we were trying to get classified as a senior care facility. We finally got around the red tape by dropping any pretense of offering care, and with a precisely worded contract that indemnifies us against—well, pretty much everything." He shrugged. "The Town & Country is not a nursing home. It is . . . a senior residential facility that does not discriminate against those for whom old age has had debilitating effects."

There was another thing that I had begun to wonder but wasn't entirely sure how to ask. "What about . . . gay people?"

Skip looked a little startled. "Oh." Then he looked at Dad. "Your dad isn't—" He cleared his throat. "Because . . . I mean, we aren't really set up for that."

"No," I said, "Dad's not gay."

And, as if to punctuate the point, Dad slammed the menu down on Skip's desk and said, "I'll have the fish-and-chips and a Scotch and soda."

HERE'S THE THING about my hometown. It will always break your heart. When I first talked Levi into moving to Boise with me a few years ago, so I could take the state job and be closer to my dad, I warned him. "Levi, this is not going to be like Portland."

Levi had grown up in Sacramento, and he insisted that every gay kid felt constrained by his hometown. "No gay kid likes where he's from," he said, "because that place probably didn't accept him. There are probably queers in Paris who felt suffocated."

In fact, Levi ended up liking Boise—it had good restaurants for a city its size and friendly people. Most of all, Levi liked what it lacked: rain and pretentiousness. Portland was gloomy, crowded, and expensive. Boise was laid-back and outdoorsy, and housing was affordable. "What's not to like?" Levi said, and for the first month he had that look people sometimes get when they move to Boise, that crazed, *how-are-we-getting-away-with-this, can-you-believe-how-livable-this-city-is* look.

Still, I warned him to be careful. "You'll get complacent, and then bang, some ignorant, reactionary shit will stop you cold. Like, for instance, at Dad and Ellen's house." But when we visited them, Dad and Ellen were on their best drunk behavior, and they even kept the volume turned down on the Fox News.

It was true, Boise was far more progressive than the city I'd left at eighteen, but all the bike trails and vegan bakeries in the world couldn't change the fact that real ugliness existed out there, just beyond the city limits. It was like we lived in two different places—cosmopolitan, techie Boise, and backwoods, scary Idaho.

And sure enough, six months after we arrived, Levi and I were walking home from dinner when a big Ford pickup rolled up. We both tensed. The driver's-side window rolled down, and a dude in a ball cap leaned out and said, almost as if asking for directions, "Fags." Then he rolled up his window and drove away.

To his credit, Levi laughed off the asshole in the pickup truck. ("Duh," he said.) He even developed a catchall phrase for such things: *so Idaho*. "That's so Idaho," he said when a religious group put up a billboard near our apartment comparing homosexuality to pedophilia. Or, when a couple stared at us holding hands in a restaurant, "Why do they have to be so Idaho?" And when that old corrupt bigot Trump won the Republican nomination: "No way half of Americans would vote for someone so Idaho, *would* they?"

It's not fair, of course, besmirching a whole state, but it doesn't take too many Confederate flags in truck windows and MARRIAGE IS BETWEEN A MAN AND A WOMAN bumper stickers to make you forget being fair.

So, when I told Levi that I could *not* put Dad in the Town & Country, I couldn't imagine a better description.

"It's the most Idaho place in Idaho," I said.

Levi laughed. "That almost makes me miss Boise."

I felt a buzz in my stomach. "You could come visit," I said, trying to sound casual.

Levi didn't say anything.

"Mrs. McIntyre on the first floor asked about you the other day," I said. "I told her you were doing great. She said, 'I didn't realize you guys stayed in touch after you stopped . . . you know.'"

Levi laughed. "Well, the smart ones don't." We sat there quietly, breathing on the phone.

Then I changed the subject again. "They don't even take gay people at the Town & Country. The guy looked apoplectic when I asked."

Levi was quiet for a moment. "Why would you ask him that?"

I couldn't answer. Why *would* I ask that? I pictured Dad in that back bedroom, his skinny old legs and butt, thickening stomach and chest. The man was built like an ice-cream cone. Was it where I was headed, that body? Was that me in there, too? Me, almost forty, with no children——just like Mom had feared——and no boyfriend, no one in the world but Dad. And when I reached Dad's age, the Town & Country age, who would be there to take care of me, the way I was taking care of Dad?

"Jay?" Levi asked, still on the line. "Are you okay?"

I could hear Dad banging around in the kitchen, no doubt looking for food. "Yeah," I told Levi. "I'm fine. I'm just——"

I looked up then. Dad was in my bedroom doorway, in nothing but his underwear, holding a bottle of extra virgin olive oil. "Is this the only lube we have?" he asked.

ELLEN ALWAYS CALLED Dad "that old son of a bitch." Dad called her "that salty broad." Levi used to say that Ellen had the voice of a leaf blower, but he did appreciate that we were rarely in the door five minutes before she yelled from the kitchen, "Cocktail, honey?"

I called her one day and told her how Dad had declined even more since moving out of her house, and this seemed to soften her a bit. "Poor bastard. I was afraid that might happen."

I told her about the nursing homes we'd visited. "You can't put your dad in a place like that. He'll die. Right after he burns the place to the ground." I didn't tell her about the Town & Country.

Somewhere during this conversation, she invited us over for

dinner and I saw, at last, an opening. I'd read that with severe dementia cases, you could sometimes settle them back into an old routine and they'd regain some of their sharpness. If I could get Ellen and Dad back together, maybe . . .

It was rich irony. I once had hated Ellen, had suspected Dad of seeing her even before Mom died. She was cranky and crude, and obviously not the mother I missed so deeply. But here I was, seeing her as my last chance, and when she admitted that she had "missed the old so-and-so," I knew I had one chance to get this right. I helped Dad get dressed—his best slacks and a nice button-down shirt. Parted his gray hair and slicked it down. "Where are we going?" he kept asking.

"Ellen's house."

"Is Ellen your girlfriend?"

"Ellen is *your* girlfriend."

He looked proud of himself. "Well—" he said.

"Yep," I said, "quite the cocksman."

On the way, I stopped for flowers. "You wanna pick 'em out, Dad?"

"I don't bring women flowers," Dad said. "There's only one thing I bring a woman."

"Okay, then." I ran into the store and grabbed a bottle of wine and a bouquet of flowers. I even stopped to look at a rack of little plush toys. Ellen had a houseful of figurines and stuffed animals, many of them wearing T-shirts that said GET WELL or HANG IN THERE. But in the end, wine and flowers seemed like enough.

I was halfway across the parking lot when I saw that Dad was no longer in my car.

The grocery store was on a busy street. There were bars in both directions. I put the flowers and wine in the car and set off searching for him. It was twenty minutes before I found him. He was on drink number two in an Irish bar.

"Hey . . ." he said, clearly recognizing me but blanking on my name. He toasted me with a whiskey on the rocks.

"Dad, we have to go. We're going to see Ellen, remember?"

"Is Ellen your girlfriend."

"No, Dad. Ellen is *your* girlfriend. I'm gay!"

A few people turned, amazed and moved (and a few surely disgusted) to be witnessing a forty-year-old man coming out to his seventy-three-year-old father in a dive bar.

Finally, I got him outside, but he was already drunk. Getting him into the car was like trying to seal a live mouse in an envelope.

Ellen was half-potted, too, by the time we arrived. She'd hit the rum early and was understandably pissed that we were late. "Tell that old cocksucker he can rot in hell for all I care."

"That's a little harsh," I said and handed her the flowers. "These are from Dad. He feels terrible."

"Why doesn't he give them to me himself if he feels so terrible?"

"He's feeling a little shy," I said. In fact, I had left him sound asleep in the passenger seat, hoping to smooth things over and then bring him in. "He wanted me to apologize."

She seemed dubious but said she would warm up the dinner that had gotten cold.

But when I went out to the car, he wasn't there. It was Ellen, standing on her porch, who pointed him out, banging on the door of the woman across the street. Perhaps I should have been pleased that he'd finally remembered something—the amorous sixty-year-old neighbor—but at that point I was fairly certain my life was over.

Dinner was cool and short, and Dad slept on the drive home. I could barely stir him when we got to my apartment. He'd wet his pants again. This happened every few weeks, after he'd had too much to drink.

"Come on, Dad," I said. I threw his arm over my shoulder, and half carried him into the building. He smelled awful. He tried to push me away.

"Let me go!" he said. We walk-wrestled down the hall.

He smelled like stale piss. "Damn it, Dad, stop fighting me!"

Finally, I got him through the door and into his smoky bedroom. I dumped him on the bed, next to his ashtray and porno mags, a little harder than I needed to.

I undid his wet pants and started wriggling them over his bony legs. That's when I realized he'd shit himself, too.

"Let me go," he said again.

FOR A WHILE, when you first come out, that fact feels like the main aspect of your identity. You're not a student or a Capricorn or an optimist. You're a gay. In some ways, I think, this can be a relief. You don't have to confront any other failings, flawed thinking, lack of confidence, trouble communicating. Or the loneliness. Because of your family, or your religion, or a general lack of cultural acceptance, you can always fall back on a handy excuse: *This* is why I feel so alone. But over time, this fact recedes again, and you are simply who you are.

The night I came out to my parents, my mom finished crying, apologized, and told me that she loved me no matter what. Then she went to bed—probably to cry some more. I wandered into my old bedroom, still covered in sports posters. I wished I hadn't told them, that I'd just moved away and lived my life somewhere else, on the beach in Southern California, or riding motorcycles in Spain. I listened to cassettes for a while, headphones on, sitting across from my bedroom mirror, sulking and staring at my pimply face—Dad's face, as I'd always been told, but without some quality that his face had. His willfulness, an ease with his appetites.

I went out to use the bathroom and found Dad fixing himself a cocktail at the bar in the dining room.

"Want one?" he asked.

Dad had never offered me a drink before.

"No, thanks," I said. Then: "Okay, sure."

He looked like he was trying to find something to say, and I imagined it would be a deeper inquiry into precisely what I had and hadn't done with my new perverted hobby—perhaps the exact number of dongs I'd slopped.

He finished mixing us whiskey sodas and then he turned to face me. "Look, I don't know anything about"—he waved his hand—"whatever you're getting yourself into here." He was a bit soused, at the point where it sounded like his voice was being poured from a decanter. "In fact, I don't know shit about shit. But I know this: If you find something in this world that makes you happy—do that."

WE LEFT FIRST thing in the morning and arrived at the Town & Country at 4:00 p.m., in time for happy hour. The car's tires crunched on the gravel lot.

We went through the hotel lobby into the lounge. I settled Dad at a table, in a big leather chair. The room was dusk-lit, already full of dressed-for-dinner old people squinting at huge menus. The menus were so big in part because the font was massive, at least 20-point. I sat with Dad a minute. He looked around, taking it all in.

Our waitress came over and brought us two waters in old café glasses. She had on a blond Marilyn Monroe wig. Like all the waitresses, she was in her sixties. They all wore blond Marilyn Monroe wigs. Up close, the wigs looked ridiculous, too low on their foreheads, but also familiar somehow, and then it hit me—they looked a little like the current president.

That's when I realized how brilliant the Town & Country was—the whole thing. Brilliant. The last whiff of a made-up world my father believed he had grown up in. This Idaho, this America, this Town & Country, with its ridiculous subsidized $2 meat loaf and 75-cent glasses of Miller, its four channels and rotary telephones and no blacks or gay people, none of that trans-nonbinary nonsense. This is where he wanted to live, in a man-ufactured Idaho motor hotel of nostalgia and denial. And this is how we have chosen to go out—as a country—smoking and drinking and straight-fucking our way right into oblivion.

"I have to go fill out paperwork now, Dad," I said. "And then I'm gonna get you settled and leave, okay? You might not see me for a while."

"Where are you going?"

"Well, tonight I'm going to Portland to see Levi. Do you re-member Levi?"

He looked at me. Nothing.

"He was my boyfriend," I said, "but I messed it up. Now I'm going to try and fix it. What do you think of that, Dad?"

He stared at me, not comprehending.

"But I'll get up here as much as I can. And Ellen said she'd come visit."

He looked confused and opened his mouth to say something.

"No, Ellen is not my girlfriend," I said. "I'm gay, remember?"

He looked back down at the giant menu and just then the platinum waitress arrived back at our table. "Hiya, sweetie," she said.

"Hiya, doll," Dad said back.

I stood and told the waitress, "I'm going to finish filling out the paperwork, and then I'll come back and get him settled in his room."

She nodded to me and said, to Dad, "Have you had a chance to look at the menu, darlin'? You know what you want?"

"Oh, I know what I want," Dad said.

"I'm gonna like you, aren't I?" the waitress said. "So, what can I bring you to eat, sugar?"

Dad looked at the menu again. "Salisbury steak, au gratin potatoes, Seven and Seven."

"You betcha," said the waitress.

I turned to leave. "Okay, Dad. I'll be back." And I started to walk away.

"Wait!" Dad said, but when I turned, it wasn't me he was talking to. It was the waitress. "Can you make that a double?"

The waitress smiled, the light from the kitchen suddenly behind her so all I could see was her silhouette and the glow of that blond wig. "We always do, honey."

Cross the Woods

OH, THAT PETER PAN hit-and-run prick. Thoughtless asshole. Not that she was surprised. Marcus was a bolter, a runner; he *always* left in the dark. She used to tell friends it was like dating Houdini. Maggie could cuff him, straitjacket him, lock him in a steamer trunk, and at 3:00 a.m., the idiot commitment-phobe would still find a way to tiptoe out into the night, belt undone, shoes in hand.

"Yeah, I'm not big on *good mornings*," he said early on, shorthand for I'm probably going to keep fucking other women.

So it wasn't that she was surprised to wake up alone. She knew last night what she'd known when she met Marcus, that he was immature, a bartender self-described as "not that into relationships." That was okay two years ago. In fact, after eighteen months of shotgun marriage to Dan and another year of separation, reconciliation and divorce, the last thing Maggie had wanted was another lousy husband. And so Marcus's casualness had been the point: the ease, the lack of commitment. She had a kid, a career, college—no time for much else. Why shouldn't sex be like ordering a pizza. Just send Marcus a text: How are you? or answer his: What up? For a while she'd even convinced herself that seeing Marcus kept her from making bigger mistakes.

But it got old after a year, Marcus's nine-o'clock-one-knuckle knock, right after she'd put Dustin to bed. Or at least it got old for Maggie, who came to dread those mornings alone, waking up like this. Especially when her own feelings began rising, and she began noticing a certain grace in Marcus's movements, a kindness in his eyes. Shit. You didn't fall for someone like Marcus. Maggie knew better. She was a lab assistant getting her master's degree in pharmacology. As she told her sister, it was like she kept going into a bar over and over, ordering dopamine shaken with nor-epinephrine and oxytocin while Marcus kept ordering straight testosterone.

No, honestly, what bothered her—this morning anyway—was that it bothered her. She'd known exactly what she was getting last night. A pizza. To feel his weight for a while, to lose herself after the sadness of the last few weeks. Once more with Marcus inside. So why did waking up alone now make her feel like such a failure . . . as a feminist, or an existentialist . . . or what? After a year apart, couldn't it be enough to just get laid? To smell him in her bed, see the indentation in the other pillow, to think, *Good. Right. Move on.*

Instead, she felt on the verge of tears, certain she would spend the rest of her life alone, a pathetic, bitter single mother—*such a bullshit cliché*—her thoughts looping into a women's magazine quiz she'd taken during the whole Marcus conundrum ("Will He Ever Commit?") and then, worst of all—flashing on her mother's pet word, *used*. Of all the stupid words.

Maybe it was just the time and place that had made everything feel so empty, the circumstances of last night, the shock of seeing Marcus for the first time in months, having him just show up at the wake like that. ("Your dad probably would've hated that I was here, huh?") He looked great in a suit, my God, those cyclist's shoulders and hips; and then the Jameson started flowing, and the toasts and stories, and it was nice to laugh and Marcus half-apologized for not calling when he saw the obituary and he muttered something about growing up a lot in the last year, and hell, even if it was bullshit, it was . . . nice bullshit, and when they were walking to their cars she practically willed him to say something, anything, so when he looked over in the parking lot and said, simply, "Well . . ." that was all it took; she was helpless, incapable of clearheaded action, because at that moment there were only two things in the universe: alone and Marcus. And last night she could not do alone. He followed her home. She paid the babysitter. And . . .

Maggie sat up in bed. Surely there was some lasting benefit from last night, some residue. Yesterday it had been a year since she'd had sex and now it had been six hours. That was something. But did being touched have any weight the next day, any value? It wasn't like she could feel his hands anymore, like she could feel anything. Except sadness. A yawning sense of being alone. Maggie opened her nightstand for some Advil, and she noticed, in the corner, on the floor behind the bathroom door, in a heap, a gray suit jacket.

That's when she heard faint voices coming from the kitchen. She got out of bed, pulled her robe on, and went downstairs.

In the kitchen, Dustin stood on a chair across from Marcus. They were eye to eye, each holding neckties. They were a foot apart, shirtless, and they had the ties looped around their bare necks. Marcus was in his boxer shorts, Dustin in his Transformer pajama pants.

"Do what I do," Marcus said. "Like looking in a mirror." Shoulder blades jutted from Dustin's tiny pale back.

"Cross the woods," Marcus said.

"Cross the woods," Dustin said.

"Over the hill," Marcus said.

"Over the hill," Dustin said.

"Around."

"Around."

"Behind."

"Behind."

"And through."

"Through."

"Perfect. Now turn around and show your mom."

Dustin turned. He beamed, surprised to see his mother in the doorway. "Look," he said, "I'm wearing Grandpa's tie."

The tie was blue, with little red sailing flags. It hung past Dustin's feet. He must've gotten it out of the box in the living room that Maggie's stepmother sent home with her. It was looped in the sort of unmanageable knot that Dustin always got in his sneakers.

Maggie wondered then if there wasn't just one ache in the world: sad, happy, horny, drunk, sorry, satisfied, grieving, lonely. If we believed these to be different feelings but they all came from the same sweet, unbearable spring.

Marcus had made coffee. He handed her a cup. She put it to her lips until she could speak again. Finally, she said to her son, in a half-whisper, "It looks so good on you, baby."

To the Corner

SWEET SEPTEMBER UP IN the Boone—twenty past last bell on the first day of school, 2008, and a pumpkin-colored school bus makes its way down Boone Street, laying middle-schoolers along the porch-couch-weed-lot-crap-board houses of West Central— Twilight Zone, Felony Flats, the West Centy.

At the second-to-last-stop, KJ and crew come off the bus slinging backpacks, headed straight to the corner—the spot they haunted all summer—barely out the sighing bus doors when shirts come off, ribs, guts, pecs, clavicles jutting beneath brown-black-white-beige casings. *D. All the above,* Studio calls them—four boys hit the chain-link kitty-corner from the Family Suprette, where they sag and scrape, low-hang lean, all of them eyeing the only girl who gets off at their stop, ink-haired lovely seventh grade Rah-something—who won't even look their way—until KJ sighs a single word: *Damn.*

Mmm.

S'right.

Rah-something turns the corner and the four heads swing the other way, birds on a line—KJ says: *Doug B, your backpack look like My Little Ponies—*

All chill up in the Boone.

Summer still, says A-Sym—so-called because of his one droopy eye, scar, crooked smile.

Should cancel school when the bump hit eighty.

That's some sensible shit.

Cars go by—skids and rides, buckets, trucks and bikes, the minivans of parents picking up kids from Holmes, the elementary school this crew graduated from two years ago—*Holmes homes* narrating traffic like they did all summer: *I'd drive that* and *Imagine if your moms look like her* and *Put some wheels on that sled* and *Why do all Priuses look constipated?*

Nah, all chill up in the Boone.

ACROSS THE STREET, old gray brocade curtains part and a head eases out, like a turtle: a silver-haired old white man squinting over bifocals, watching the boys on the corner, through the grimy storm glass mouthing the words: *Well, I will be goddamned.*

Inside: a dark living room, midcentury American (first time around) and tall, craggy Leonard Darvin pulls away from the window, repeating for emphasis: *I. Will. Be. God. Damned.* He thought for sure that when school started those kids would leave that corner, but no, here they are again. *Are you kidding me!* Leonard rants among relics—bookshelves bloated with dusty hardcovers, a blue sectional, two clamshell club chairs, console TV, hi-fi—*What a waste!* All summer he watched those wastrels gather on that corner and loiter, their very existence an affront to the careful steps of his own life: Korea, GI Bill, college, marriage and kids, squire circle in the Knights of Columbus, copy desk at the afternoon newspaper, then city desk reporter when the morning paper ate the afternoon, then back to the copy desk, and before he knew it, a buy-out retirement and part-time job as a reference librarian, full retirement and full grandparenthood, an easy glide until last year, when Marjorie died and everything just stopped. There's nothing in life he likes less than self-pity and yet he can't seem to fight it off: a *what-was-it-all-about* refrain plays in his head. When Marjorie died, he stopped reading, stopped fishing, stopped opening curtains, stopped doing everything he loved except the garden. And he gave even that up this summer. Maybe that's what he hates about those boys on the corner, that they've somehow skipped to an ending they haven't earned. That they're born with the knowledge he has only now discovered: that it's all rigged, for nothing, that we're all just standing on corners, waiting for dirt—

No, Leonard says aloud. *Bullshit.* He can't recall a single moment that he spent with the lack of initiative those boys across the street show every day, just . . . *standing there.* But it's not laziness that bothers him, or that they sometimes mess with traffic, or that they might be drug dealers or their single mothers might be on food stamps—if Michael is correct. It's not any of that right-wing, phony, up-by-his-bootstraps bullshit that Leonard's son spouts. (*Don't forget who paid for those bootstraps, Michael.*) Nor is Leonard the sort of jerk who sees kids on a corner and worries about neighborhood property values the way his daughters do. (*Oh, he sees his girls calculating their small inheritance.*) No, it's the sheer waste of time, of health, of potential. That's what offends him. Grim determination has kept Leonard living in West Central Spokane for fifty years, through boom and bust, and bust and bust and bust, rumors of gentrification becoming stale jokes, his brothers in Seattle and Portland tripling their money while his home's value remained as flat as the land it sat on. He was resolute

through regular bouts of vandalism and theft, junk cars parked
in front of his house, feral cats in the hedges, neighbors going
the rental route with single-coat-paint remodels—through it all,
Leonard held tight. For fifty years, he engaged the neighborhood
kids, shot baskets with them, asked after their families and homework, hired them to rake leaves or to help with his big garden.
Last spring, he even tried hiring one of the corner kids, Timothy,
but one day the boy just stopped showing up, disappeared off the
corner (*He's probably in jail,* Michael said) and then Leonard was
done with them, done with all of it, done caring.

For the first time his depressed neighborhood depressed him,
especially those saggy-pants shirtless boys on that corner.

Don't go looking for trouble, his daughter Emily said during one
of his rants about the kids on the corner. *If they're harassing you,
call the cops.* Middle daughter Saundra, who yells as if her father
lives at the end of a wind tunnel, saw it as an opportunity to
move things along. *Dad, maybe it's time to think about assisted living!*
But the harshest reaction came from Michael, the eldest, whose
every solution comes from this talk radio Rush person, and who
squinted out the window and said, *Two of them look white,* as if that
had something to do with it. And then Michael showed up with a
small dark box, with two chrome latches, and said, *Look what I got
for you, Dad,* opening it slowly, *for your protection,* like some sacred
relic: a small black-and-chrome handgun.

A gun? Christ, Michael.

It's just a .22. In case those gangbangers give you trouble.

Back when he was a newspaper reporter Leonard covered a
house fire in this neighborhood, in what, '75? Woman fell asleep
with a lit cigarette and *Foom!,* up went her house. Leonard was
finishing a shift as night cop reporter and caught it on the scanner,

rousted a shooter and they met at the scene, fire crew pushed back
by the heat, the photographer snapping away: flames framing the
back of this stone-faced woman with a blanket wrapped around
her. That's when, from this raging house fire, a little kid walked
out, four years old, just strolled right out of the inferno and up
the sidewalk in scorched pajamas and smoking hair, easy as if he
was coming to catch a school bus, and a firefighter scooped the
kid and only then did the mother begin to howl and weep, two
other kids dead as coal in that burning house, but her four-year-
old walking out calm as Jesus, and nobody had seen anything
like it, a miracle for sure, but at Mass that Sunday, Leonard had
to fight to keep his praying mind from asking (*If You could do
that, why not have all three kids walk out*), wrong wrong wrong,
he scolded himself, but too late, like a crack in a foundation.
Every night for a month after that he stood over his kids' beds
and prayed for their safety, and vowed to love them so much it
would hurt, and he did, and it did, and he's proud of them, and
quietly proud of himself for putting four kids through college
into good, decent lives (two teachers, a radiology tech and Michael in sales) and he'd have put the fifth through college, too, if
not for that druggy boyfriend of hers, and yes, he loves his kids
and he loves his kids' kids and if he's around that long, he will
love his kids' kids' kids, but *really*—his son's solution to some
shirtless, saggy-pants teenage boys hanging across the street is
to bring him a gun? A goddamn gun?

No, he loves his children as much as those nights he stood praying above their beds, but sometimes he suspects they might be the
ripest assholes in the whole world.

Leonard slides into the bedroom, where he's finished boxing
up Marjorie's clothes. A year, that's what everyone advised. So,

he waited. It'll be a year next week—Michael and his wife want to have everyone over for dinner, to what, commemorate—oh, what he'd give to miss that dinner. Leonard has written MARJORIE on the boxes of clothes, as if they could belong to someone else. The girls picked over most of her things during the last year, magpies. The rest of her stuff takes up just four boxes, one less than he bought. That extra box bedevils him, its emptiness a howling taunt: all the time they didn't have. Or perhaps he should fill the extra box with his own clothes, which hang in the closet, morose and alone, work shirts and Sansabelt slacks, twill pants and Sunday jackets, hats, belts, ties: half a closet, half a life.

On the stand next to Marjorie's side of the bed are pictures of grandkids and a frame with a small, stained glass Jesus. *Divine Mercy* it reads in script on the bottom. Sunlight used to glow in little Jesus' robes in the mornings. Marjorie seemed to sense some shift in Leonard after the miracle of the house fire—of course she did—he quit the Knights of Columbus and stopped ushering at Mass, fixated, in the words of Graham Greene, on *the appalling strangeness of the mercy of God*.

You need to trust your faith, Marjorie used to say.

But what if you were my faith?

And the anger? Where does that come from? That it was indecent, even cruel of her to go first? He can't imagine driving these boxes to Goodwill: MARJORIE, the boxes say, and he will leave his Marjorie among the used clothes and couches and drive to dinner at Michael's house, all those children and grandchildren, strangers really, watching him. And then he'll begin a second year without her. Christ God.

On a shelf in the half-empty closet, above his clothes, sits Michael's shiny black gun box; the latches gleam at him like unblinking eyes. He feels like his kids are trying to tell him something he isn't hearing, something drastic: *Those gangbangers . . . looking for trouble . . . maybe it's time.* The latches of the gun box glitter in agreement. Or maybe the gun box is suggesting something else. He covered such things as a reporter, of course; he has seen the spatter.

A cop told him once: in the mouth is the best way to do it.

ON THE CORNER, the boys pool their money and send Doug B to the Suprette for Skittles and Red Bulls—feast at the fence, traffic from the elementary school dying down, cars dwindling until eventually a lone Subaru turns onto Boone and KJ drifts away from the fence—rubs his ass above his pants and limps out into Boone Street, almost to the divided yellow—so the short-haired lady in her sporty wagon *got-to-go-on-around*, all the way into the other lane, the three on the fence hooting her along, *Go on 'round now,* and *Best get to the REI.*

Subaru Lady throws a harsh sideways at KJ—*Damn,* he says— but she goes around because what's she going to do, stop and yell at some rocked-out kid in the street, line of white-drawered ass above his jeans? Nah, cars never stop, might sometimes honk, but they never stop, always go around—an experiment KJ runs over and over as if looking to disprove this thing he knows.

You gonna get run over one of these times, Doug B says.

Yeah, man, why you always do that? asks A-Sym.

But Studio knows why KJ does his street-stroll, same reason he crosses Boone wherever and whenever he wants, though Studio would never say it out loud, go all school counselor on them— this street is the thing Kelvin James can control, not his shit-bird stepdad or his lazy mom or the Russians who want to fight him, or the substation cop who thinks KJ is a banger, what, some kind of middle-school kingpin (*You slinging today, chief?*)—nah, it's just *his* fence, *his* corner.

The fourth kid, Doug B, is several pounds of wit and wisdom behind the other three. He makes no such observations. He just watches KJ and thinks, *Dude, how do you get your chest like that?*—Doug B crazy-in-love with KJ, and sometimes he wonders if that makes him gay—*Dude, you're too boring to be gay,* Studio said—which is why they tagged him Doug B, a name that upset him greatly. (*My last name's Weller and anyway, what other Doug you know?*) But right now, Doug B could care less about his lame nickname or whether the others think he's gay or boring or both—his only concern is how it is he can do fifty pushups a day, just like KJ advised, and still have a chest like a Boone Street pothole.

Seriously KJ, Doug B says, *how you do your chest like that? You break down and buy that P-90 shit off the TV?*

KJ shakes his head. They all watch the infomercial. *Nah, man, I ain't bought it, I just watch the commercials. It's common sense. Go after different muscle groups, keep 'em guessing. That's all the P-90-X is.*

Studio has a thought: *Hey—you think P-90-X is its Muslim name?*

Studio chose it from the Honors English Summer Reading List, *The Autobiography of Malcolm X*, then gave it to KJ to read and KJ passing it on to A-Sym.

Yeah, KJ says, *maybe it was P-90-Little till it put on a bow tie and joined the nation.*

P-90 Brian is my slave name. I'm P-90-X now.

They come off the fence laughing. It's how Studio got the nickname, breaking them up like that, like the laugh track on old Nick-at-Nite shows: . . . *taped in front of a live studio audience*. Laughter breaks and rolls like a wave coming ashore. Even Doug B is laughing—although, just as the others suspect, he doesn't get the joke.

P-90 Brian, A-Sym repeats.

Yeah, says Doug B—

—Then something catches their eyes up the street. KJ squints. *Blight?* And sure enough, riding up on a new mountain bike, skidding sideways to a stop, all braces and big grin, is Blight.

No way! Look who's up in the Boone!

Where you been, man?

You steal that bike, Blight?

Nah, I found it in your girlfriend's ass.

When Timothy first crashed the Boone, they called him Red Hedge, then Whack—skinny red-fro-skin-and-bones living in that lady-wasn't-even-his-mom's crap-nasty-smelling house—KJ and the boys would be scraping the fence and Timothy would walk by on his way to the Suprette for some cereal for the random little kids in that smelly house and they would tease him, *Where you goin', Red?* Or *what up, Whack?* Then Studio had him last year in seventh grade honors math at Glover Middle and he told KJ, *Man, that dude is fun-NEE*, the only quality that matters on the corner, and one day that winter Timothy stopped at the fence and suggested they change his tag from Whack—white/black to Blight—black/white. And like that, Blight was born. And their four became five.

Then there was the shit show at his house last spring, cops coming in after Blight got knocked around by *the-dude-crashing-with-the-lady-wasn't-even-Blight's-mother*, prompting KJ to say what

they all knew, *Man, we* all *a little ghetto, but that shit Blight's livin'
in? That's just wrong.*

After the cops came Child Protective Services—the butterflies,
KJ calls them, master of free association (social workers = social
butterflies). He had his own experience with the butterflies, a
home visit and a week of foster care before an abusive stepbrother
was evicted from his house. But even the butterflies must've recognized real shit when they saw it, because they yanked Blight
out of that house and threw him in with the fosters for good.
Now here he is three months later, and Timothy looks great—
real haircut, taller and thicker, arms and chest filling out. Court-
ordered, Medicaid-paid, rubber-banded orthodontia grill.

Blight, Doug B says, *man, you all tall and shit.*

And A-Sym: *How you like it up in the Sac?*

It became their thing this summer, saying *up in the*—mostly
to screw with the substation cop who likes it when they talk like
characters from *The Wire—Hey, yo! We be up in the Boone las' night
and seen some* shit *go down*—the others trying to keep a straight
face as KJ goes full-gangster on the suggestive substation cop—
*That Russian crew hangin' up in the Broadway Foods be slingin' the rock
n' shit.*

And now everything is *up in the*—all of them *up in the Boone,*
Studio *up in the Honors,* A-Sym *up in the dojo* where his dad takes
him for karate, Doug B *up in the special ed* (Doug B: *I ain't in special
ed, I work with a learning specialist is all*).

And Blight? *He up in the Sac now,* and he hears it right away. As
for Sacajawea Middle School, the more affluent junior high on the
South Hill where his foster parents live, he's not sure what to say.
He shrugs. *Nah, it's good. I mean, it's fine.*

What about the girls? I hear they smokin'.

They alright. I already had most of 'em. And the moms. I'm working my way through the teachers now.

They come off the fence laughing again, Blight's lips parting over his braces of that juggy rim at his own joke.

You kill me, Blight.

You got to hook us up, man, get us up into that South Hill ass.

Not me, Studio says. *Them Sac girls so stuck up you need a Sherpa to talk to 'em.*

They all bust up again, even Doug B, who doesn't know what a Sherpa is. *Sherpa,* he says.

How them fosters treatin' you, Blight?

Nah, it's all good.

You look like you eatin'.

That lady loves the Top Chef, *always trying out new food. Hummus and capers.*

The fuck's a caper? Like a crime?

Nah, like a little olive. But without a hole.

So rich people get the whole olive and we get the ones with holes?

Blight laughs. *Nah, man, a caper's tiny, like a bb. And my foster parents ain't rich.*

How many in the house?

Six. All boys. They're all pretty cool. The lady can't have kids so they started takin' 'em in. Nah, it's okay. And it is, okay. Calm, none of the edge he felt living down here. And yet, at the same time, he misses . . . what? Something? This.

KJ nods. He knows what it is to miss things you shouldn't.

Much as they missed Blight over the summer, they were glad he got out. He got a shit deal: mother sketched off with an air force dude when Blight was little, dad moved in with Rebecca, then the dad went on a bug-eyed tweak and ended up in jail for stealing tools out of garages, left Blight in a house with no family, stuck babysitting those random kids, Rebecca's three-by-three: three kids by three dads, plus Blight—in fact, that's what Blight is doing back here—with school starting he was thinking about the oldest after him, Bowen. So he rode his bike past the house for the first time since June, hoping to catch the kids walking home from school, but the curtains were closed on the house and Timothy isn't supposed to stop—not that Rebecca was so terrible— he liked her most the time, until she'd get depressed, then the curtains would stay closed, and the house would go to shit and he'd end up getting the kids ready for school himself, making meals while she bugged off on oxy or crystal or booze, whatever the new guy was into—and a few times she even made Timothy (what would you call it) . . . cuddle? Is that even the right word? That's what freaked out the social workers, even though Timothy told them it was okay, she didn't seem to want sex (to his shame, *he* kind of did) just someone to hang on to, and he didn't blame her for it—she's only ten years older than him—but he wishes he could've taken Rebecca's kids with him when he left, especially Bowen, who's eight, and who got the baton in the shit relay when Timothy left, stuck taking care of the others. (*But that's just your guilt talking,* his counselor said, what she calls Timothy's *got-out guilt.*)

That's who Blight hoped to see today—Bowen and the other two randoms at Rebecca-the-lady-ain't-his-mom's house—his little white-boy/black-boy/white-girl half-step-not-brothers-and-sister.

You guys seen Bowen around here today? Blight asks.

Nah, man. KJ turns to the others. *Any of you see little B walking home from school today?*

I seen him a few days ago over at Bongs, Doug B offers. *Seemed good.*

Timothy pictures Bowen digging in cushions for quarters to buy a single diaper for the baby. Or a single smoke for Rebecca. Bongs is the store to go for open-pack singles.

He must've gone by already, Blight, Studio says. *Sorry, man.*

Timothy nods. Studio is the guy he misses the most. He's even smarter than Timothy, or quicker anyway—a genius if he had to guess—and he thinks about a phrase he read once, *native intelligence*—Studio's dad being Colville, although Studio isn't enrolled in a tribe himself; anyway, he doesn't think that's what native intelligence means—and while Blight likes all the guys, A-Sym with his good-natured, crazy-ass crooked face, big sweet time-bomb KJ, even dull Doug B—Studio is the guy Timothy wishes could come to Sac and take the honors classes with him, like they did at Glover.

Hang here, KJ says, *maybe the lady-ain't-your-mom will send Bow to the store again.*

Blight feels for the cell phone in his pocket—he should really check in with his Foster Mom, but he doesn't want them to see he's got his own phone, seems shitty somehow—*Nah, I should get going.*

Why don't you just go on up to the house? Doug B asks.

Dude, KJ says—Doug B is so stupid sometimes—and it gets heavy on the corner.

Blight shrugs. *I'm not supposed to have contact with Rebecca unless I'm with my Guardian Ad-litem.*

Even heavier now, the other guys wondering what went on with that lady—it's quiet, but the others can tell when Studio is building to something.

Be a good rap name, he says finally, *Guardian Ad-Litem. Court-appointed rapper.*

Laughter peals again.

Rollin' in my Toyota Tercel/makin' sure them kids be well.

KJ doubles over again and Blight covers his braced teeth—laughing hard as Studio goes off—*Yo, check your frustration/I'm just here for visitation*—and man, they're laughing, so easy up in the Boone, sweet September, seventy-seven on the bump on the first day of school, September, two thousand and eight—and damn if this isn't the best place and time to be alive—

—and that's when they catch movement across the street—that buggy old guy, Leonard, whose wife died last year, old gray stork Leonard is coming out his front door carrying something—and they all look up. Timothy smiles. He did yard work for Leonard last spring, nice old guy always brought him sandwiches and Dr Peppers while he weeded, which is how Timothy first got a taste for Dr Pepper, working in Leonard's garden—but something is off, something is wrong—Leonard doesn't seem to recognize him.

Gentlemen, Leonard says, his gray hair like blown wire as he strolls across the street with a box, *I have something for you*—

The old man angles across the street and sets the box on the curb. He smiles at them, little tufts of white hair coming out his ears, too, big bug-eyed glasses, question-mark spine.

And here they are, six of the nine thousand people *up in the Boone,* felony flats, the Twilight Zone, misdemeanor meadow, West Central, the West Centy, on a natural peninsula carved by the curling Spokane River canyon, which makes a loose U around this neighborhood and frames it to the south, to the west, to the north, while on the east, Monroe Street's cop shop, courthouse and jail form a gate, so it's the one neighborhood you can't escape—and if you believe the cops and real estate agents, this might be the worst strip in the city, maybe the state—but you know what: fuck 'em, it's also the most alive, everybody on the street, all that bagged-beer chronic drama playing out on porches and sidewalks, outdoor couches and strip-weaved lawn chairs, in weedy lots and parks and out front of the Vietnamese grocery, on corners like this one—

—where a lonesome old widower reaches down in the cardboard box he brought from his house and five boys lean forward a little—

—to see the old man come up with a handful of belts.

I have gifts!

He holds out belts like a deacon at one of those snake churches, a nest of black and brown. *All summer I watched you gentlemen struggle with your trousers, and I thought, What kind of country is this, where smart young men can't afford belts? We can send spaceships across the galaxy, shrink a computer to the size of a billfold but we can't keep our young men's pants up?*

His grin is playful as he holds out an old-man belt for each of them. *No man should have to go around with his underwear out for the world to see.*

The boys cock their heads in a *Dude's-fuckin'-with-us* fashion, Doug B tugging at his khakis.

And look, I brought shirts, too! Leonard kicks over the box and they spill out: button shirts! Stripes and whites and patterns and that baby blue of fat guys in cubicles: must be ten dress shirts in there.

No one should go without a shirt in America, Leonard says. *There are two things you need to know to make your way in this world. Education is the great equalizer. And clothes make the man.* He reaches down and grabs a shirt with a pattern that looks like old wallpaper. He holds the snake-nest of belts and this shirt out for the biggest kid, clearly the leader.

And sure enough, KJ comes off the fence, chooses a belt carefully, woven brown leather. He pulls his jeans up over his white undershorts, tugs the belt through the loops. He takes a shirt, too, the most ridiculous one, a swirly curly, big seventies collar, and puts it on. It strains his chest and arms, but he manages to button it all the way to the top. *I should tuck this shit in, huh?* and he tucks it and yanks his pants up over hips to his navel, cinches that brown leather belt around the rumpled waistband of his pants and turns to his crew. They're laughing their asses off, KJ looking like a substitute teacher, and now they're all grabbing belts and hoisting pants and tucking shirts and maybe tomorrow, Studio thinks, when they dress like this at school, it will catch on, and within weeks, it will seep up to the high school and onto the internet and onto streets everywhere, or maybe they're already doing it in Queens or Quebec or Qatar, and in a month every kid in the world will intuitively know that *this is now cool,* cinching and tucking and buttoning—old man style—Urban Outfitters and American Apparel picking up on it just as the substation cop sends out an intel memo that her *Spokane street gang is now wearing Sansabelt slacks and crushed fedoras,* but that's all in the future because for now it's still a sweet September day on a slow corner up in the Boone—

—where a laughing KJ and crew have followed Leonard across the street and into his house, front door wide open, A-Sym pulling curtains—*Let a little light in, Leonard!*—sun busting on dusty wall-to-walls, and into the bedroom where Leonard has taken all his clothes out of his closet and spread them out on the bed,

KJ and crew chugging Dr Peppers and going through Leonard's whole wardrobe, *Check it out* and *Look at this*—

Take it all, Leonard says, *anything you want,* tams and ties and loafers and belts, the old man standing in the doorway smiling, wistful (*You shall be witness . . .*) and that's when Blight breaks off from the pile of clothes and sidles up to the old man: *You remember me, Leonard?*

He looks over at the boy, and maybe he was thrown by his height and hair—but yes, the big eyes, the reddish Afro (but tighter now, and the kid is so much taller)—can this be the same young man who worked in his garden last spring? He gave that kid books and cans of soda, and they talked about school. He was in honors classes, English and U.S. history and algebra, and Leonard told him to suck as much out of that school as the cheap bastards would give him and yeah, it IS him—

Timothy? Leonard asks—the kid's grin going off with a flash of braces, and it IS him, here, now, looking not just older, but like he's crossed over into some other territory, and Leonard realizes he was hurt by the kid disappearing like that, hurt by everyone good leaving at once. *By God, Timothy! How are you?*

Good. I got moved into foster care. I'm on the South Hill, at Sac now.

Ah, that's a good school. Will you go to Ferris or LC?

Ferris.

Takin' honors classes still. College prep?

Yes, sir.

That's good. Outstanding. Keep that up. Out of the gardening business, though?

Timothy shrugs.

And before he really considers what he's saying, and that it commits him to tomorrow and after, Leonard offers something he hadn't planned: *I could still use someone to clear the beds. Rake leaves. Trim the hedges.*

I could come on Saturdays.

A stone in his throat. Goddamn. Leonard had a whole farewell speech planned for these corner wastrels, commencement address, goodbye benediction, about how it's short, life, how you're young and you think you know everything, but really, you don't know shit until you're too old to do anything about it, and just when you get comfortable it bleeds away from you, all that you worked for, THAT'S why you can't waste a day of it, *not a single God-damned day, gentlemen*—because one day, before you know it: *Foom!*

Is it okay if I bring my little brother? Timothy asks. He imagines having Bowen meet him here on Saturdays, letting him have the money they make, good way to start easing Bow out of that house.

Leonard is staring at the shiny black gun box in the closet. *Hmm? he* says to Timothy; did the kid say something about having a brother come? *Oh, of course, yes,* he says, *bring anyone you want.*

And KJ and crew are completely decked out now, crisp and buttoned, caps jaunty, belts tight. But Timothy is looking past them, to one of the boxes marked MARJORIE. Leonard's eyes follow. And the little glass Jesus on top of the clothes in the box. Christ God, the appalling mercy. The corner boys laugh and model for each other while Timothy helps Leonard hang the rest of his clothes back up in the closet.

Famous Actor

THE FAMOUS ACTOR WAS rubbing my tit with his elbow.

He'd swept into the party not five minutes earlier, in old jeans and a plain gray T-shirt, and plopped down on the couch next to me, facing the other way. He was having a chat with a guy leaning on the arm of the sofa. I heard him say, "Twelve pounds of muscle," and I heard him say, "Dude sandbagged that route," and I heard him say, "No, man, the Ducati Mach 1 came out in limited release in '64. I know because I have one"—all while rubbing my left boob.

I looked around the party: forty or so people clustered in threes and fours, pretending not to look at the Famous Actor (even here in Bend, we know not to go goony around celebrities), but no one went more than four or five seconds without stealing a glance at him. Nobody but me seemed to notice what his right elbow was up to.

After a few minutes, he stopped elbow-fucking me and turned so that we were face-to-face. It was weird staring into those pale blues, eyes I'd known for years, eyes I'd seen in, what, fifteen or sixteen movies, in a couple of seasons of TV, staring out from magazine covers. He muttered something I couldn't quite hear.

I leaned in. "I'm sorry—what?"

"I said"——he bent in closer, so that his mouth was inches from my left ear——"the universe is an endless span of darkness occasionally broken by moments of unspeakable celestial violence."

I was pretty sure that wasn't what he'd said.

He laughed as if even he recognized what an insane thing that was for someone to say. "You ever think shit like that at parties?"

I tend to think about crying at parties, or I wonder if someone might try to kill me. But I didn't say that. I don't very often say what I think.

"Hey," he said, "this is going to sound like a line, but . . . do you maybe want to get out of here?"

He was right. It did sound like a line. And I did want to get out of there.

"Okay," I said.

I disliked him from the moment I decided to sleep with him.

IN ONE OF his first movies, *Fire in the Hole,* he plays a scared young soldier. I can't even remember which war but it's not Vietnam. It's maybe one of the gulf wars, or Afghanistan, or something. It's a truly awful movie, but somehow too earnest to really hate. Still, you know you've made a bad war movie when they don't even show it on TNT. At the time he was cast, the Famous Actor was still known as the kid from the Disney Channel. I think the role in that war movie was supposed to launch him as an adult actor. But you got the sense that people watched the movie thinking, *Wait, what's the kid from* The Terrific Todd Chronicles *doing carrying a rifle, for Christ's sake.* Still, I guess it did turn him into a real adult actor because he started doing more movies after that.

We made our way through the party. He didn't ask how it was

that I didn't need to tell anyone that I was leaving. I was glad I didn't have to explain that I wasn't actually *invited* to the party.

There were a few people I knew standing outside and I wondered what they would say about him leaving with me. The Famous Actor climbed in the passenger seat of my Subaru. He sat on my makeup bag, held it up, then tossed it into the backseat. He had a small hiker's backpack with him, which he sat at his feet. "Must be weird to go to a party in Bend, Oregon, and end up leaving with me," he said.

I shrugged. "There's always a party at that house. Everybody knows about it."

"No, I didn't mean the party. I just meant this probably wasn't how you figured your Friday night would go."

"This is my Wednesday," I said. I explained that I had Mondays and Tuesdays off from the coffee shop, so I always thought of Fridays as my Wednesdays. He looked at me as if he couldn't tell if I was crazy or if I was fucking with him. It's hard to explain, but I can make myself distant, make my face as blank as possible.

"Huh, funny," he said. He stared out the window as I drove. He hadn't buckled his seat belt and my car bonged at him.

"You know that thing I said at the party—about the universe being an endless span of darkness? It was really a comment on how it gets old, everyone looking at you like you're going to say something profound. Sometimes I play off that expectation by saying something totally crazy." He laughed at himself. "You know?"

My car bonged at him again.

When he dies in *Fire in the Hole,* you can tell it's meant to be the emotional peak of the movie. The soldiers are walking through this destroyed city and a sniper's bullet zips into the spot where his neck meets his chest, just above his body armor. He slaps at the wound like he's been stung by a bee, and only then does he seem to realize what's happening to him. That he's dying. It should be a profound moment. Those washed-out eyes get all wide and he frantically reaches around his back to feel whether the bullet has gone all the way through. His line is something like, *Sarge! Did it go through? Did . . . it . . . go through?* And then he just falls over. It's hard to say what's wrong with it, but it became one of those unintentional laugh lines. Like: Sure, war is hell, but it's nothing compared to Terrific Todd's acting.

He pulled a cigarette pack from his pocket. "You mind?" American Spirits. Naturally. I can't remember the last time I dated a guy who didn't smoke Spirits. Every guy in Bend smokes them. He blew the smoke to the roof of the car, which answered by bonging at him again about his seat belt.

The Famous Actor explained that he'd been making a movie nearby—I knew this, of course; everyone knew they were filming a post-apocalyptic movie called *The Beats* in the high desert, and we all knew the cast. Someone had told the Famous Actor that Bend was known for its rock climbing, so he'd called a climbing guide and they'd gone bouldering that day. Then the guide invited him to the party. I knew the guide he'd called. Wayne Bolls. Wayne's website is covered with pictures of celebrities he's climbed with, like an old New York dry cleaner. Star Fucker Tours, we call it in Bend. *We put the climber in climbing.*

"It's so great to get away from the bullshit," he said. I guess the bullshit was Hollywood, and wealth and fame—pretty much everything that everyone else in the world totally craves. He took a long drag of that cigarette. "But hey, Bend's a cool town, huh?" I nodded. That's the worst thing about Bend. Its coolness. That and its size, how everyone thinks they know you. He picked a piece of tobacco off his tongue. "For me it's just a treat to be around normal people." I made a noise that must've sounded like a laugh. "What's so funny?" He took another drag of his cigarette. "I'm serious."

He seemed genuinely hurt. "I don't see why people have so much trouble believing that famous people just want to be normal."

IN HIS LAST movie, *New Year's Love Song,* he is one of like a hundred celebrities paired off in parallel love stories. He was cast as the manager of a rock band that is doing a concert on New Year's Day in New York. The band is supposed to be a modern-day Fleetwood Mac, I guess—two young guys and two young girls—but without the talent and the hard drugs that made Fleetwood Mac so interesting. The cute singer is married to the drummer and, as the band's tongue-tied manager, the Famous Actor needs to keep the press from finding out they're divorcing until after the concert—although they never really make it clear why that would matter. The singer is played by the girl from that Nickelodeon show *You Can't Fool Tara!*—it was billed as a kind of Disney-meets-Nickelodeon thing; this was right after her whole sex-tape scandal, so the movie was meant to redeem her image, or something.

The movie ends with the Famous Actor's band manager character stumbling out onstage in Rockefeller Plaza and telling the singer that he's always loved her in front of, like, a jillion people. But here's what I don't get: Why do we find that romantic? Are men such liars that it's a turn-on to have that many witnesses? It's one of those movies that make you sad to be female, that make you want to stab yourself in the ovaries. It's truly a hateful movie, but I was still teary at the end, in a completely involuntary way, the way crying babies are supposed to make women lactate. "I want to start every year from now on with you in my arms," the Famous Actor says to the singer on the stage, in front of everyone in the world. There should be a German word for wanting to gouge out your own teary eyes.

"I like your apartment," the Famous Actor said. He walked around like someone sizing up a hotel room. He ran his hand along the spines of the books on my shelf and crouched in front of my albums. "Vinyl," he said. "Cool." When he got to a band he approved of, he would say the name. "Love this old Beck. Ooh, Talking Heads. Nice. The New Pornographers. Yes."

I put my keys on the kitchen table and looked through my mail. There was a late notice for a credit card bill, a late notice for a water bill, a solicitation for a fake college, and a postcard from my ex. The postcard showed some old 1960s tourist trap in Idaho called the Snake Pit. On the back he'd written, "Expected to see you here." It's this thing my ex and I have: we send each other old postcards and write shitty things on them. I sent him one from Crater Lake on which I wrote: "The second biggest a-hole in Oregon." We never really broke up; he just moved to Portland with his band. Not that we had this great relationship. He always said I needed help. I always said he was a pig who fucked any girl who would have him. But I'll say this for him: he was not a liar. He told me all about it every time. He'd get back from some gig in Ashland or Eureka and say, "Dude, I got something to tell you." After a while I'd get anxious even seeing his name on my phone because I thought he was going to tell me about some new girl he'd junked. But I couldn't seem to break up with him. When he finally left for Portland, I wasn't sad, just more deadened, the way I get. Sometimes I think our real problem wasn't his infidelity; it was his honesty. We send old postcards just to say—Hey. Still here. I wondered if he'd be jealous if he saw who was in my apartment.

The Famous Actor plopped down on my couch. "It's so great to just be in, like, a fucking apartment! Right? You know? A real place? With, like . . . walls . . . and furniture and books and a TV and real posters and . . ." I wondered if he was going to name everything in my apartment, room by room: dresser, nightstand, alarm clock, toothbrush, antibacterial soap, Tampax . . .

I opened my fridge. "You want a drink?"

"I'm in recovery," he said. "But you go ahead." He held up his pack of American Spirits again. "This okay?" I said it was fine and he lit up, took a deep pull of smoke, and let it go in the air. "No, this is nice," he said again. "Just what I needed." He pulled another piece of tobacco off his tongue. Or actually, I suspect that he pretended to pull a piece of tobacco off his tongue. He leaned his head back onto the couch. "I just get so fucking tired of . . ."

But he couldn't seem to think of what it was that made him so fucking tired.

IN *AMSTERDAM DEADLY*, he plays a UN investigator who goes to The Hague to testify in the trial of a vicious African warlord. As soon as you see the cast you know he's going to fall for the beautiful blond South African lawyer defending the warlord. The actress is that girl from *My One True,* and because she's as American as Velveeta she got knocked pretty bad for her South African accent, which sounded like an Irish girl crossed with a Jamaican auctioneer. Still, she and the Famous Actor really do have chemistry. Watching that movie is like watching the two best-looking single people at a wedding reception; not a lot of drama about who's going to fuck later. But if the romance in that movie is okay, the politics make no sense. The dialogue is like someone reading stories out of the *New York Times*. The Famous Actor has a speech near the end where he yells, "If the Security Council won't pass this joint resolution, then I will get these refugees across the border to the safe zone myself!" Not exactly *Henry V*. I think sometimes movies, like people, just try too hard.

We had straight missionary paint-by-numbers sex: some foreplay, exactly enough oral to get us both going, then he pulled a condom out of that backpack he carried and rolled it over his dick. It was ribbed, which I could see he believed was thoughtful of him. There was nothing weird or obsessive or porny about the sex. Or particularly memorable. First sex is always kind of awkward; you don't yet know what the other person likes. Everything's basically in the right place, but it doesn't feel right, or it takes a minute to find.

First sex is like being in a stranger's kitchen, trying all the drawers, looking for a spoon. There was one point where he was over me, his eyes closed, head back, weight on his arms like he was doing a push-up, and it was kind of weird—like, Oh, hey, look, Terrific Todd is boning someone. Oh, wait it's me. But I shouldn't make it sound like the sex was bad. It was fine. Really, the only disappointing thing was how much stomach fat the Famous Actor had—I mean, really, when you have that much money, how hard is it to do a few sit-ups? Of course, that might have been intentional, too, part of his normalcy campaign.

Afterward, we were lying on my bed naked, and he was smoking another American Spirit. He smoked so many I wanted to buy stock in the company. "That was great," he said. "And thanks for not taking a selfie or anything weird like that."

I must've made a face like, Christ, are you kidding me?

He sat up. "Oh, you'd be surprised how often that happens. I know actors who have, like, a contract they have women sign before they'll have sex." He named two actors, both of whom had been in movies with him. "I mean, can you imagine?" he asked. "Making a woman sign a contract before you fuck?"

He offered me his cigarette. I took a small drag. Those organic cigarettes tasted like dog shit.

"That's the part I really don't think people get." He picked another fake tobacco bit off his tongue. "You know? About fame? How dispiriting it is, how dehumanizing? It's like you're this . . . product. Right? I mean: I'm not some product. I'm a fuckin' person." He slapped his little intentional belly fat. "Right? Why can't people understand I'm just a regular guy?"

"I think people understand that," I said.

IN *BIG BRO*, he plays a guy in a fraternity whose older brother is a Wall Street trader who shows up after his divorce to act out some *Animal House* fantasies, only to find that frats now are full of serious students. The actor who plays the Wall Street brother had recently left *Saturday Night Live* and you can really tell the difference between someone used to making live audiences laugh and someone who falls into a giant birthday cake and reads lines like, "Oh boy! Here we go again!" to a Disney laugh track. Still, *Big Bro* was the Famous Actor's breakout. It must've made $200 million and it's watchable in part because the Famous Actor seems so easygoing and likable in it (in other words, exactly like no fraternity guy ever, in the history of the world). People saw him differently after that. I think, when an actor exudes such charm, we assume the character must be closest to his real self. But there's no reason to think that; he could just as easily be the selfish loser who raids his senile dad's retirement account in *Forty Reasons for Dying,* for instance. We just want to like people, especially famous people.

It's really not possible to sleep next to someone the first time you've had sex together. That's something I'd like to take up with Hollywood if I ever get the chance: how they always cut from the kissing couple to them lying peacefully in bed postsex, snoozing with smiles on their faces. I'd like to grab some screenwriter by his ears: "Hey, you go fuck a stranger and then try sleeping afterward!" We were lying there on our backs, staring at the ceiling. He was smoking another cigarette. Our legs were touching. "If you want me to go, I can call for a ride," he said.

"Only if you want to," I said.

"Cool," he said. "Yeah, cool. I'll stay. I like it here. It's chill." I didn't say anything. He sniffed. "I think people would be surprised at how hard it is for someone like me to find a place where I can just . . . you know——*be*? Where there's not some PA constantly buzzing around asking if I want a Sprite."

"You want a Sprite?"

He laughed a little, took a pull of smoke, and when he started to reach for his mouth, I watched him closely. He looked like he was picking something off the end of his tongue again, but I'll be damned if I saw any tobacco bits there. He looked right at me with those Pepsi-blue eyes.

"Sometimes I daydream about hiding out someplace like this.

Just saying, Fuck you to the fake industry stuff and just dropping the fuck out. Not tell anyone either, just chill in Bend, Oregon, for a month, go out to breakfast, rock climb, maybe get a bike, read poetry in the park, go to parties like last night, hang out with someone cool like you? Know what I mean?"

"Yes," I said. I didn't say the rest of what I was thinking, which was: Who doesn't daydream of that, of not having a job or any worries, playing around all day, riding a bike and reading poetry and having sex? The difference is that most of us would starve to death in a week.

I started to imagine the Famous Actor hanging around my apartment for the next month like some unwanted houseguest. A month becoming two, and three, him smoking forty cartons of organic cigarettes and never finishing that book of poetry he was supposedly reading, me coming home every day to Terrific Todd marveling still at all the normal shit in my normal apartment— *dish soap, spatula, salt pig, can opener!*—that band of fat around his middle getting bigger and realer all the time.

He leaned over, got his tennis shoe off the floor, put his cigarette out on its sole, and put the butt in the pocket of his jeans. Then he propped himself up on one elbow—the one that I had gotten to know so well earlier. "Hey, can I ask you a personal question?"

That seemed like such a guy thing to say right then. Hey, remember a few minutes ago my dick was inside you? Well, now I was wondering if I could ask you something . . . personal?

"Sure," I said.

"It's just . . . I can't get a read on you."

I didn't say anything. I get that a lot from guys. Also, it wasn't technically a question.

"I just keep feeling like . . . I don't know . . . like you think I'm . . . kind of a douchebag or something."

Also, not a question.

Toward the end of *Big Bro,* after this huge party where Snoop Dogg inexplicably shows up with a bunch of hookers, the rest of the frat pulls the Famous Actor's character aside and tells him that his big brother has got to go. He's nearly gotten them all expelled and they're all flunking classes and in danger of losing their fraternity charter. It's probably the most moving scene in the movie, the Famous Actor telling his brother he's got to leave. "Hey, Charlie, these are my brothers now," the Famous Actor says, "but they'll never be . . . my brother." Chastened for his boorish behavior, the older brother slinks away sadly. Of course, he doesn't really go away, but shows up three minutes later with Mark Cuban to save the day at his brother's oral presentation in his business class.

"I don't think you're a douchebag," I said to the Famous Actor.

"No, I think you do." He sat up higher.

"It's not that," I said. "It's just . . ." What are you supposed to say—after years of therapy to untangle your difficulty in forming relationships, your self-destructive behavior, the depressive periods, and suicidal thoughts? And some narcissist just expects you to pillow-talk it out?

"Seriously," he said, "I need you to tell me what you think of me."

What I thought of him? That his insecurity was infinite? Instead, after a minute, I said, "You'll always be my brother."

YOU HAVE TO wonder how a movie like *Big Bro 2* even gets made. In it, the younger brother has graduated from college and been hired by the older brother's company, which has somehow morphed from a Wall Street firm in the first movie to a tech company in the second. They're about to unveil this new kind of biocomputer, but an evil tech company called Gorgle wants to take over the brothers' company, so the old *SNL* comedian has to gather all the old frat guys together to use their special skills to defeat— Ugh, you know, it actually hurts my head to even think of the plot of that movie. The best thing I can say about the second *Big Bro* is that the Famous Actor is barely in it, and only because he's clearly fulfilling some line in a contract that required his presence in a sequel. The *SNL* guy's career had stalled, and most of those frat guys would've starred in animal porn just to work again, but the Famous Actor had gone on to become the Famous Actor by then. He seems truly apologetic in the six or seven scenes he's in—like, I'm sorry, America. I really am sorry.

He had that same sorry look on his face as he sat on the edge of the bed and looked back over his shoulder at me. "You know, I think you're not being very generous."

"Sorry," I said.

"I mean, maybe you're the asshole. Did that ever occur to you?"

"Yes," I said.

He turned away. "You can't know how weird this fame shit is. It's like you're see-through. Everyone assumes they know everything about you, but you know what? Nobody knows a fucking thing about me!" He stood and rubbed his forehead. "Always trying to be what people want—after a while, it's like you can't even trust yourself anymore. You're always second-guessing, like, Wait, how do I talk again? Is this how I react to things or how I want people to see me react? And when no one's watching, you feel totally fucked—like, Am I even here? You don't know how hard that is—to not know yourself!"

He really seemed to think famous people were the only ones who didn't know themselves.

"Then I meet someone like you, someone I might genuinely like, someone I don't want to think that I'm a celebrity dickhead . . . and what do I do?" He laughed. "Act like a dickhead."

He walked across my bedroom to my dresser. Behind a pile of clothes there was a picture of me with my sister, the last picture of us before she disappeared. He picked up the picture and stared at it. In the picture I'm eleven and Lana is thirteen and we're standing in front of the hammer ride at the county fair. We have huge grins on our faces and Lana's giving the thumbs-up because we're so proud of riding that scary ride together. Three months later she would run away from home. We never found out what happened to her, if her body is somewhere or if she's working as a hooker in Alaska or whatever. She could be in the Taliban, or she could be in the circus, or she could be a housewife, or she could be rotting in a field in Utah. That was the hardest thing for my parents—just never knowing. Our house was a tomb after that. My parents were never the same. The Famous Actor stared at the picture a moment and then put it down. He turned and faced me.

"So, if I've been a little self-absorbed, I apologize."

"It's fine," I said.

"No," he said. "It's not fine." He was getting worked up again. "You can't just say, It's fuckin' fine and then keep acting like some zombie! You can't fuckin' do that! You have to give something back! You can't just sit there in judgment thinking that I'm an asshole and not give me the chance to show you I'm not! I mean, am I asking too much? For a little human interaction!"

"What's my name," I said.

He stared at me for a few seconds. "Aw fuck," he said.

IF I WERE trapped on an island or something and I could have only one movie to watch, but it had to be one of his movies, I'd choose *Been There, Done That*. It's telling that my favorite of his movies is one where he's just a supporting actor. I think it's hard for even good actors to carry a whole movie. He's great as the gay brother of the heroine, who has come back to her family's home in 1980s Louisiana with her black boyfriend. He has several opportunities to go too broad with the gay brother, or to go all AIDS-victim-TV-movie-of-the-week or something, but he's really restrained. And when the gay brother ends up being the most racist person in the family, the Famous Actor turns in an extremely nuanced and smart performance. It's even a little bit brave. I suspect it's what happens when you work with a great director. But I also think there's something deeper that he managed to find within himself in that movie.

He snapped his fingers and pointed at me. "Katherine!"

I shook my head.

"But it's something with a *K* sound, though, right? Caroline or Cassidy or . . ."

"Sorry."

He had his eyes closed, concentrating. "You work at a bar."

"Coffee shop."

"Well, fuck me," he said. "Fuck me fuck me fuck me." He opened his eyes, as if suddenly finding out someone he'd known for years was not who he thought they were.

"You had a lot on your mind," I said. "And your elbow."

He shook his head—like, Can you believe me?

"Don't worry about it," I said. "I suspect it's harder to not be a douchebag than people think."

He gave a little laugh, but I think, of all the things I said, that might've hurt the most. The condescension and truth of it. I felt okay then, in control of things.

"Well, thanks for understanding, Katherine," he said, "or whatever your name is."

I just smiled.

He reached into his backpack for his phone. "I should probably—" He turned on his phone and it buzzed and buzzed. He began reading text messages. "Oh shit."

"Girlfriend?"

"What?" He scowled. "No. No. I have an earlier call tomorrow than I thought. I'm gonna have someone come get me."

"Sure."

He pressed a number and put his iPhone to his ear. "Hey. It's me. I'm at this girl's house. Yeah, in Bend. I know. I know. Hey, is there any way . . ." He didn't have to finish the sentence. I guessed there were a lot of sentences he didn't have to finish. "Yeah. Cool. Just a sec." He looked up at me. "Hey, what's the address here?"

In *Been There, Done That,* he has a great scene where he has a beer with the black boyfriend, who, it turns out, is super religious and has a problem with gay people. It ends with the two of them laughing together, two otherwise decent men confronting their old biases. As Hollywood pat as it sounds, the scene comes off as entirely genuine.

I have to say, right before he left, it felt that way in my apartment, too. Genuine. Like we'd come through something. He took a quick shower and came out dressed in the same jeans and gray T-shirt.

He bowed. "Well, nameless queen of Bend, it was a pleasure to meet you tonight. Thank you."

I'd put a T-shirt on.

"Can I kiss you goodbye?"

I said he could, and I stood up.

It would be hard being with an actor. Figuring out what's real. That goodbye kiss he gave me—honestly, I don't know if I've ever been kissed like that: one hand behind my neck, the other on my waist. It was a great, generous kiss and I felt myself opening up to him, more than I had in bed. In fact, the kiss was so good I started to think about that laughter in *Been There, Done That*. I mean, clearly, the actors in that movie weren't really laughing in that scene, but in a way, they sort of were. I guess in acting, you become the very thing you're portraying. In sex scenes, if you act turned on, you get turned on. Act like something is hilarious, it becomes hilarious. And that's how that kiss was—

My God, if that kiss wasn't real, I don't even care. I'll take fake over real any day. I've seen real.

Maybe it's that way with our lives, too. Normal people. I mean, we're all acting all the time anyway, putting on our not-crazy faces for people, acting like making someone a cappuccino is the greatest thrill in the world, pretending to care about things you don't, pretending not to care about things you do care about, pretending your name isn't Katherine when it is, acting like you have your shit together when, the truth is, well—

I didn't want to look out the window as he left—it seemed like such a stupid movie-cliché thing to do—but I couldn't help myself.

I looked out. He gave a small glance over his shoulder toward my window, but I think the light was wrong and he couldn't see my face. Then he flicked at his hair and jumped into the passenger seat of a blue Audi, which zipped away. I imagined his Big Bro driving the car. I imagined the Famous Actor lighting up a Natural American Spirit while the car bonged at him to put on his seat belt. He hated seat belts. It was three in the morning. I wasn't tired.

I looked around my apartment.

The Famous Actor was in a serial killer movie, too. It's called *Over Tumbled Graves* and he plays this young cop, the love interest of the girl detective hunting a serial killer. It might be the only movie of his that I've never seen—because of Lana, I guess. If you suffer night terrors and insomnia you learn to avoid serial killer movies. Not that I begrudge him being in it. We all make choices. And he generally makes good ones. I just read that he is getting a franchise superhero in one of those reboots. And that he's engaged to the girl who is going to play Blue Aura in the same movie.

I'm glad for him. He's been through a lot the last year. It wasn't even two weeks after the post-apocalyptic movie finished production in Bend that I read that the Famous Actor was going back into drug rehab. Of course, I might have been the least surprised person in the world.

The morning he left, I rubbed lotion on my arms so that I wouldn't start scratching. I went back to bed, but I couldn't fall asleep. I had to be at the coffee shop at six. I repeated the steps: Get out of bed. Keep moving. Take care of yourself.

I got up to take a shower. That's when I noticed my medicine cabinet door was slightly ajar. I opened it all the way. He had cleaned it out. The Zoloft I take for depression. The Ativan I take for anxiety. The Ambien I sometimes take to sleep. But not just that. He took the Benadryl and the Advil and the Gas-X. He even took the Lysteda I sometimes take when I get these ungodly heavy periods. I can't imagine what he thought he was going to do with that one. Two days later I got a visit from a nice young woman from the production company. Interesting they'd send a woman. Smart, I guess. I signed the nondisclosure documents without negotiating. She gave me a check for six thousand dollars. All I had to do was promise never to mention his name. But what's a name anyway?

That morning, as I stood there, staring at that empty medicine cabinet, I felt the strangest sense of pride in him. Warmth. Love, even. Well, look at you, I thought, you *are* normal—as normal as the most fucked-up barista in Bend, Oregon. Relax, Terrific Todd, wherever you are, you're one of us.

Balloons

MRS. AHEARN-ACROSS-THE-STREET OPENED HER screen door, pulled me inside and kissed me. It took a second to place the taste, but then I got it: bean with bacon soup.

"My mom said I should check on you," I said after she finished kissing me.

Her eyes were watery. She leaned in and kissed me again, even harder. She pushed my mouth open with her bean-with-bacon tongue. She grabbed my butt with both hands. Then she backed up again, like she'd just thought of something.

"You know who's got a great ass—" she said.

"Who?" I said.

"—your brother."

I had no idea what to say.

CHECKING ON MRS. Ahearn-across-the-street was one of the phony jobs my mom made up for me in the summer of 1994, after my first year at Spokane Community College. She was always looking for ways to sneak me money without having Dad cranking on me for not having a job. They were like a sitcom sometimes.

"He's a late bloomer," Mom would say.

And Dad would say, "Don't you have to bloom to be a late bloomer?"

And Mom would say, "Maybe he has a learning disability."

And Dad would say, "I know he has an *earning* disability."

So Mom offered me twenty bucks a week to check on Mrs. Ahearn-across-the-street.

We always called her that. We'd say, Mrs. Ahearn-across-the-street backed into our mailbox, or Mrs. Ahearn-across-the-street left her car running all night. She was about my parents' age. Forty-something, fifty-whatever, I don't know. She wasn't *creepy* old, but she was definitely old. And if she wasn't exactly pretty, either, then she was like . . . the ghost of pretty. Mom always said it was "tragic" how Mr. Ahearn died of cancer and left her a widow so young. But I always thought that a small part of Mom envied it, the drama, I guess.

"WHAT DO YOU mean check on her," I asked the first time Mom brought it up.

I was in my room playing *Mortal Kombat* on the Sega.

"Just go over there and see if she needs anything," Mom said. "Danny did it all last summer, out of the goodness of his heart. He still asks about her."

The goodness of his heart. It was widely acknowledged that my older brother Danny was both a saint and a genius. He was in law school at the University of Washington. I was getting C's in community college.

"But . . ." I looked up from my game. "What does Mrs. Ahearn-across-the-street even need?"

"I don't know, Ellis. Take out her trash. Shop for her. Rake her leaves."

"So if I rake her leaves, do I get more money?" I asked. "Or is that included in the twenty? I mean, is there like an hourly component that kicks in?" My mom left my room without answering.

AFTER SHE KISSED me and said that about Danny's ass, I asked Mrs. Ahearn-across-the-street if she needed anything from the grocery store.

She blinked a couple of times, like she was clearing something away, and then she disappeared into the kitchen. She came back with a twenty-dollar bill, a Safeway coupon and a shopping list. Her eyes were still watery. The coupon was for Swanson meat pies, four for three dollars. There were only two other things on her shopping list: bean with bacon soup and Canadian Mist whiskey.

"I can't buy you whiskey," I said.

"I'm a social drinker," she said.

"No, I mean, I'm not twenty-one."

"How old are you?"

"Nineteen."

She stared at me like this couldn't be true. "Ah Jesus," she said. Then she said it again, "Jesus." And she took the twenty back.

DANNY ANSWERED ON the first ring. "Hey, it's Ellis."

"What do you want?"

I didn't know how to ask what I wanted to ask.

"Mom has me checking on Mrs. Ahearn-across-the-street," I said.

He was quiet for a long time.

We were both quiet for a long time.

Finally, I said, "Don't you think I should get extra for raking leaves?"

He hung up.

I TOOK OFF my headphones. Upstairs, my parents were arguing again. "He should get a job is what he should do," my dad was saying. "Danny had two jobs at his age."

"Every kid's different," Mom said. "Ellis will find himself."

"He should find himself a job."

"Kids grow at different paces."

"I worked from the time I was twelve years old," Dad said, a sentence I think he had been saying out loud every day since he was twelve years old.

I put my headphones back on.

I KNOCKED ON the screen door.

"It's unlocked," said Mrs. Ahearn-across-the-street. I came inside. She was sitting in a chair watching a game show, a meat pie and a glass of whiskey on the TV tray in front of her.

"Where do you want your mail?" I asked.

"Kitchen table," she said.

The kitchen was a mess. I put empty soup cans and macaroni boxes in a grocery sack and cleared a space to set her mail. I took the trash out the back door. "Ellis," she said. "About the other day . . . I wouldn't tell your parents about that."

I wasn't sure if she meant *she* would not tell my parents, or that *I* should not tell my parents.

Either way was fine with me. "OK, cool," I said.

I GOT BETTER grades that fall. I talked to a girl in my English comp class, and we started studying together. I began applying to four-year schools. Once a week, I checked on Mrs. Ahearn-across-the-street. She didn't try to kiss me again. I raked her leaves, took out her trash. Once I cleaned a bird's nest out of her eaves. Mom had me bring carved pumpkins to her house, and two days later, when some kids stomped them into her porch, I cleaned up the mess.

Then Danny announced he was coming home for Thanksgiving—and he was bringing his new girlfriend. Mom loved to brag about Danny's new girlfriend. She showed everyone the picture Danny had sent of the two of them at Pike's Place Market. His girlfriend had giant boobs. "Isn't she pretty?" Mom would ask. And I would think, Nope, she just has giant boobs.

THE DAY I found out Danny was bringing his girlfriend home, I went shopping for Mrs. Ahearn-across-the-street: soup and laundry detergent, hamburger and Hamburger Helper, cheddar cheese and meat pies, but without the coupon.

"Danny's bringing his girlfriend home for Thanksgiving," I said from the kitchen as I put her groceries away.

I looked around the corner into the living room. She was in her chair. The bottle of Canadian Mist was on the TV tray, next to a glass. The TV was on *Family Feud*. She slumped a little, staring down at her lap.

"I'm sorry," I said.

AFTER I FINISHED putting the groceries away, I came in and sat in the other chair, which must have been her husband's.

"What's she like?" Mrs. Ahearn asked.

"Giant boobs," I said.

"Figures," she said. She offered me the bottle. I had never had whiskey. Or any alcohol. I took a sip. It was a taste I'd never even imagined before, so I couldn't say if it was good or bad.

On the *Family Feud*, Richard Dawson asked the family, "What is something . . . you fill with air?"

"Lungs," I said.

"Tires," she said.

But the number one answer was balloons.

"Balloons!" Mrs. Ahearn said, with wonder. Then she laughed, like—who could have ever imagined it! *Balloons!*

That's the thing, I guess—how impossible it is to know a thing before you know it. What whiskey will taste like. What it's like to kiss someone. Probably even what it's like to lose a husband. And sometimes, after you learn something for the first time, maybe you don't know any more about it than you did before.

"Can I ask you something, Mrs. Ahearn?"

"Sure," she said.

"How's *my* ass?"

"Not bad," she said. And she offered me the bottle again.

The Way the World Ends

1
IMPENDING DOOM IN THE
GOLDEN TRIANGLE

The skies open as if a seam has torn. Rain strafes the silt loam fields and hanging dogwoods of Central Mississippi. It slashes windows, streets and parking lots and floods cypress swamps. Rain surges all morning until an icy wind hardens it to sleet and, by afternoon, a swirling, greasy snow.

Snow in Central Mississippi? In March? Confused students scurry across campus, backpacks covering heads. Classes are canceled, departmental meetings, sporting events—everything is put on hold. Streets, parking lots and sidewalks empty. Then in the afternoon, it stops, and the campus is eerie and quiet, a premonition.

During this short break in the storm, three strangers set out on separate treks across the cold, unforgiving expanse of campus. By end of day, they will be pushed to the edge, made to face oblivion together in the same refuge.

The first, Anna Molson, is replaying a job interview she just completed—wondering aloud to her sister if it went as badly as she thinks, or if this is just more of her midlife pessimism, this sense of doom she has about the world, and about what once would have been called her "prospects." She just turned thirty-seven. After six years in the Arctic, her longtime boyfriend is encouraging her to find a job back in the States so they can have a baby. Her parents are encouraging her to freeze her eggs. Even now, Anna's sister is encouraging her to "get a younger hairstyle."

Anna Molson isn't sure how much more encouragement she can take.

"So, you don't think you got it?" her FaceTiming sister is asking.

Anna holds up her phone and stares into her sister's face as she hurries across campus. "I don't see how," she says. "And this felt like my last chance."

"I know it feels like that, but it's not." Claire is feeding her daughter, Anna's niece, shoveling tiny spoons of mashed sweet potatoes, like coal into a furnace. "Maybe you should just move home without the job. Get pregnant and see what happens."

Anna laughs. "I have a pretty good idea what happens."

On-screen, her sister laughs, too. She leans forward and squints. "Seriously, though, Anna, what have you done with your hair?"

"Nothing!"

"Right. Like . . . ever?"

"It's humid here! And it's been storming all day!" Anna holds up the phone for Claire to see the wall of black clouds behind her. On cue, the wind picks up and the sleet starts to come down again. "In fact, here it comes again. I gotta go."

For just a moment, in the bottom of her iPhone screen, a tiny figure appears, a man walking behind her, the storm above him like a giant kite.

Rowan Eastman is a scruffy thirty-eight and might be forgiven for suspecting ownership of that black cloud. Raised by a single, mercurial mother, Rowan grew up believing disaster was just a gin and tonic away. Even now, as he listens to hold music on his own phone, Rowan has a powerful sense memory: at seven, walking home in a snowstorm after his drunk mother crashed their car. Rowan had just read a book about avalanches, and he worried the snow would bury them. "Aw, you read too much, Rowie," his mother said. Then she made him stick out his tongue. "See, we can eat our way home." Thirty years later, walking alone across the Mississippi State University campus, Rowan opens his mouth again. Flakes melt on his boozy tongue.

The airline hold music continues to play in his ear, and Rowan adapts the shapeless melody to a Johnny Cash song he's been humming all day, a song from the stack of country-western albums that was the only remnant of his father by the time Rowan was old enough to know that he was supposed to have a mom *and* a dad.

"*They're bound to get you,*" he sings now, as the snow picks up its pace again. "*They got a curfew . . . and you go to the . . . Starkville city jail.*"

The third person is just leaving his apartment. Jeremiah Ellis is a twenty-year-old college junior late for his work-study job at the Butler Guest House. Jeremiah thought about skipping altogether because of the storm, but he needs the money, and anyway, he hasn't skipped anything since sixth grade Sunday school. So, he zips up his coat and tells his roommate the disturbing news he's just received: there is an emergency meeting tomorrow for Spectrum, the campus gay and lesbian group that he joined three weeks ago. There, Jeremiah must decide how to vote on a big issue: whether the group should go forward with its plan to stage the first-ever MSU Pride Parade, despite the fact that the reactionary Starkville town council has just rejected their permit.

"Yikes," his roommate Garren says, game controller falling to his lap. "How you gonna vote?"

"I don't know," Jeremiah says. "I've only been out for three weeks. It would suck to get arrested for it so soon."

Garren nods. "What'd you expect, though, man? I mean, who moves to Mississippi to be gay?"

Jeremiah laughs and zips up his coat. He starts for the door but pauses for Garren to say that thing he's begun saying whenever Jeremiah leaves the apartment. "Hey, be careful out there."

And with that, Jeremiah steps into the tempest.

As this once-in-a-century storm strafes Mississippi's Golden Triangle, these three strangers lean into the same icy wind, deep in their own thoughts and engaged in the endless human struggle to keep moving forward in the face of certain cataclysm.

It's like Rowan Eastman's mother said years earlier, after driving their car into the ditch: "Aw, stop crying, kid. It ain't the end of the world."

But . . .

What if it is?

2

INTREPID SCIENTIST ANNA MOLSON MUST WARN THE PRESIDENT

Wind howls, snow swirls, and Anna Molson rushes toward the Student Union Building, where a young man holds the door. "Best get out that storm, ma'am."

She steps inside and shakes the sleet from her coat. "Thank you."

"Crazy-ass weather," the student says.

"Yes," she says. "It is." All day, people in Starkville have been saying how unseasonal the weather is. How crazy-ass. It is something she, of all people, doesn't need to be told.

And it's not just the snow. The high today in Starkville is thirty-eight degrees Fahrenheit. (Or, as she would record it in her professional life: 3.33333 Celsius.) At the Tiksi Arctic International Hydrometeorological Observatory, where, until recently, Anna has been monitoring permafrost data and reading Scandinavian mystery novels, the high today is also, coincidentally, 3.33333 Celsius. (On the Fahrenheit scale, a mind-boggling *forty-eight degrees above average*.)

The same temperature in the Arctic and in Mississippi? In March? No wonder folks can't get their minds around what's happening. Anna imagines a spaceship hovering over campus, vaporizing buildings with lasers, the locals looking at one another: *Well, that's unseasonal.* Of course, words are destined to fail compared to hard data. Alarming? Catastrophic? Crazy-ass? If only there were a word as precise as 3.33333—those threes going off into infinity, irreversible, into the endless nothingness of space.

Anna looks around the Student Union Building: twenty kids wait out the storm bent over laptops, buried under headphones.

Sometimes, when she returns to the States like this, Anna has the urge to grab people and shake them from their stupors. *Don't you see what's happening?* Melting polar ice, deforestation, acidifying oceans, calving glaciers, sea levels rising, epochal floods and storms, mass extinctions, ancient diseases released from the permafrost. A complete collapse of delicate environmental systems on every level. Not in some hazy future—*now*! Just look at the news: hurricane follows hurricane on the East Coast as the West burns and coral reefs die and island nations slide into the sea. Anna has the urge to yell at strangers (*Who cares who won* The Bachelor*!*) or her sister (*You want me to get bangs?*) or her parents (*Freeze my eggs?*). Back in civilization she always gets the urge to scream at a whole distracted world.

At times like this she feels like the intrepid scientist in an old disaster movie, the one nobody ever listens to: *Mr. President, if my calculations are correct—*

In the Student Union Building, Anna gets coffee. Starbucks is, unsurprisingly, the only thing open in this storm: commerce's cockroach. She sits at an open table.

A moment later a bearded man about her age plops down at the table next to her, hands on either side of his cup. He holds it up in a friendly toast.

She tips her own cup in response.

"Guessin' y'all ain't from Starkville," the man says.

No, she says, she is from Oregon, here interviewing for a job.

The man nods. He has glassy brown eyes and thick facial hair that goes too high on his cheeks. She puts him five minutes of grooming from being handsome.

"And how was it?" he asks, his drawl thick and drippy, making the words run together—*Anhowwadit*.

"The interview? It was okay." In fact, it was exhausting, awful: meetings with the handful of faculty and students who braved the rain, and, an hour ago, a stressful final interview with an associate dean eager to get home before the storm got any worse. After noting her lack of teaching experience, he closed her file and said, "Thanks for coming down. Have a safe flight home." And that was it, prospects doomed, interview over, except for a pro forma dinner later tonight with some professors—assuming they don't cancel because of the weather.

"English Lit?" the scruffy man guesses.

"Hydrology," she says, and explains that, until ten days ago, she was working on field research projects in the Arctic, in Greenland and in Russia. She's here interviewing for an assistant professorship in the Geosciences Department.

"That so?" He smiles. "A climate scientist? Well." He leans sideways toward her table, confiding, "Don't try convincin' folks down here that the planet's heatin' up . . . long as we freezin' our asses off."

Anna smiles, and for the six-thousandth time, explains that an overheated planet will manifest itself in many ways, polar areas warming, temperate areas seeing an increase in storm patterns. She forgets sometimes how to talk normal human being. "It's common," she says, "mistaking weather for climate. Weather simply reflects climate in a certain time and place."

"A certain time and place," he says, "I like that. Yeah, that's good." He pulls a flask from an interior pocket in his jacket and holds it up, eyebrows rising with it.

"No, thank you," Anna says.

He shrugs and pours a healthy shot into his own cup of coffee. "Mind if I ask another question—"

She shrugs. What the hell.

"Something I always wanted to ask one-a-you climate zealots—"

She doesn't flinch at the word.

The man leans in conspiratorially, narrows his wet eyes. "How long we got?"

She laughs, surprising herself with the bitterness of the sound. Stupid. What's she supposed to say? Five years? Five thousand? In geological time, it's the difference between a quarter second and a half second.

"Eleven years, four months, two days," she says.

He points at her with his coffee cup. "That's good. But, what, ninety-seven percent-a-you-all believe the world is doomed, right?"

She doesn't bother correcting him. This focus on end-of-civilization scenarios is silly, people imagining it will be like an adventure movie, everyone starring in their own apocalyptic single-shooter game. These are wildly complex systems on the verge of sudden, epochal change. And while a tiny percentage of scientists might argue that human activity isn't the *primary* cause, none would debate that the rise in greenhouse gases and corresponding global temperature is going to have devastating effects on human civilization. That it already has.

"Okay, here's my real question." The man leans in. "If that's the case, why do y'all even go to work? Why not just empty out all-a-y'all's bank accounts, get a bunch-a-cocaine, rent a suite in Vegas, and go out in a big ol' science orgy?"

Anna smiles. "I take it you've never been to a climate conference."

The man's eyes sparkle. "Why, you're funny, Dr.—"

She offers her hand. "Anna Molson."

He shakes it. "Seriously, Dr. Anna Molson. Why go on mea-surin' raindrops and countin' whales and all that shit when these people"—he gestures around the Student Union—"don't care one whit, and you know damn well it's probably too late? I mean, don't y'all sometimes ask yourself: *Why go on?*"

It surprises Anna how much this question stings. Like a trap-door has given way in her chest.

Among climate scientists, it's called "*pre*-traumatic stress dis-order" but the feelings are no joke: anger, hopelessness, depres-sion, panic—a recurring nightmare in which you see the tsunami on the horizon but can't convince anyone to leave the beach. She knows scientists who have become drunks, who have dropped out and moved to the desert, who have committed suicide.

Does she sometimes *ask herself, Why go on?*

No. She asks herself that question every single day.

Anna lets out a deep breath. "I didn't get your name."

"Rowan," he says, "Rowan Eastman."

"Well, Rowan Eastman. May I?" She gestures at his jacket.

It takes him a second to understand. "Oh, sure," he says, and he produces the MSU flask, flips it expertly like a Boy Scout handing over a knife.

She pours some whiskey in her coffee. Then a little more. More. She takes a sip. Better. She is surprised to have been so rattled by his question. Maybe it's just the condescending mis-ery of today's job interview. (*Thanks for coming down. Have a safe flight home.*) Well. Screw you, associate asshole dean. Screw you, Mississippi, screw you, impending doom, pre-traumatic stress disorder, bangs and blizzards, and frozen eggs, thawing ice caps, screw it all! That's what this improvised Irish coffee tastes like—a warm cup of screw you.

"Can I tell you about the first project I worked on?"

Rowan nods.

"Before arriving in Greenland, I imagined I'd be studying somewhat fixed systems—you know, sun is hot, ice is cold, glacial thinning is linear and predictable. But right away, we observed something strange. The Jakobshavn glacier was melting even in the winter, with temperatures still well below freezing.

"We worked with NASA for two years, outfitting an old DC-3 to drop probes all over the ice. Pretty soon we had our answer." She holds up her coffee cup. "Warm water was coming from underneath, melting the glacier from below, the way a warm drink might melt ice cubes. Human activity had not only raised temperatures; it had rerouted ocean currents, meaning that even our most pessimistic estimates were off. Three meters of rising sea levels we expected to take eighty years . . . might take half that time. So, Rowan Eastman, you ask how many years we have left?

"None. It's happening . . . right . . . now." She waits for this to land. "And I realized something working on that project." Anna stares past him. "This profession I was in? The better I did it—the worse it was going to be."

Rowan just stares at her. The hum of the Student Union Building is the only sound for a while.

Anna smiles. "Do you know what it was called, that project?"

Rowan shakes his head.

"Ocean Melts Greenland."

Rowan laughs. "OMG. That's funny." And, after a moment, he says, "Mind if I ask another question?"

"Is it going to be as cheerful as the last one?"

He smiles. "Why Mississippi?"

"You don't mess around," she says. Her parents asked the same thing, dripping with Pacific Northwest condescension—as if Mississippi were the backwater of all backwaters, as if there wasn't ignorance in places like Oregon, too. In fact, sometimes the smug self-satisfaction of Portland (*I am* saving *the planet in my brand-new Tesla*) is the worst thing she can imagine.

"A boyfriend," she says. "Salvaging a relationship." Like she and Bashir were a shipwreck at the bottom of the Atlantic. They got together in grad school—two people convinced they could maintain a long-distance relationship while continuing their important, separate work on different continents. With so much time apart, they came to a tacit understanding: fidelity without militancy. Anna pictures it as a formula balancing basic integrity with the need for intimacy. Bashir calls it the Molson-Reed Axiom to the Golden Rule (Don't Do Unto Others Unless You Absolutely Can't Help It, and If You Do Unto Others, Use a Condom).

For six years, they pulled off this arrangement while making the most of the weeks they spent together. They exchanged old-fashioned letters and grew adept at Skype sex. (Him: "You're freezing." Her: "Yes, I'm naked in a Quonset hut on a glacier." Him: "No. I mean, on-screen, you're freezing.")

In Greenland and Russia, she indulged a few work crushes, drunken kisses, fumbling with two senior researchers, one man and one woman—but she was pleased not to have disrupted the basic Anna Molson-Bashir Reed Axiom, or the box of condoms underneath her bunk. She assumed similar behavior on Bashir's part. But he was working at the Sea Level Solutions Center at Florida International University, and Miami apparently offered more temptations than were found in her assorted Arctic weather postings. Finally, he admitted he'd been sleeping with someone. In fact, he'd been sleeping with *several* someones. "In fact . . ."

"Yeah, I get it," Anna told him.

Bashir insisted these flings were not what he wants but were simple acts of loneliness. Frustrated dread over the very thing they always talked about—having their important work ignored by the world. Bashir doesn't *want* those other women. *She* is the one he wants. In fact, he wants her to move home and have a baby. Now.

Oh, the existential ache of those particular words—*home* and *baby* and *now*. Where is home? When is now? Babies? Future? Give up a job she once saw as a calling to work on a relationship that suddenly feels so insecure—in Miami of all places, where in the coming decades, flooding will create two million refugees?

So, a compromise: she told Bashir she would look for a teaching job in the States, something close to him. And he would stop doing unto others and they would talk about starting a family.

Anna finds herself surprised that she has told the bearded man this whole sordid story. "And so," she says, "here I am."

"Here you are," Rowan says. "In a certain time and place."

She smiles. "Yes, interviewing for a job in Mississippi because it's as close as I could get to my shit boyfriend in Florida."

"It's like a country song," Rowan says. "Movin' to Starkville for the man what cheated on ya."

Anna laughs. "Or maybe coming to Mississippi is my version of running off to Vegas and blowing all my money on cocaine."

"You forgot the orgy part," says Rowan.

"No, I didn't," Anna says.

Something shifts between them. Neither one looks away. Finally, Rowan Eastman swallows and holds up the flask. "Another?"

"May as well," she says and hands over her cup. "There's no way I'm going to get this job anyway. Apparently, they interviewed some guy with twice as much teaching experience as me."

The man with the beard finishes pouring the last of the whiskey into their cups. He waves the empty flask. "Yeah, we-e-e-ell—" He stretches the word out, speaking now without any trace whatsoever of that Mississippi drawl. "I wouldn't worry too much about that guy."

3

ROWAN EASTMAN SURVIVES
AND SCAVENGES FOR FOOD

Rowan had made it through the formal interviews with faculty and staff. He'd survived the apologetic tour of Starkville ("We just got sushi") and the underfunded Geosciences Department. He'd met the undergrads (earnest, lumpish), the grad students (harried, cynical), and then had a requisite dinner with his potential colleagues ("Sorry, we can't put alcohol on the university credit card.").

The faculty dinner was at a restaurant called Commander Cole's on the edge of the Cotton District, a neighborhood of old sharecropper shacks and plantation houses disturbingly transformed into student housing.

His dinner companions that night were an old-school geology prof and an attractive, cheerful woman who taught meteorological broadcasting. "Dr. Weather Girl" she called herself, explaining in her fetching drawl that she taught students how to stand in front of green screens and "talk tornado."

Dr. Weather Girl also brought her boyfriend, an English professor and sulking novelist with two last names, something like Anderson Henderson or Dickerson Gunderson. The novelist kept one hand on Dr. Weather Girl at all times and watched Rowan with suspicion, as if he was afraid Rowan might steal his cheerful girlfriend—which made Rowan want to get the job so he could steal the novelist's cheerful girlfriend.

Still, he survived every indignity—faculty, students, department dinner, even Dr. Weather Girl and Norman Mailing-It-In—without screwing up, without offending anyone, without indulging his smart-ass self-destructive self.

Then, the next morning, in his last interview, with an officious associate dean, Rowan blew the whole thing. They were talking about Rowan's recent project on declining whale birth rates when the associate dean muttered that he didn't want to bring in "a climate zealot."

"Zealot?" Rowan said before he could stop himself. "What's that mean?"

Stupid. He knew what it meant. The word was a test to see if he could abide some harmless Mississippi backwardness. The students at MSU were no doubt as bright (and as dim) as kids from Connecticut and California, but some would need to be brought along slowly. (*No, Zebidiah, according to carbon dating and, well, everything, the world is a bit older than six thousand years.*) If he got his dander up over a little snake handling or the Ten Commandments or the worship of AK-47s or a phrase like *climate zealot*, he could no doubt make trouble for this dean.

Rowan tried to save the ball from going out of bounds. "Hey, I'm here to teach *science,* not *political* science." But it was too late. He'd blown it. Like always. And he needed this job. He'd left a tenure-track position at UMass in 2012 to go to work for the National Oceanic and Atmospheric Administration, studying the effects of warming seawater on northeastern whale populations. He measured acidity and temperature levels in the traditional breeding waters of right whales, *Eubalaena glacialis*, one of the rarest baleens left in the world, nearly hunted to extinction. The research had been physical—careening around in boats, scuba diving—and the most fulfilling work of his life.

Then, in early 2016, his mother was diagnosed with esophageal cancer (proving the veracity if not the efficacy of those warning labels on cigarette packages), and Rowan took a leave from NOAA to return home to Boston to help her through chemo and radiation.

The events that followed were unrelated, except in the desktop of his mind, where they shared a file called COLLAPSE 2016–2018:

- An ignorant orange grifter was elected president and turned science denial into an official government position.
- Rowan's grant wasn't renewed, and the Provincetown project was spiked (the money apparently needed to buy assault rifles for xenophobic coal miners somewhere).
- He struggled to find another job.
- His mom died.

She had raised him alone, this brash, larger-than-life woman who used to list on forms that asked for his father's name: "Business, None Yr." His father had left nothing behind but a box of old albums—1970s country, mostly. Everything else Rowan got came from his mother (including her dreamy blue eyes, her love of booze and her difficulty with relationships). She was what used to be called "a character," meaning she showed up hammered for school events, hit on his teachers, and once blew his college tuition money on a trip to Mexico. She made up adorable nicknames for his girlfriends, "Trampy-pants" and "IUDear," and always made sure to call the newest girlfriend by the last girlfriend's name. Even after Rowan escaped to college and grad school, to his own life, she exerted more influence on him than he would have wanted, and more than he wanted to admit.

But then she got sick, and before Rowan could get his mind around it, his mother was dead. This devastated him in a way he couldn't explain. He felt bereft, his entire being altered, a moon without its planet.

His ensuing job search did little to alleviate the darkness. The government in 2017 was backing out of its *fact-based obligations* and there seemed to be thousands of academics and environmental researchers like him out looking for work. Rowan taught adjunct classes at a community college. He sat around listening to his dad's records, preparing his mother's house for sale—only to find out she'd borrowed heavily against it and owed more than it was worth. He drank, gained fifteen pounds, quit shaving. As his fortieth birthday approached, he toyed with adding a line to his CV: *second PhD in abject failure, dissertation pending.*

Even when things seemed to be going well—like this interview at Mississippi State—self-sabotage was never far off, as when the associate dean asked about his research, and Rowan explained that, before he lost funding, he was the project hydrologist on a team that studied how changing weather patterns had decimated two northeastern right whale pods. It was quiet in the dean's office, and not long after that, they had their disastrous exchange about him being a "climate zealot."

Rowan tried several times to correct course: "But even if I hadn't lost my funding, I would've wanted to return to teaching. It's my life's work—inspiring young people. I consider myself a natural teacher."

He sometimes imagined his mother in various situations, not like a ghost, exactly, but more like a sports commentator, and he pictured her just then, standing next to the associate dean, in one of her scandalously short dresses, holding a highball and cigarette. He could almost hear her smoky laugh—*A natural teacher? Rowie, are you high?*

"And I've always wanted to work in the South," Rowan said. And, surprised to hear his voice crack, he added, "My father was from down here." At that show of vulnerability, the associate dean simply stood. So, Rowan stood, too. And they shook hands. "Well, thanks for coming down," the dean said. "I hope you have a nice flight home."

It was the fifth university job he'd interviewed for; he'd whiffed on all five.

Even his *nice flight home* wasn't meant to be.

That afternoon, monsoon winds and rain blew in. "All the flights in and out of Jackson are canceled," explained Jeremiah, the sweet, nerdy kid who manned the desk at the Butler Guest House, the on-campus motel bricked up against the concrete walls of the stadium.

And so Rowan stayed another night in Starkville. This time there was no faculty dinner, no meteorology babes with clingy novelist boyfriends. He scavenged for food: some popcorn Jeremiah got him and a vending machine granola bar. He walked through the rain to the saddest liquor store since the last sad liquor store, where he grabbed a fifth of Jim Beam and a souvenir MSU flask. He took his booze and his flask back to the Butler Guest House.

In the morning, the storm had worsened, and the entire Jackson airport was closed. No getting out of Memphis either. The airline help desk had a three-hour wait. Outside, the rain turned to sleet. Rowan filled his flask and wandered around campus, getting pelted and speaking in the drawl he'd been practicing. "How y'all doin' today?"

By the time the sleet became snow, Rowan was a little bit drunk, catching snowflakes on his tongue. He stepped into the campus Starbucks to get warm, and that's when he saw her, this tall, intelligent-looking woman in glasses and a winter parka getting coffee.

He decided to try his accent on her—"Guessin' y'all ain't from Starkville—"

Only to find out she was here interviewing for the same job.

They bantered, shared a moment, a look, a pessimism, a flirtation, *a certain time and place—*

Time to come clean, he thought.

"Yeah, we-e-e-ell," he said. "I wouldn't worry too much about that guy."

And now, in a certain time and place, these two job candidates, greased by Jim Beam, are laughing at the coincidence. She has a great smile, this Anna—making the components of her face (angular cheeks, unruly eyebrows, hastily arranged ponytail) come together into what one might call beauty. He even likes that her teeth aren't *too white*—this is someone who might enjoy a cup of coffee, a glass of wine, someone who might even be a fan of his off-brand male imperfection.

"So . . . you are the guy who interviewed for my job," she says.

"Technically, I was here first. *You* interviewed for *my* job." In fact, he'd had a good feeling about Mississippi State. Before he flew down, he'd sat around his mother's house, listening to that stack of crackling skipping country music. Those sad, twangy records: Conway Twitty, Merle Haggard, Loretta Lynn, and especially Johnny Cash—the more he listened, the more Rowan began to feel the music in his bones. He could live here. Life is hard, the songs seemed to say, but at least it's funny, and it rhymes.

With Anna now, he resorts to his fake drawl once again. "Well, Miss Molson, I don't suppose y'all would wanna get another bottle of whiskey and follow me on back to the Butler Guest House, maybe get drunk and have us a sloppy ol' make-out session before your faculty dinner?"

She laughs. "I really should tell you something, Mr. Eastman. In case you do get this job and end up living in Mississippi. *Y'all* is used only for plural second person. For a group. So, if you were propositioning a *group* of people, you would say, 'Do *y'all* wanna go get drunk and make out.' But to inappropriately proposition just one person you would say, 'Do *you* wanna go get drunk and make out?'

"And yeah, sure. Why not?"

JEREMIAH ELLIS OFFERS REFUGE
TO DESPERATE SURVIVORS

In the Butler Guest House, at the Desk of Endless Suffering, Jeremiah sits behind a computer screen ignoring his half-written Special Topics in Poly-Sci paper. Instead, he edits a selfie on his iPhone, messing around with different filters. The storm has canceled everything and only two job candidates are staying in the Butler Guest House, so the reception desk is strangely quiet for a Friday night. This means Jeremiah has found himself with plenty of time to work on the important stuff—a new social media strategy.

He attempts a knowing-starlet pose—photographed from above, glasses off, cheeks sucked in, eyes gamine-like, open wide. He captions the picture, *work study = work slutty*, and tries different filters. He wishes personalities were like this: that you could just slide into a *vivid warm* version. A *dramatic cool* Jeremiah.

Finished, Jeremiah considers the photo. He's not sure. His *Come on* face looks more like, *Come on. Seriously?* It is a look his roommate Garren calls: Jere*myass*.

He texts the photo to Garren, and to his sister in Benton— What do you think? They've both urged him to make his social media presence "more out." (Or as Garren once put it, "Go gay or go home.")

But Jeremiah has always been more careful, an analytical kid, a process-and-rule follower, which is probably why it took him all of high school and nearly three years of college to admit, even to himself, that he liked men. Raised Baptist in a small Louisiana town, he grew up assuming he'd be married before having sex of any kind. And while the religion mostly fell away, he isn't quite ready to go full bathhouse.

In the one earbud he is allowed to wear at work, Rihanna preaches burning something, love on the brain, the kind of boldness that Garren urges—Jeremiah singing along in the empty reception area: "*What you want from me—*"

Garren has been Jeremiah's best friend since winter quarter of their freshman year when they met in an honors history seminar and played together on an intermural basketball team called Five Guys with One Ball. They moved in together the next year. Garren was the first person that Jeremiah came out to—exactly three weeks ago. They were playing Super Smash Bros. in their apartment, and Jeremiah blurted out: "So I think I might be gay."

Garren looked up from his controller. Four seconds passed. "Might be?" he finally asked. Garren is a short, smart white kid from Hattiesburg with glasses and terrible hair. Jeremiah is a short, smart black kid from Shelton, Louisiana, with glasses and terrible hair.

"*Am* gay?" Jeremiah said.

"How long have you known?"

Jeremiah didn't know how to answer that. How does a person know *what* he knows, let alone *when* he knows it? He felt like a detective on a cold case, sifting through memories, hunches and suspicions (suspect owned two pairs of red shoes and likes *Glee*) but he finds nothing conclusive. Sure, he'd wondered, felt urges, crushes, but his feelings were fluid, changing day to day. And not knowing how other people felt, he didn't know what was *normal*. Heck, doesn't everyone get a dizzying crush on their male chemistry teacher?

Then, last month, the campus film club showed the movie *Milk* in conjunction with Spectrum, the gay and lesbian group on campus. Jeremiah loved the film—and was especially moved when Sean Penn delivered Harvey Milk's iconic speech about hope ("You cannot live on hope alone, but without it, life is not worth living."). He'd never thought of being gay as a political act. But, as the credits ran, he felt emboldened, and he approached one of the Spectrum leaders, a charismatic senior named Trevor Blankenship.

"I feel like I'm coming to terms with some stuff," Jeremiah said.

Trevor gave him a knowing look. "Well, you have support here."

Trevor hugged him, and when they pulled back, their faces remained close. Jeremiah shocked them both by quickly kissing Trevor. "It was like a bomb going off," Jeremiah told Garren. The kiss lasted only a second before he felt a hand on his chest, Trevor gently pushing him back, Jeremiah apologizing and hurrying off, Trevor calling after him, "It's fine!"

Garren had listened quietly to this story. "That's it?" he said finally.

"Well, yeah, so far," Jeremiah said. "I've only been out—" He checked his watch. "Forty minutes."

Garren's brow furrowed, and he looked back at the TV. For a moment, Jeremiah worried if his revelation would ruin their friendship. But then Garren said the same thing he'd been saying to Jeremiah for two years. "Dude, we gotta get you laid."

Of course, Garren was also a virgin. "We gotta get *you* laid," Jeremiah said.

"Well, obviously," Garren said. "But see, this helps *me*. I'm going to look so sensitive and progressive with a gay roommate."

"Will you though?"

And like that, they were back to the same shit-talking Super Smash bros. In fact, Garren became Jeremiah's strongest ally, talking him into going to the next Spectrum meeting. Jeremiah was surprised to find only fourteen other students there. Turned out there were only seventy-nine Spectrum members total—on a campus of twenty-two thousand students. But there had to be more gay kids than that at MSU, didn't there? Were people just more closeted here, or was it a self-selecting thing: Did gay students intuit the conservative heart of Central Mississippi might not be the best place for them?

At the meeting, Jeremiah was encouraged to join the Pride Parade committee by a persistent woman who admitted she had an ulterior motive: she wanted broad racial representation on the parade committee. "And since you're—" She stared at him. "Uh, Jeremiah, what exactly *are* you?"

Gay! would have been the correct Harvey Milk answer, or a RuPaulian *Fabulous!* But Jeremiah went with his old middle-school retort: "A mishmash, I guess." Back in the Benton Middle School days, he'd list his rainbow grandparents in a single word: *Blackfrenchalgeriannative.* Maybe now he could trade that whole hyphenated bayou identity sampler for an emphatic *Gay!*

When Jeremiah got home, he told Garren he was on the parade committee. His helpful roommate volunteered to help him make a penis float. "Yeah, I don't think it's that kind of parade," Jeremiah said, though, as always, he appreciated Garren's enthusiasm.

And now, as if on cue, Garren texts back about the *Jeremyass* selfie:

You look hot as hell, Garren writes. Then: Gonna be rainin' dick soon.

Not really dressed for dick-rain, Jeremiah writes back.

How's work? Garren texts.

Oh man, crazy times at the Butt-Plug House

Four days a week, Jeremiah works here on the Desk of Un-
ceasing Misery at the Butler Guest House, the on-campus motel
for visiting parents, interviewing professors, and guest speakers.

Today, he braved the storm to find the BGH empty except for
two job candidates. In Room 2: Miss Anna Molson (tall, nerd-
pretty, like a woman who gets a movie makeover and rips off her
glasses to reveal she's been stunning the whole time) and in Room
4: Rowan Eastman (dad bod and the kind of unruly beard that
white guys can get away with but would make Jeremiah look like
a terrorist hobo).

But this is where it gets crazy: Dr. Dad Bod and Dr. Makeover
are interviewing *for the same job*! And they apparently bumped
into each other at the Starbucks! Nothing in the otherwise exten-
sive *Butler Guest House Manual* about what to do in *that* situation.

And now they're hanging out in his room, a fact Jeremiah discovered when he went to clean the coffeepot in the common area
outside their rooms and he saw Dr. BeardyMan putting out the
DO NOT DISTURB sign and Dr. LadyLady sitting on his bed.

He texts Garren: Never guess what the bearded prof is doing

What

The OTHER PROF

Fa reals

Dude put out the Do Not Disturb

They interview for the same job and then bone-in pork chop?

Right?!?!

Kinda hot tho

Yeah, cept er'body having sex but Jeremyass

Garren-teed ain't havin sex neither, yo

Jeremiah is texting back (Not exactly a news flash) when he looks up to see two other professors duck out of the storm and into the waiting area in front of the Butler Guest House. The man is shaking water off a closed umbrella.

Jeremiah recognizes him: Henderson Anders, the novelist and English prof who taught a Contemporary Fiction of the South class that Jeremiah and Garren took together as sophomores. The class turned out to be wildly entertaining, in no small part because it took very little prompting to distract Dr. Anders from his lectures and send him on a profanity-laced tirade about other, more successful southern authors who wrote "cloying, derivative bullshit."

With Dr. Anders is the pretty young weather teacher always on the campus TV station. She brushes the sleet from her coat. Shelves of shimmery brown hair descend either side of a perfect middle part and frame eyes that seem lit from within. She is carrying a picnic basket. "Whew!" she says. "I wasn't sure we were going to make it."

"Oh, hey, Jeremiah," Dr. Anders says. "This is my girlfriend, Dr. Nancy Poole." Dr. Anders has a bottle of red wine in one hand. His other hand is square in Dr. Poole's back.

"We were supposed to take a job candidate to dinner," Dr. Poole explains. "Anna Molson?"

"Oh yeah, she's back there," Jeremiah says.

"I've been trying to call her phone, but I think it's turned off. With this storm, everything is closed. So, we thought we'd just bring some food and a bottle of wine and find a place here to talk."

Jeremiah wonders if he should tell them why Anna Molson is not answering her phone. He imagines pulling out the thick *Butler*

Guest House Manual and looking in the index for the unlikely heading "Sex, Guests Having (p. 13)."

But Dr. Anders changes the subject. "Hey, I saw your name on the Pride Parade flyer."

"Oh. Yeah." Jeremiah laughs nervously and feels his face heat up.

"It's unconscionable," Dr. Anders says, "those fundamentalists at the city rejecting your parade permit."

For a moment, Jeremiah had fantasized the parade as his own personal coming-out ceremony. In his imagination it would be like one of Harvey Milk's rallies. He'd step outside his apartment, and a crowd would be there (mostly men with moppy '70s hair and tight jeans), and he'd go all Sean Penn on them: "You've got to give them hope!"

At the Desk of Infinite Awkwardness, Dr. Poole shakes her head. "I hope you know how much support you have within the faculty."

"Thanks," Jeremiah says. He tells them that the parade committee is meeting tomorrow to vote on their options: (1) postpone the parade while they appeal, (2) have the parade only on campus, or (3) defy the town council and march downtown without a permit.

"You have to march," says Dr. Anders. "Make the bastards arrest you."

"Yes!" Dr. Poole says. "March straight downtown and put it right in their old, bigoted faces."

Jeremiah smiles at these well-meaning white liberals telling a shy brown kid to go antagonize a bunch of small-town southern police officers. He thinks about his grandfather, who rode with the Freedom Riders in the 1960s and who used to say things like, "Whatever you've got to live for, you have to be willing to die for, too."

Is Jeremiah willing to die for a pride parade? He wouldn't mind actually having a year or two of *being gay* before getting beaten up for it. Or arrested. It's easy for these professors to push *his* civil disobedience, but he's the one who would have to go out into the job market next year with a conviction on his record. How does that tend to turn out?

And what would his old scripture-quoting grandfather, with his stories of facing down dogs and fire hoses and sheriffs, say, if he discovered Jeremiah's "to die for" cause was a gay parade? Would he sit up in his grave and yell "Abomination!"?

When the parade permit was rejected, Jeremiah had felt both relieved and demoralized. He joked with Garren that maybe he should've stayed fake-straight. Statistically, he's done better that way, having kissed three girls in his life and only one guy, the aforementioned Trevor Blankenship, who, because he has a boy-friend now seems uncomfortable around Jeremiah. (Seventy-nine gay people on campus and he's already alienated two?) At least as a fake-straight, he got some good high school dance pictures out of the deal.

Garren, who never lets his lack of knowledge of a particular subject dull his expertise, had the answer. "It's the whole 'coming out' myth," Garren said. "I think you have to do more than just announce you're open for business. Think about it, if ten percent of people are gay, then you have to work ten times harder."

There must be gay bars in Memphis and Birmingham, Garren suggested cheerfully, but besides not yet being twenty-one, Jere-miah isn't ready for that; he'd feel like a freshman wandering into a graduate seminar.

Of course, there was another alternative, but every time Jer-emiah looks at Grindr, it makes him feel oily, and he's not quite ready for the weirdos and glory holers, the spankers and yankers, the secret married closeted football coaches, state troopers, and insurance agents.

That's why, in his soft-focus imagination, the parade had sounded like the perfect way to come out—in the open, with sunlight and rainbows, signs and songs and speeches and . . . sigh, sweet Trevor Blankenship at his side.

Jeremiah looks up from these thoughts to find the professors hovering above the Desk of Endless Banality, like they expect something from him. He wonders if he should give his Harvey Milk speech now. (*You've got to give them hope! And a parade permit!*)

"You were going to call Dr. Molson's room," Dr. Poole reminds him. "Let her know we're here with dinner."

"Oh, right," Jeremiah says. "Sorry!" He picks up the phone. But of course, Dr. Molson isn't in her room. She is in Dr. Eastman's room, no doubt staring at this very moment at his PhDick.

Yes, this situation is definitely *not* in the *Butler Guest House Manual.*

"Um, okay . . ." Jeremiah hangs the phone up. "You know what, I think I'll just go back and knock. 'Cause, uh . . . the phones have been . . . and . . . the storm . . . I'll be right back."

A small courtyard separates the Desk of Perpetual Wretchedness from the guest rooms. Jeremiah runs across it—the snow a stinging sleet now—and enters the guesthouse. He walks through the common area to Room 4. The DO NOT DISTURB sign is still on the door. He listens outside the door: Laughter. Music.

He puts his ear closer, against the door.

Shit. Marvin Gaye?

Marvin Gaye + Do Not Disturb = middle-aged people having sex.

Although, as he listens, he recognizes the song as "Mercy Mercy Me," which is less sexy than, say, "Let's Get It On," but it is still Marvin Gaye, the only singer who can make *Fish full of mercury* sound almost hot.

What to do? Jeremiah stands there a full minute until the song finishes. He listens for sex sounds, but all he hears is more laughter; then Dr. Molson says, "Okay, that one was easy, but you looked so cold."

Then Dr. Eastman says: "I got one!" And before Jeremiah can knock, a new song starts—Lou Reed singing about the last great American whale.

Maybe they aren't having sex yet. Maybe geoscience professors get off playing environmental songs first. Finally, Jeremiah knocks. But behind the door, they don't seem to have heard over the music.

"I don't know that one!" Dr. Molson says.

"Off with it then!" Dr. Eastman yells, while Lou Reed mutters about shitting in rivers and dumping battery acid in streams. Dead rats washing up on beaches.

Yeah. No way sex is going on in that room, Jeremiah thinks. He leans in to knock even harder.

And that's when the door from the courtyard opens, and Dr. Anders and Dr. Poole step into the guest room atrium with their food and wine. Dr. Anders still has his free hand on Dr. Poole's back, as if Dr. Poole is a puppet that Dr. Anders operates.

"Is everything okay, Jeremiah?" Dr. Poole asks. (Jeremiah looks at Dr. Anders to see if his mouth moved.)

"You were gone a long time," Dr. Anders adds.

"Oh, yeah, sorry. She must have gone somewhere—"

Then another door opens—Room 4—and Jeremiah turns to

see Dr. Eastman step into the hall wearing nothing but a pair of blue boxer briefs.

He is carrying an ice bucket and looking back over his shoulder as he pretends to run in super slow motion. "Must . . . get . . . ice . . . before . . . glacier . . . melts!"

Dr. Eastman slo-mo turns to see Jeremiah and the other two professors outside his door. He stops, straightens, and lowers the ice bucket to cover his crotch.

The door to the room is wide open, and inside, they can all see Dr. Molson, barefoot, wearing pants but no shirt or bra. Her back is to them, and she has a drink and is dancing—possibly worse than Jeremiah has ever seen a human being dance before—to a song by the Pretenders. She belts out the lyrics in a voice as unfortunate as her dance moves—

"*I went back to Ohio—*"

Finally, Dr. Topless turns to Dr. Boxer Briefs. "Oh and get more popcorn—"

For a moment everyone freezes—

Weather is climate in a certain time and place.

In this time and place, two mildly depressed scientists interviewing for the same job have been caught in some kind of deviant envirosexdeath party by an overlooked genius of southern literature (his grotesque, generationally damaged characters speaking to themes of a perverted American history) and a meteorology professor who teaches her students to stand in front of a green screen and cheerfully narrate the death of the planet.

In the middle, like the referee at a wrestling match, or the host at a swingers' club, stands young Jeremiah Ellis, who thinks: *My God, I really am the only person on the planet not having sex, aren't I?*

5
CIVILIZATION DEVOLVES INTO
A DEBAUCHED HELLSCAPE

Even in disaster, there is the endless human capacity for adaptation. Consider: after a few seconds of awkwardness (Dr. Poole: "Oh my!" Dr. Eastman, looking for his pants: "We were just—" Dr. Anders: "We'll come back—" Dr. Molson, hurrying into her bra: "No, just a sec—"), a surprising acceptance settles over the intrepid survivors.

Jeremiah returns from the Desk of What-the-Hell-Did-I-Just-See with four wineglasses and a corkscrew. Dr. Eastman and Dr. Molson are fully dressed and sitting with their guests in the guesthouse commons as if nothing has happened.

They share the snacks Dr. Poole brought, the wine Dr. Anders brought, and the last of Dr. Eastman's whiskey. Soon, they are laughing—

DR. MOLSON: "So mortifying—"
DR. ANDERS: "Really, it's nothing—"
DR. POOLE: "Job interviews are stressful—"
DR. EASTMAN: "These wontons are terrific—"

Anna explains how she and Rowan met and were drinking together to blow off job-interview steam, and how they eventually invented the game Strip Name That Tune, Environmental Edition, and that Rowan was losing badly, having failed to identify so many songs that Anna had to go easy on him with Marvin Gaye.

"Thank you for that," Dr. Anders says.

Rowan and Anna talk about the motivation behind their wild afternoon—the storm and the grim associate dean who made them both feel like they had no chance for the job ("Yes, he can be abrupt," Dr. Poole confirms).

And then they share their sense of screw-it-all frustration about the blithe reaction of their fellow Americans in the face of overwhelming evidence (some of which they have personally gathered) of environmental doom.

"Honestly, after a while, you feel like saying 'I give up. It's not worth it,'" Dr. Molson says. "So to have Rowan say, 'Screw it, let's get drunk' . . . well . . ." She laughs and doesn't finish the thought.

"I get that," Dr. Poole says. "You bang your head against a wall, yelling, 'We have to do something,' and half the country still votes for corrupt, science-denying assholes."

"It's like we're eager for the end now," Dr. Anders adds. "Like, as a nation, we've decided to just go ahead and blow our kids' inheritance."

"Yes!" Dr. Eastman picks up on this metaphor: "Like a mother who borrows against her worthless house to sneak booze and cigarettes while she's getting cancer treatments, and then dies leaving a house worth half what she owes on it."

The others note the personal turn of the metaphor.

"Meanwhile," Dr. Molson says, "we put pressure on women to have kids, to freeze their eggs. Why? Seven billion people on the planet, each new baby a tiny climate disaster unto himself." She tells them about a Swedish study that found that each American child brought into the world means another *fifty-eight metric tons of carbon dioxide*. To offset the carbon footprint of one more American baby, 684 teenagers would have to become impeccable recyclers who gave up air travel for the rest of their lives.

"*He's* got kids," Dr. Poole says, with a slight hint of accusation, pointing to Henderson Anders.

"They hate me," the novelist says.

"Well, at least that's something," Rowan says.

Jeremiah finishes setting the table with napkins, water glasses, and a pitcher of water. He tells them he'll be at the desk. He looks around the room and feels like he's glimpsed some secret adult truth, the ain't-no-Santa-Claus cynicism with which these scientists view the world.

They are effusive in thanking Jeremiah. He says he will check back to see if they need anything. Three more hours on this shift.

Jeremiah returns to the Desk of Complete Confusion to work on his Poly-Sci paper, but he can't concentrate. Every twenty minutes he crosses the courtyard to check on the guests—and in this way, he picks up shards of conversation, like a time-lapse lecture on the horrors of climate science. He learns, among other things:

- Catastrophic two-degree-Celsius increase is likely baked in, the last four years the warmest on record, and only a miracle, a disaster, or some unforeseen technology will keep the planet from a disastrous *four-degree*-Celsius increase.
- As humans burn fossil fuels at a catastrophic rate, carbon dioxide levels are rising to their highest concentration in *fifty million years,* and greenhouse gases to a level that hadn't been seen in the fossil record in *four hundred million years.*
- Dire projections of global sea level rise vastly underestimate the truth, and polar glaciers and the Greenland ice field melt

are occurring far faster than previously thought. As Dr. Molson says, "A city like Miami is basically toast."

· We are well into the sixth great extinction, possibly worse than the comet that wiped out the dinosaurs, and, as Dr. Eastman says, "Polar bears are done, and whales, and, really, all the big fauna. Including us."

Each topic is more disturbing than the last for Jeremiah, the final blows coming when he delivers a fresh bottle of wine that he has liberated from a cabinet in the Alumni Events office.

· There is no historical precedent, and therefore no response to such a disaster (this turns out to be the theme of a short story that Dr. Anders is writing) because literature, even dystopian literature, is humanist, with civilization (love, kindness, intelligence) serving as baselines for equilibrium, when in fact, human civilization may be "nothing more than a clever infection."

But this nihilistic lecture on impending environmental doom—by turns edifying and terrifying—is only half of what Jeremiah witnesses that night in the common area outside the guest rooms across the courtyard in the Butler Guest House at Mississippi State University in Starkville, Mississippi, United States, North America, Earth. In addition:

· The couples grow progressively louder, shouting about politics and the environment, going on tangents that suddenly sprout leaks of personal confession: "Seriously!" Dr. Anders screams at one point. "Why don't I just dig up Faulkner and rebury him so that I can move on!"

On a normal night, Jeremiah would call campus security, as he often has with fraternity alumni guests. But with the storm, the empty guesthouse, and the grim prospects for humanity, Jeremiah thinks, *Aw hell, let them have their end-of-the-world fun.*

And so, they have their end-of-the-world fun. In addition to the rest of Dr. Eastman's whiskey and the three bottles of wine, Dr. Anders remembers he has some edibles in his car, and he ventures out in the rain, and they suck on some weed-laced Jolly Ranchers, which quiets the party a bit.

Then a laptop is procured and the music returns, at first with the same environmental theme as earlier (sans stripping), but after "Big Yellow Taxi," they decide massive planetary collapse calls for dance music, and the volume creeps higher until it crosses the courtyard, and Jeremiah finds himself tapping his foot to a Donna Summer song at the Desk of No Fun Whatsoever.

Dance music invariably leads to dancing, and in the last hour of Jeremiah's shift, he sees every combination of dance floor coupling across the courtyard, boy-girl, girl-girl, even, at one point, boy-boy, although, afterward, when the two men refuse to kiss, Drs. Poole and Molson boo so heartily that Dr. Anders grabs Dr. Eastman and they re-create the famous D-Day sailor photo.

By this time, the adults are trashed. Jeremiah sits out at the Desk of Ungodly Patience doing homework for an hour after his shift ends before finally asking them to wind down the party. He doesn't want to lose his job. He's gotten in trouble only once at the BGH, and that was when a group of visiting football recruits got hold of some beer and broke a few windows after he went home, his supervisor Lame Jimmy explaining that his shift doesn't end until "lights-out" and all is quiet.

But this party is far from lights-out. Dr. Eastman has explained that he inherited a healthy stack of 1960s and '70s country music from his father, and he calls up an old Johnny Cash album, *At San Quentin,* to play a song about the night Johnny got arrested by the police, right here in Starkville. "I never knew my father," he admits. "So, when I was a kid, I used to picture Johnny Cash."

They toast Rowan's dad and begin singing "Folsom Prison Blues" at full volume, loudly confessing to shooting a man in Reno just to watch him die.

Is a song admissible in court, Jeremiah texts Garren.

Rappers hope not, Garren texts back.

The profs see him lurking on the edge of the party with his phone. "Jeremiah! Come sing with us!"

"Come dance, Jeremiah!"

No, he has a big day tomorrow.

The professors offer him wine, and when he says no, a pot Jolly Rancher. Jeremiah confesses that he doesn't drink or use drugs.

"Wonderful!" they say, and "That's great!" and "Good for you!" For a good five minutes, four trashed adults go on about how swell it is that Jeremiah doesn't get trashed.

In fact, Jeremiah asks, "Is there any way you could bring the party down a notch?" He explains that he isn't supposed to leave until "all is quiet," and he has this Spectrum meeting tomorrow morning at 9:00 a.m. and if he could just—

"Right! Spectrum! The parade!" Dr. Anders grabs Jeremiah by the shoulder and yells at a volume completely unnecessary for both topic and proximity: "You gotta convince them to march straight downtown!"

Dr. Anders then proceeds to tell Drs. Molson and Eastman

about the MSU Pride Parade and how Jeremiah is on the committee that applied for a parade permit and how the old Christians
on the Starkville town council denied them—the only parade
permit denial in town history. And how Jeremiah will be voting tomorrow about whether to postpone the parade, contain it
to campus, or march right through downtown and challenge the
Starkville police to do something about it.

Among the drunken, depressed professor cohort, the vote is
unanimous: "You gotta march downtown!" And "Make them
throw you in jail."

Their sloppy encouragement reminds Jeremiah of the time his
dad and his uncle Mo got hammered at his Grandma Jean's wake
and then took turns giving him terrible life advice. *(Biggest thing
is, never let go of a grudge!)*

Inexplicably, Dr. Eastman has adopted what he appears to
think is a Mississippi drawl, and he tells Jeremiah, "Y'all gotta
fight, my man."

"Yeah, I'll try to remember that," Jeremiah says.

Dr. Anders has a spittle string between his lips like Uncle Mo
sometimes gets. "Don't let the assholes get you down, J-dog."

Dr. Poole cries, "Be strong, Jeremiah."

Dr. Molson says, "You know, I'm a little bit bisexual myself."

"Okay then," Jeremiah says, and he exits. All is definitely *not*
quiet, but there is no precedent for this night. Since two faculty
members are here, he hopes he won't get in trouble for leaving.

Back at the Desk of What the Hell Does It Matter Anyway,
Jeremiah fills out his last log report. He shuts down his computer and sits quietly for a moment, thinking about this strange
night. He feels sick, like a kid who has heard more than he was
supposed to hear. It's not like he's been unaware of the dangers

of climate change. It's the level of their pessimism, the *surety* of it, that stings.

Environmental doom has always been aimed at personal behavior: recycle, don't eat beef, drive a hybrid. But this. This is different. This is not about fixing the problem; it's about giving in to it. Their nihilism devastates him. It's one thing to hear adults say there's no Santa. But to hear there's no Future? Swift kick to the soul.

Jeremiah unplugs his phone from where it's been charging. Four times a day, he must recharge this little device, this cord connecting him to the rest of the world. What does it take to make this marvel of innovation and science? At what cost? And, if these scientists are right, what will happen when these things shut down—when it all shuts down?

His sister has finally written him back, saying that his earlier profile pic was Hot, hilarious, perfect!

There are also three new messages from Garren: You coming home? Get picked up by a serial killer? Be careful out there.

Deena and Garren. These people who love him . . . and his love for them . . . it's overwhelming . . . what did Dr. Molson say, seven billion people on the planet . . . each new baby a tiny disaster . . . and yet we love our people so much . . . what becomes of them?

In church, they always insisted that the meek will inherit the earth, but Jeremiah has been meek for a good twenty years and this clearly falls under the heading of false advertising.

It's all so disheartening. Why bother voting or marching or . . . anything. He wants to yell at his small-town red-state high school science teachers for leaving out a few pertinent details—like the fact that *the planet is fucked*. The religious kooks are right: we really are living in end-times. It's as if he's only ever seen the pieces and, now, he sees the whole broken puzzle.

Hopeless, Jeremiah thinks.

Yep. That's the word.

He puts his head in his hands.

When he can sit up again, Jeremiah texts Garren: On my way. He texts Deena: Love you, Sis. He writes a note to the morning supervisor, Lame Jimmy. Then he grabs his coat and stands to leave.

Jeremiah glances once more through the window across the courtyard. He can't quite see what's going on, just bodies moving, dancing, or maybe it's devolved into something else, something he doesn't want to know, like coming across some channel of twisted professor porn. *Do not see that. It cannot be unseen.*

Finally, he leaves the Desk of Blissful Ignorance.

Outside, the storm has subsided. The temperature has risen, and whatever snow fell earlier has melted. Tree branches and leaves are strewn everywhere. It is a cool but mostly clear Mississippi night. The moon even flashes from behind a cloud for a moment as Jeremiah walks alone. He cuts across campus, stepping over branches and debris—wet papers, an MSU banner, some construction tape—all blown around in the storm. He passes the stadium, the highway, the cemetery. A few cars go by, but otherwise, he doesn't see a soul. Seven billion people on the planet, and tonight, he is the only one. He reaches the apartment he shares with Garren, in an old sharecropper house where families worked in the cotton fields until they died. One of Jeremiah's great-great-grandfathers was a sharecropper, the son of slaves. There is a family story of an uncle who was lynched for nothing more than sleeping beneath a farmer's apple tree.

Jeremiah thinks that word *hopeless* again.

He stands outside. Stares up at the endless sky.

6
JOHNNY CASH INEXPLICABLY APPEARS IN AN OTHERWISE DYSTOPIAN CLIMATE CHANGE STORY

Another spring night, another time and place, and Johnny Cash finishes playing at the country showcase at Mississippi State University. As so often happens with Johnny that year, the strung-out singer can't sleep after performing; he's too high, too horny, too raucously curious. The instruments are loaded, and the rest of the musicians, including his future wife, June Carter, go back to the University Motel to get some rest before moving on to the next town. Johnny sets out alone, a paperback book in his back pocket. He wanders from party to party, on campus and off, closing them all down until he finally gets a ride back to the motel.

He still can't sleep, though, and at 2:00 a.m. he leaves his room and ambles away from the motel to get some cigarettes. He wanders down a residential street, lined with magnolias, and steps into a yard to pick "a dandelion here, a daisy there." What happens next will make its way into a minor song in the Cash canon, "Starkville City Jail," from the second of Johnny's four live prison albums, *At San Quentin*.

A patrol car pulls up and shines a light into the yard where Johnny is either picking flowers or relieving himself, and he finds out the hard way that there is a curfew in Starkville. He is arrested for public drunkenness and vagrancy. And, as Johnny sings, *you go to the Starkville City Jail.*

He bonds out six hours later after paying a thirty-six-dollar fine.

Years later, a reporter named Robbie Ward will track down the man who claims to have been Johnny's cellmate that night in 1965. Smokey Evans was fifteen and was in jail for public drunkenness when the singer was brought in. He didn't sleep at all that night, according to Smokey. Johnny paced around, raging and yelling and kicking at the bars so hard he eventually broke a toe. The last thing he did before he left the cell was hand over to Smokey his battered black shoes. "Here's a souvenir," he reportedly said. "I'm Johnny Cash."

That morning in 1965, Johnny walks down the center aisle of the tour bus, disheveled and exhausted. His fellow musicians barely notice. That's just John. But June Carter sees that he's limping a little, and when she looks down, she wonders why he is not wearing shoes.

Fifty-three years later, Jeremiah Ellis lies in bed in the same town wondering what it will be like for him to be arrested and taken to the Starkville City Jail. After all, he will not just be some kid breaking the law; he will be a gay, mixed-race kid breaking the law, the great-great-great-grandson of slaves, an uppity Negro to some old southern sheriff's deputy with a secret nostalgia for anti-miscegenation laws or a target for some bigoted inmate.

Maybe he shouldn't go to the meeting at all. Maybe he has no business being in a Pride Parade; you could argue that a person should have to be openly gay longer than three weeks to get to express pride over it. And what if those cynical professors are right—what if the world is headed for cataclysm? In the face of *that,* what does it matter if seventy-nine gay people (and that's if everyone shows up) put on a stupid parade in a city where they're not even wanted? Maybe he just should follow the professors' lead and get drunk. Cut loose. It's like he's been saving his life up—for what? He should live a little while there's still time. Maybe Garren is right (stupid and crass, but right), and he should spend more time worrying about getting laid. Let it *rain dicks*.

Is this the way the world ends?

Of course, it's an impossible question, a paradox because it is both a complete certainty and utterly unknowable, as undeniable and incomprehensible as the beginning of the universe or the creation of life.

Yeah, that's it, ain't it? says Johnny Cash. *Thirty-six dollars for picking flowers and a night in jail? You can't hardly win, can ya?*

But there are things that we *can* know:

On his last album, *Ain't No Grave*, Johnny Cash will sing that no grave can hold his body down. Unfortunately, this will turn out to be wishful thinking, and he will die of complications from diabetes in 2003. In 2005, his old cellmate Smokey Evans will die, too, from injuries sustained in a fistfight. Smokey will leave his prized possession, Johnny Cash's black shoes, to his nephew in Georgia, but the shoes will go missing not long after that.

Nancy Poole will find out she is pregnant, and she and Henderson Anders will get married in a little ceremony at city hall. They will have twins, a girl and a boy. The first few years of marriage will not be easy, though, and they will divorce four years after the twins are born. But Henderson will feel lost without his family and will agree to seek counseling for his lifelong depression and control issues. The couple will reconcile and eventually remarry in a lovely ceremony on campus, little Eudora Anders serving as the flower girl for her parents, little Faulkner Anders the ring bearer.

Rowan Eastman will end up getting the Mississippi State job

when the department's first choice turns it down. He will finally find a home in Starkville. The sushi is surprisingly good, and there's a fine group of progressive-minded people. The students are smarter than he assumed, and his climate zealotry won't be an issue. In fact, he will organize the first-ever Central Mississippi Climate Conference and will become faculty adviser for an environmental group on campus. He will remain friends with Nancy and Henderson Anders until they divorce, when Rowan screws it up by asking Nancy out. (When Henderson finds out, he punches his friend in the face, a sequence of events that will show up barely fictionalized in Henderson's novel *Starkville*.) But Rowan will apologize, and, slowly, over time, he will begin to step out of the long disaster-filled shadow of his mother—until he meets a woman just like her, a country music fan and bartender named Carla, whom he promptly marries.

Anna Molson will decide not to have a baby, or to freeze her eggs. She will decide not to get her hair cut. She will not move to Mississippi—in fact, when the associate dean offers her the job, she will simply say, "I've decided to stay in my current position." She will not tell Bashir about "that night," and they will decide to continue their careers *and* their long-distance relationship. In what they call their recommitment ceremony, Bashir will remove the Tinder app from his phone. (Her: "Um, I think that was Uber Eats." Him: "Oh, right, sorry.") Eventually, when Anna moves on to a new project, Bashir will move to Siberia to be near her.

More importantly, Anna will go back to her research with a renewed sense of purpose. In two years, her paper on Siberian ground temperature variance, solubility, and melt-rate will catch the attention of an international team working on new techniques for carbon capture—the groundbreaking technology of taking carbon dioxide waste from energy plants and out of the air and pumping it straight down into volcanic rock, where it quickly forms a solid, either calcite or ankerite. While only tested in small, isolated instances, the technology has the potential to cleanly dispose of billions of tons of carbon dioxide—if it can be reproduced on a large scale. Among Anna's contributions will be suggesting the Siberian Traps as a potential site, her research showing that the cold temperatures speed up and stabilize the solidification process so that even the more transportable but unpredictable liquid carbon dioxide can be stored and buried. The massive size of the traps, some seven million square kilometers, roughly the same as Australia, make this the first real candidate for large-scale carbon capture, and when Anna's team is awarded the prestigious Crafoord Prize, the *New York Times* sends a reporter to Siberia to interview her. She points out how the Siberian Traps were likely formed during the last major extinction, the Great Dying, some 250 million years ago, when 96 percent of marine species and 70 percent of land species were destroyed, in part because of massive volcanic activity in Siberia.

"Wouldn't it be ironic if this place that once destroyed life now helps save it?" she is quoted in the *Times*. "The challenges before us are mind-boggling, of course, but this is one small step, and it gives me hope."

7

WITH A WHIMPER AND A BANG

As so often happens after a storm, the quality of air the morning after the great climate orgy is breathtaking. The clarity and richness, the way the air is imbued with moisture, and the colors—the sky a soft white-blue, like a thing forgiven. Trees and plants pop with every shade of green, and the buckeyes defiantly flower in what look like tiny red peppers. It's as if the whole once-in-a-century storm were just a dream, a scary story told around a campfire.

Is it any wonder we are pulled so quickly from our sense of doom, from sorrow and desperation, in such a world as this? Who could believe that in such overwhelming beauty exists such fragility? Jeremiah feels a stirring as he crosses campus and sees this beauty all around him.

Anna Molson is mostly feeling the fragility. Her mouth is so dry she wishes there were a drier word than *dry* to describe how dry her dry mouth is. She's not sure where she is. She sits up and hits her head on a keyboard tray. She is apparently . . . under a desk. She's not sure whose desk.

She looks down and sees with horror that she is wearing nothing but a man's T-shirt and underwear. At least it's her underwear. That's good. The T-shirt is blue and has the words CUBA and PARADISE OF THE TROPICS on it.

"Everything okay, Dr. Molson?"

She looks up to see Jeremiah standing in the doorway of the Butler Guest House reception area.

"I think so." Now she vaguely remembers leaving Rowan's room after a drunken debate about where she should sleep. "I got locked out of my room. I came out here to see if you had a spare key in your desk. I must've fallen asleep." She tries to remember what time that was. Four maybe? "What time is it?"

"Six-thirty," Jeremiah says. After a mostly sleepless night, he has come by the Butler Guest House to clean up before Lame

Jimmy starts his shift at seven, and he has found Dr. Molson sleeping under the Desk of Morning Regret.

He nods toward the courtyard and the common area by the guest rooms. "Is it . . . safe to go back there? I should clean up before my boss comes in."

And suddenly, shame joins her headache and dry mouth, Anna wondering, how much did Jeremiah see—and how much *was* there to see? She's never done anything quite like *that* before— even though she's not entirely clear all *that* entailed, or with *whom* it entailed. She does remember Bashir texting at some point, How was the faculty dinner? She felt the buzz of her phone just as she and Dr. Poole were starting a slow, grinding striptease for the two cheering men. She remembers stopping the dance, reading Bashir's text, and thinking of all the lies he must've told while he was sleeping with half of Miami. She texted back, Uneventful, tossed her phone aside, and went back to helping Nancy Poole out of her shirt.

"Why don't you let me go back there first?" Anna tells Jeremiah. She is still half under Jeremiah's desk, and she looks around for something to put on. Jeremiah says he knows where they keep extra graduation robes, so he grabs one for her and she puts it on.

"Thank you," she says.

The common area is a mess of wine and whiskey bottles, potato chips, popcorn, and strewn clothes.

Anna pushes on Rowan's slightly open door and sees the other three sleeping it off—Rowan alone in one queen-size bed, Henderson and Nancy curled up in the other. (In her own drunken logic, she remembers looking for a key in Jeremiah's desk, thinking that if she slept in her own room, she could tell Bashir that she hadn't "slept with anyone.")

Jeremiah comes into the common area with a broom and cleaning supplies.

"I'm so sorry for this," Anna says. "It really got out of hand."

"It's fine," says Jeremiah as he picks up the pieces of a broken wineglass. "If we can just get this all cleaned up before my boss comes in."

"We should've been more considerate," Anna says again.

"It's really fine," Jeremiah said, "I'm glad you had fun."

Fun. Jesus.

Jeremiah pauses with the broom. "But can I ask you something?"

"Of course," she says.

"Is everything as awful as you made it sound last night?"

Anna tries to figure out how to explain last night—the collision of middle adulthood and the current, depressing state of politics, of the world, and her own late-thirties malaise, Bashir and the Molson-Reed Axiom to the Golden Rule, her eggs dying—all of it.

"I think it's a stressful time, and I guess we felt the need to cut loose a little," Anna says.

"I don't mean what happened here," Jeremiah says. "I mean what you were talking about. You all sounded so defeated. I went home last night, and I couldn't stop thinking the word *hopeless,* over and over—that people are an infection and babies destroy the planet and how everything we do just makes it worse."

Anna stares at this earnest boy, his thick glasses, crooked Afro, button shirt, baggy jeans. She feels the final weight of her full shame. "Jeremiah—" she begins.

But he wants to finish. "I'm not very old," Jeremiah says. "I haven't figured out who I am. And in two hours, I'm supposed to go vote on whether our stupid little gay club should march through town so a bunch of backward people can line up to call us fags and tell us we're going to hell.

"But I guess it seems to me"—Jeremiah pauses, choosing his words carefully—"that you shouldn't give up hope until you've done everything you can."

This hits Anna like a fist, and she pictures students in other cities protesting the now-weekly school shootings, with their perfectly reasonable request to apply some basic common sense and rational thought, to *do something,* to enact some basic gun laws—and how demoralizing it must be to see those same adults shrug helplessly at the backward, illogical politics, to act as if it were all unavoidable.

"So, I guess that's what I wanted to ask you," Jeremiah says. "If you think we've done everything we can?"

It is this second question that takes Anna's breath away. *No,* she thinks, *we haven't done a goddamned thing.* Not really. We present at conferences, and we write papers and we make placards and we march on a specified day and then we go back to work, back to TV, back to lives of gossip and distraction. And to be asked this question by this kid, here, in Mississippi, where people died fighting for basic civil rights? It's more than she can take. Anna begins to cry.

"I'm sorry—" Jeremiah starts.

She straightens, walks over to Jeremiah, and hugs him. She thanks Jeremiah and says: "There is so much more to do."

Rowan Eastman hears a noise outside his room then and stirs awake. He sees Henderson and Nancy in the other bed and tries to put the night together in his mind—*Wait, did I kiss Henderson?* He wishes he hadn't been so drunk and stoned so he could remember sequences instead of just random flashes. He decides to go find Anna and make sure she's cool with everything that happened and maybe ask if he can see her again, although it puts a lot of pressure on a second date when the first one ends with a half-naked tangle of strangers.

He moans as he climbs out of bed and walks out of his room into the common area. There are four rules of thermodynamics that govern matter in the known universe, but after that day, Rowan will propose a fifth, *Shit can always get weirder,* when he comes out and sees, amid the empty wine bottles and strewn clothes, Anna, inexplicably wearing a black graduation gown, in a deep embrace with the work-study kid, Jeremiah. It is too much for Rowan, and he turns and goes back to bed.

And this is the way the world ends:

Jeremiah Ellis gives a rousing speech that morning at the Spectrum committee meeting, telling the gathered students, *You don't give up until you've done everything you can,* and the parade committee votes unanimously to march right through campus and straight into Starkville, with or without a permit. Under pressure from all sides, the town council eventually grants a permit, and a month later, the streets of Starkville are filled with more than twenty-five hundred people marching for gay pride, carrying rainbow banners and balloons, waving MSU cowbells decorated with rainbow tape. Even more people cheer from the streets. They come from Birmingham, from Memphis and Jackson, and Jeremiah takes his place among them, marching in the front row with Trevor Blankenship and the other organizers. His roommate Garren marches a few rows back, wearing a STRAIGHT-BUT-SENSITIVE-AS-SHIT T-shirt of his own making. Jeremiah keeps looking over his shoulder, smiling, on the verge of tears as he takes in the faces, the rainbows, the sheer love—stretching block after block, through traffic lights, down streets, as far as he can see. There are protestors, of course, the last gasps of the superstitious and reactionary, those frightened of change, but their shrill voices are drowned out—for now—by the crowd's chanting and singing, and by Jeremiah, who yells every few minutes, seemingly apropos of nothing: "You've got to give them hope!"

ACKNOWLEDGMENTS

THESE STORIES FIRST APPEARED, in somewhat different forms, in the following places: "Mr. Voice" *Tin House* and *Best American Short Stories 2015;* "Fran's Friend Has Cancer" *Ploughshares;* "Magnificent Desolation" *The Spokesman-Review* and Selected Shorts; "Drafting" *Mississippi Review;* "The Angel of Rome" (written in collaboration with Edoardo Ballerini) Audible Originals; "Before You Blow" *The Spokesman-Review;* "Town & Country" Scribd Originals; "Cross the Woods" *Esquire;* "To the Corner" *Harper's Magazine;* "Famous Actor" *Tin House, Best American Short Stories 2017,* Pushcart Prize Anthology XLI; "Balloons" *Washington Square Review;* "The Way the World Ends," Amazon Originals Warmer Series.

Thank you to my wife and first reader, Anne Walter; to my agent, Warren Frazier; my editors, Jennifer Barth and Millicent Bennett; and everyone at HarperCollins, especially Jonathan Burnham, Sarah Ried, Liz Velez, Amy Baker, Jane Beirn, and Chantal Restivo-Alessi, who helped get permission for the cover photo. And to Italian film icons Roberto Russo and Monica Vitti, *grazie mille* for allowing us to use that wonderful image. Thank you to Katy Sewall, for giving this book such a great read, and to a slew of other writers, friends and editors who, from 2013 to 2021 selected and contributed to these pieces, including Cheston Knapp, Jennifer Haigh, Andrew Milward, Amy Grace Loyd, Heidi Pitlor, T. C. Boyle, Meg Wolitzer, Tyler Cabot, Yael Goldstein Love, David Blum, Julia Sommerfeld, Spencer Gafney and Carolyn Lamberson. Monica Mereghetti and Carlo Maffini were a huge help with the Italian and Latin in "The Angel of Rome," and a special *grazie amico mio* to Edoardo Ballerini for helping me bring those characters to life.

THE COLD MILLIONS
JESS WALTER

1909. Spokane, Washington.

The Dolan brothers are living by their wits, jumping freight trains and lining up for work at crooked job agencies. While sixteen-year-old Rye yearns for a steady job and a home, his dashing older brother Gig dreams of a better world, fighting alongside other union men for fair pay and decent treatment.

But then Rye finds himself drawn to suffragette Elizabeth Gurley Flynn and her passion sweeps him into the world of protest and dirty business. As a storm starts brewing, questions of love, sacrifice, brotherhood and betrayal emerge, threatening to overwhelm them all . . .

> 'A beautiful, lyric hymn to the power of social unrest in American history . . . funny and harrowing, sweet and violent, innocent and experienced; it walks a dozen tightropes'
>
> Anthony Doerr, author of
> *All the Light We Cannot See*

> 'A brilliantly multifaceted panorama of early twentieth-century America . . . Walter is a writer whose work deserves a wide readership'
>
> *Sunday Times*

> 'A work of irresistible characters, harrowing adventures and rip-roaring fun . . . One of the most captivating novels of the year'
>
> *Washington Post*

BEAUTIFUL RUINS

JESS WALTER

THE NUMBER ONE *NEW YORK TIMES* BESTSELLER

The story begins in 1962. Somewhere on a rocky patch of the sun-drenched Italian coastline a young innkeeper, chest-deep in daydreams, looks out over the incandescent waters of the Ligurian Sea and views an apparition: a beautiful woman, a vision in white, approaching him on a boat. She is an American starlet, he soon learns, and she is dying.

And the story begins again today, half a world away in Hollywood, when an elderly Italian man shows up on a movie studio's back lot searching for the woman he last saw at his hotel fifty years before.

Gloriously inventive, funny, tender and constantly surprising, *Beautiful Ruins* is a novel full of fabulous and yet very flawed people, all of them striving towards another sort of life, a future that is both delightful and yet, tantalizingly, seems just out of reach.

'Intelligent and thought-provoking, but also a lot of fun. Reading hours fly by and reaching the final page feels like a genuine wrench'

Sunday Times

'Magic . . . A monument to crazy love with a deeply romantic heart'

The New York Times

'Hilarious and compelling'

Esquire

He just wanted a decent book to read ...

Not too much to ask, is it? It was in 1935 when Allen Lane, Managing Director of Bodley Head Publishers, stood on a platform at Exeter railway station looking for something good to read on his journey back to London. His choice was limited to popular magazines and poor-quality paperbacks – the same choice faced every day by the vast majority of readers, few of whom could afford hardbacks. Lane's disappointment and subsequent anger at the range of books generally available led him to found a company – and change the world.

'We believed in the existence in this country of a vast reading public for intelligent books at a low price, and staked everything on it'
Sir Allen Lane, 1902–1970, founder of Penguin Books

The quality paperback had arrived – and not just in bookshops. Lane was adamant that his Penguins should appear in chain stores and tobacconists, and should cost no more than a packet of cigarettes.

Reading habits (and cigarette prices) have changed since 1935, but Penguin still believes in publishing the best books for everybody to enjoy. We still believe that good design costs no more than bad design, and we still believe that quality books published passionately and responsibly make the world a better place.

So wherever you see the little bird – whether it's on a piece of prize-winning literary fiction or a celebrity autobiography, political tour de force or historical masterpiece, a serial-killer thriller, reference book, world classic or a piece of pure escapism – you can bet that it represents the very best that the genre has to offer.

Whatever you like to read – trust Penguin.